DRAGON RIPPER

Book 1 of "The Detectivists"

This is a work of fiction. The characters, incidents and dialogues in this book are either products of the author's imagination or are used fictitiously. Any resemblance to actual events or persons, living or dead, is completely coincidental.

No part of this book may be reproduced or transmitted in any form or by any means, electronic or mechanical, including photocopying, recording, or by any information storage and retrieval system, without permission in writing from the author.

DEL SOL PRESS.

THE DETECTIVISTS – DRAGON RIPPER

Copyright © 2020 by Melanie Bacon
All rights reserved.
Printed in the United States of America.
Del Sol Press, 2020 Pennsylvania Avenue, NW,
Washington, D.C., 20006.
•

www.delsolpress.org
ISBN-13: 978-0-9998425-8-4

Our books may be purchased in bulk
for promotional, educational, or business use.
Please contact Del Sol Press by e-mail at editor@delsolpress.org.
First Edition: September 2019

10 9 8 7 6 5 4 3 2 1

For Michael

"Where there is no imagination there is no horror."

- Sherlock Holmes

Chapter One

I prefer to visit opium dens at dawn, when citizens both good and bad tend to favour their beds. Hence the black fog of night had already begun paling to steel when I neared Whitechapel alley, anxious to procure the usual morphine dosage for the ailing horses in my charge. But no sooner had I turned the corner into the alley than I encountered Astraia Holmes for the very first time, kneeling in the blood of a dead prostitute just a few steps from the entrance to my routine narcotics purveyor.

Long ago I learned to never closely examine the various fluids and offal littering our more disreputable thoroughfares (I'm always happier not knowing the precise source of the squish in which I step), and as a consequence I almost fell over the woman kneeling on the ancient cobblestones of the alleyway. Despite the fact I carried a kerosene lantern I did not at first notice the blood puddles seeping into the street in front of her.

Tripping over persons collapsed under the influence of gin, drugs, or general despair is not that unusual an occurrence in the East End, and as I saw no starving children heaped about the place I prepared to move on. But then I realized her clothing and kneeling posture were not those of the standard derelict one typically finds sprawled in the street. She wore a respectable, subdued grey walking dress— perfectly tailored, impeccably clean except for the several inches above the hem now mounded in alleyway muck despite its unfashionably short skirt length (almost to the top of her ankle boots). A piquant straw hat sat rakishly on her head. Immaculate snow-white gloves on slender hands gripped a magnifying glass just a few inches above what I now realized for the first time was a great deal of dark fluid.

"Do you need help, miss?" I asked this strange person, unhappily comparing her fashionable guise to my soiled and tawdry appearance, conscious of my own hatless windswept locks, bulky handbag and seedy mended gloves. I wore one of my work gowns, no doubt stained with all manner of God knows what. Had I even washed my face?

"If you could refrain from stomping through the evidence, I would be most grateful," she said in a high, almost girlish whisper, the kind of voice one usually associates with giggles and nonsense.

I glanced down and gagged when I saw I indeed stood in a pool of blood, in a street awash in the wet sticky stuff. And now I could smell it, the coppery odour rising even above the ordinary stink of Whitechapel alleyway filth. Desperate to escape the sanguine liquid I rushed horror struck toward the steps of Mr. Wu's opium den (Mr. Wu being a conscientious business owner who took pride in the relative cleanliness of his establishment).

I tugged at the tightly locked door handle, to no avail. I pounded on the door, but no one answered my entreaties. Mr. Wu's shop of evil was closed for business. Which meant I would have to pay full price through the police medical supplier for horse morphine, a serious bite into my paltry budget. Unless Little Joey would agree to introduce me to another opiate distributor...

"Come here for a moment and bring your lantern, if you please," ordered the woman in a most officious tone.

"Are you addressing *me*, miss?" I asked. Glancing around, I saw no one else whom she could be soliciting. However, Whitechapel is renowned for its abundance of residents who habitually converse with themselves. As a rule, I do not respond to rude or peculiar persons, but my curiosity had been whetted. Did she always carry a magnifying glass in that little lacy reticule dangling from her wrist?

"Of course," she snapped in her light girlish voice. "And do try not to step in the blood."

Skirts lifted so I could better gauge where my footsteps fell, I endeavoured to tip-toe around the red-tinged ordure of the street in response to the haughty woman's demand, my sturdy industrial lantern providing most of the light illuminating the gruesome locale. The filigreed lantern with its tiny flicker of light at her feet would have better served to illuminate a doll house than a blood pool in an opium alley. Clearly someone had died here, though what that had to do with either of us I could not say, but I was willing to assist her by providing additional light. On my way to her side I slipped twice in the slimy muck but managed not to fall in it, a happenstance which both surprised and gratified me.

The kneeling woman was not impressed. "Do you think you could take a look at this without sprawling in it, and tell me what you see?"

"I will attempt to do so." I glanced down to examine that which she assiduously studied, but I have always had poor night vision, even with artificial light.

"I can't see anything," I complained.

She moved her dainty lantern closer to the spot she wished me to inspect. On a small, relatively unsplashed section of the pavement, someone had traced a complex glyph. In blood.

3

I lowered my own lantern to the place and described what I saw. "It appears to be a pictograph of some kind," I said. "Smeared a bit, there at the edge."

"The smear is no doubt from one of the police constables' boots, caused when they conducted their so-called investigation. I suspect they did not even notice the thing, otherwise they would have clomped through it like they did every footprint and other possible clue that might have been on the ground. You do not believe the design could be just a natural result of the blood spatter phenomenon creating a false pattern?"

"I do not think so. Despite the horrific medium used, the tracery appears most exquisite, almost a work of art," I said. "Like oriental calligraphy, perhaps."

She nodded. "That is what I believe also, but I like to have my hypotheses confirmed by a second observer and my usual assistants refused to accompany me into this alleyway. Do you by any chance have a camera nearby?"

I shook my head. "No. Sorry."

Failing to respond to my sarcasm, she nodded and stood. "Come look at this."

Daintily, almost like a spirit, she glided beyond the frightening calligraphy to stand before the brick wall of Mr. Wu's building. Raising her lantern to the structure, she pointed her magnifying glass toward a section near the door. "What do you see here?" she asked, holding her glass implement to the wall as aid to my inspection.

I followed her, not half so ethereal. I have always been a clodhopper of a girl. I stared through the lens at the wall.

"The brick has been gouged," I said, removing a glove to lightly run a finger along a furrow incised into the masonry.

"You see there are three grooves, in fact, each almost a foot in length, separated by approximately three inches at the left end of the gouge and closer to five inches distance from each other at the right end," she said. "Do you have any theories about what could have created them?"

"I have no idea," I said, moving my finger over the lowest furrow, carved perhaps a half-inch deep into the brick. "But I don't believe I saw them when I was here last week."

"No, I don't expect you did," she said. "These gouges are fresh. You can see the brick dust from them on the ground, still unspoilt by the alleyway filth."

I lowered my own lantern to examine the ground and saw that she was right. "What type of instrument was used to make such delineations?" I asked. "A knife or sword?"

"No normal man could have made such deep indentations using any blade of which I'm aware," she said. "Whatever did this was incredibly powerful. The more pertinent question, I believe, is why were these cuts made at all?"

I looked around the scene. At the blood splashed all over the ground. "No, the more pertinent question is: what terrible event occurred here?"

"A woman was slaughtered here last night," she said. "The police were just leaving when I happened by."

I began to shake. I gripped the wall, my fingers clasping tightly into two of the furrows lest I swoon. "Do they know who did it?"

She shrugged. "The police believe it was Jack the Ripper."

I shook my head. "They are mistaken," I said.

She studied my face. "I agree with you." She glanced around the alley, her attention returning to the small blood pictograph on the ground. "This was some other monster altogether." She moved away from the wall, slipping the magnifying glass into a pocket in her dress. I took uncharitable pleasure to see the unattractive bulge the heavy item made in her gown. "Well, that's about all I can see here for the time being. I'll return after work with a camera, in case some of this evidence still remains." She looked up at me, again finding me wanting. "You don't appear to be carrying a sketchpad on your person either."

"No. Sorry," I said, biting my caustic tongue to keep from asking her if I really looked like Mary Cassatt, out on an early-morning landscape-painting jaunt.

She turned her back to me. "How wrinkled am I?"

"Um, not too much," I said hesitantly. "But your bustle ribbons are bloodied. And your hem."

She looked down at herself and snarled, finally noticing the red filth sopping the bottom of her dress. "Damnation! I shall have to go home and change my clothes. Letty will be furious." She examined the tiny gold watch pinned to the bosom of her gown.

"Who's Letty?"

"My companion. She is sleeping in a cab around the corner, ostensibly waiting for me. Now she'll be late for her breakfast and I shall be late for work."

"Where do you work?" A tea shops. A milliner's? Perhaps she modelled for a doll maker.

"At the new Whitechapel Library," she said. "Which will open late this morning, since I prefer not to drip blood all over the premises. Drunk Willie will have to wait an extra hour for his morning paper." She nodded to me and left, almost floating over the coppery muck, her tiny lantern twinkling beside her like a fairy light. Within seconds she was out of sight.

I stared for a few minutes longer at the mess, wondering how long it would remain here on the street. Would the police ask the fire department to come in with their hoses? Doubtful. And street cleaners seldom exercised their skills in the East End—and certainly never in the alleyways. The gore could easily remain clotting here until the next heavy rain. So perhaps the strange person I had just encountered actually would be able to take some photographs upon later return.

The dead woman. Another prostitute, as before? This seemed likely; the police estimated that over a thousand women plied the wanton trade here in Whitechapel. Did she have a family? Children who would never see their mother again. That was the scene which regularly haunted my nightmares. After pounding fruitlessly for several more minutes on Mr. Wu's door, I left the reeking lane, trying to avoid the sticky red puddles. But when I glanced back several minutes later as I walked down High Street; I saw red footprints following behind me. A cold chill consumed me until I realized those footprints were mine.

The repulsive stains faded over the course of the streets as I walked to the stable at the rear of the Leman Street station of the Metropolitan Police. I hoped I would not be called upon to perform any horse surgeries today. I hated to inflict pain on any animal, and my morphine supply was almost gone.

Happily, the day brought no emergencies to my door. I spent a few hours singing to the horses as I treated them, a pleasure I had indulged to my heart's content ever since the death of my papa, the stable's previous veterinarian. Unlike Mummy, who had wished me to sing professionally, Papa had been a fan of neither opera nor the female contralto voice. Fortunately, the horses seemed to like both. Shortly before noon I forced myself to work on more mundane matters until Police Constable Frank Froest came by the office to chew the rag, as was often his wont.

"I've had a rough morning, Maddie, and I'm ready for my tea," the dear man said, placing his helmet and truncheon atop a pile of papers on a side table. "Go wash your hands. There's a slight scent of the horse about you and that grime under your nails looks suspicious."

I set my pencil down on the table, giving the stable cat warming my lap a final caress before easing her onto the ground. I was glad to put my papers away. I had been doing accounts, an activity always depressive to the nerves. The police veterinary service had still not received the fourth quarter funds, and now we neared a new year. A tardy approach to funding was typical for the government, and frankly the reason, I believe, that so many government employees are open to bribery. I probably would have been too if it weren't that all of my clients are equine, who limit their extortion actions to slobber and snuffling for sugar cubes.

"Do the boys have any extra coal, Frank?" I asked. "We've been lucky with the weather, but I'm just about out and it could snow any time now. I'd prefer not to move my office into a horse stall just so I can stay warm enough to wriggle my fingers."

He laughed. "I remember when your father had to do that a time or two. Didn't please him by half, I can tell you."

"No." Papa had never cared for horses and only became an animal doctor when it was clear he would never succeed as a regular doctor. Papa had, shall we say, a poor bedside manner. Having to spend all of his time in the horse stalls just in order to stay warm would not have improved his temper.

I went to the pump to wash my hands, scrubbing under the nails as directed, and returned to hear the kettle whistling on the small stove as Frank carefully measured tea into the chipped but sturdy china chicken pot, Juno the cat arching and purring around his ankles. Juno liked teatime. Frank reached down to scratch her neck.

8

"I'm serious about the coal, Frank," I said, lifting the hot kettle with a cloth-wrapped hand and carrying it over to him. "Otherwise, Juno and I will have to come to you for tea instead. And just imagine how much grousing we'll do."

"We cannot have that," PC Froest said as I poured water into the pot. "I'll see what I can contrive."

I smiled. Frank Froest was a like a bull, short and powerful and utterly unstoppable when he committed his intent to something. I would stay warm this winter.

"Did you bake any of that gingerbread I like so much?" he asked.

"Of course," I said, batting my eyes at him. He laughed at the gesture as he always did when I behaved in a coquettish manner. I am not an especially feminine woman, being nearly six feet tall, deep-voiced and heavily muscled.

Frank procured the tin from my desk drawer and unwrapped the cheesecloth covering the fresh gingerbread. He sniffed greedily, then placed the bits left over from the day before onto Juno's plate for her teatime treat. "You're wasted on the horses, my dear. You should find some nice large man who'll appreciate your beauty and your fine cooking."

I have no talent in the kitchen, a fact I saw no reason to share with Frank. Happily, for both of us, I lived above the corner bakery. I took care of Tina, the Feinmans' delivery horse, and the Feinmans took care of me.

"What was so rough about your morning, Frank?" I asked after we finished our first few silent minutes of tea and gingerbread bliss.

"A consultant from Scotland Yard came nosing around, asking questions about a case we're working on in the Limehouse neighbourhood," he said. "I couldn't be rude to him, but I have no patience with civilians who intrude into police affairs."

Hopefully he'd have more patience if the intruder was me. "Frank, what do you know about the woman who was violently killed in an alley this morning?" People got killed in alleys every day, but the amount of gore in this case was unusual.

He looked at me in surprise, setting his mug down on the table. "How did you hear about that so soon, Madeleine? We are trying to keep it quiet. We don't want another Saucy Jacky panic, not now that people are finally feeling safe again."

I secured the leftover bits of gingerbread from our plates in the tin, then allowed Juno to return to my lap for her postprandial nap. "Is that why you left a river of blood in the alley when you removed the corpus? Because you didn't want to raise alarm?" I shook my head. "I encountered the crime scene this morning on my way to Mr. Wu's for horse medicine."

"The inhabitants of that area are not early risers, though no doubt the word is out by now," Frank said. "But the mess was washed away long before anyone else had time to find it."

I didn't correct him. No need to bring the bossy doll-woman to police attention. "You mentioned Saucy Jacky. Is that what they think that this was another Ripper killing? What are the similarities to those crimes?"

"A prostitute, Sarah Prentiss, was slashed to ribbons. I do not believe it is the same fiend as last year. But we have to consider the possibility."

"What do Detectives Reid and Abberline think?"

"I am not allowed in those exalted conferences," Frank said in a bitter tone. Frank's ambition was to be promoted to detective and work in the Criminal Investigation Department. "But they are intelligent men; I suspect they believe it's a different killer too, which would be even worse, wouldn't it? Having two such monsters on the loose?"

I shivered, caressing the cat for comfort. Frank's comment about two monsters hit a bit close to home.

"Why do you believe Miss Prentiss was the victim of a different killer?" I asked, pouring him his second cup of tea.

"Well, let's see. There was no mutilation. Her throat was cut, certainly, but so was her face and chest, with slashes deeper than the cut to the throat. The one to the face obliterated her nose and cheekbones; the chest wound actually broke open the ribs and sternum. There was no indication of any torture—it was just the three cuts, fast and vicious. Oh, and there's a cut on her upper arm, but that appears to be a continuation of the assault to the chest."

"Just those three cuts?"

"Just those three cuts, almost parallel to one another. The one to the chest almost split her in two. It would take an incredibly sharp blade and the strength of a titan. We have been unable to identify the weapon."

"Did the killer leave anything at all to identify him?" What I wanted to ask was, did the killer take any souvenirs? But it would be better to let Frank volunteer the details. More collegial. Less likely to rouse suspicion.

He shook his head. "If so, we missed it in the morning dark. A few men returned later with the water pump to hose the blood from the alley, but they didn't have time to look around much as the residents were beginning to stir."

I had not reckoned on the police cleaning up the crime scene to inhibit resident hysteria. Sometimes I did not give the police sufficient credit. "Did no one hear anything at all when the woman was attacked?"

"Not that I know of yet. But we'll continue to question people in the neighbourhood."

Clean up the mess, then question the people. Poor way to avoid a panic. I allowed Juno to jump from my lap, to chase prey only her keen ears could hear. "How did the police learn of the event then?"

"That's an interesting story. Your Mr. Wu, who I understand almost never leaves his place of business, alerted a bobby on patrol on Whitechapel High Street shortly after three o'clock this morning. We have Wu in jail, but he's not a serious suspect. He wouldn't have the strength, for one thing."

I thought about the slight, frail man. Impossible to conceive of him chopping a woman almost in two.

"What did he say? Can he identify the scoundrel?"

"He says he didn't see anything and didn't examine the victim long enough to notice anything more than that it was a woman. I suspect the only reason he even informed the police at all was because the corpse on his doorstep deterred his customer traffic."

"Is there a reason he needs to remain in jail if he isn't a suspect?"

He shrugged. "Probably not. If you would vouch for him, I suppose we could sign him out to you."

I could tell by the small smile on his lips that he proffered the suggestion only to tease me. Perhaps that's why I answered as I did. "That would be fine." I took a sip from the cooling liquid in my cup. "After we finish our tea."

*****

Mr. Wu and I were not particularly close. He peddled the vilest sort of narcotic; I was his customer; such was the extent of our relationship. So it was perfectly natural that he expressed surprised at being released to my security, his mouth actually falling agape when a bobby delivered him to the jail antechamber a couple of hours later and he saw to whom he owed his discharge.

"If he doesn't return to give his report to the coroner's jury you will be held responsible, Miss Barquist," the disapproving jailer told me, unshackling the stunned little man and pushing him toward my person. I frowned at the shackles, and at the bruises I saw on Mr. Wu's face. Surely such brutality had not been necessary. The man wouldn't have caused them much trouble. I doubted he weighed over seven stone.

"Mr. Wu is a witness who came forward to aid the police after a vicious crime had been perpetrated on his doorstep," I said icily. "Was it *really* necessary to shackle him?"

"What are you, his solicitor?" the turnkey said with a snide look. I could tell he wanted to hit Mr. Wu again, or at least make some other rude comment, so I hustled the Chinese man to the door.

As Mr. Wu withdrew I turned again to the jailer. "When does the coroner's jury meet on this matter?"

"Probably tomorrow; day after at the latest. Froest will let you know."

During those last few moments of discussion between the jailer and myself, Mr. Wu took full advantage of his freedom to scuttle halfway down the street. I hurried to catch up, ignoring the stares directed at me by fellow pedestrians shocked to see an almost-six-foot-tall English woman chasing an almost-five-foot-tall Chinese man down the street. Happily, my limbs were twice the length of his and he soon realized he would not be able to escape me. Also, he was not a particularly healthy physical specimen and couldn't maintain speed for long. After less than a quarter mile I found myself keeping pace with just an easy trot.

"Mr. Wu, am I going to regret vouching for you?"

Out of breath and puffing he stopped and stared up at me, suspicion in his face. "That depends. Why did you do it?"

Truthfully, I had to struggle for a moment for an answer. Why had I done it?

"Someone sliced three long gouges out of the side of your building," I said. "Do you know anything about that?"

His face went pale with dread. "No." Fear renewed his energy. He began to run.

I knew he was lying and anxious to avoid further questioning. Nevertheless, I jogged along beside him, keeping up easily even in my bulky skirts. A police constable stepped toward us as we turned onto George Yard, but I waved him away. "It's all right, PC Hemings," I said as we ran past him, giving him a reassuring smile. He accepted my words and didn't follow, but no one gossips like a copper and I knew to expect more visitors than usual tomorrow at the veterinary surgery.

My eyes scanned the crowds as I ran, a habit ingrained over the last year. I almost fell over myself in shock when I thought I saw a distressingly familiar face popping into a shop on the other side of the road, but then I forced myself to focus on the day's own troubles, as scripture says.

Surely that wasn't Bert Cranston. Surely, I had been mistaken. He could not have returned.

Mr. Wu had to stop running when we reached his alleyway due to the crowd of people milling about, morbidly curious about last night's horrendous murder. Mr. Wu and I pressed through, and as we neared his door, I noticed the doll-like woman from the morning was there again, methodically disassembling photographic equipment situated in front of the deep cuts channelled into the wall near the door.

One hand clasped to Mr. Wu's shoulder to keep him from escape, I used the other hand to tap on the little woman's back. She turned.

"Good afternoon, Miss," I said. "This is Mr. Wu... Mr. Wu, this is—?"

"Miss Holmes," the woman said in her light voice. "I'm happy to make your acquaintance, Mr. Wu." She held out her hand, but he didn't notice. He had probably not even heard her speak as he stared, hyperventilating so hard I worried he would faint, horror struck at the three furrows gouged into the wall of his building.

"Do you know what this is, Mr. Wu?" Miss Holmes asked in her officious yet girlish tone.

He whispered something I could not understand. I looked to Miss Holmes for clarification, but she shook her head. "I'm afraid I don't speak Cantonese, Mr. Wu."

He didn't respond to her. Except for his heavy breathing he did not move, not even when I waved my hand in front of his face.

"Mr. Wu is the citizen who informed the police of the despicable murder committed here last night," I explained to Miss Holmes.

"But I think we can assume he did not notice this element of the crime before, since his response is so extreme," she said.

"I concur." The man reminded me of a statue I'd seen once of Lot's wife, turned to a pillar of salt, her face eternally frozen in fear.

We waited politely for another minute for him to come out of his stupor, but this civility eventually palled. "Well, this is ridiculous," Miss Holmes said finally, pulling a tiny jar of smelling salts from her reticule. She wafted it under his nose, tapping his face lightly with her gloved hand at the same time. He jerked back; if I had not grabbed his shoulders he would have fallen to the ground.

He tried to pull away.

"Do not release him," Miss Holmes ordered. "Or he will escape into the warren of this criminal neighbourhood and never answer our questions."

"Oh, he mustn't disappear," I said in dismay. "He is required to testify as witness for the coroner's jury, since he found the body. I've vouched for him with the police."

She studied me in disapproval. "That was foolish of you," she said. She looked into the face of the frightened, struggling man. "I doubt you can depend on him to appear voluntarily."

I sighed. "I suppose I can keep him in the stable for a day or two."

"You live as well as work in the police stable?"

"No. I don't live there."

Again, he tried to pull away, but really, the man had no strength at all, probably the result of regular narcotic use.

"It is getting dark," Miss Holmes said. "Let us go to my cab and take him to your place of work to question him. You're certain it will be secure?"

"I suppose so. I've never had a horse escape, at any rate."

Hauling the bulky photographic equipment in her arms she pushed through the crowd, a tiny woman but strong and forceful. Mr. Wu and I followed her—he tried to escape just once, a half-hearted attempt at that—and it was only as I heard her give direction to her waiting cabbie to take us to the Leman Street police stable that it occurred to me to wonder how she knew the proper destination.

The cab was terribly crowded, hardly of sufficient size to hold Miss Holmes, her camera equipment, and the dozing woman I assumed to be the companion Letty, let alone the addition of a six-foot woman and an anxious opium den proprietor. I had given an instinctive professional glance at the horse before entering the conveyance. It looked healthy enough but I nevertheless hoped for light traffic so the ride would be quick.

The cab's horse began its clomping stride. I looked out the window at the traffic and pedestrians but saw no one to alarm me.

"Miss Holmes, how did you know where I work?" I noticed that the farther we travelled from the alley the calmer Mr. Wu became. Once I felt confident, he wouldn't jump out of the cab if I released my hold I relaxed enough to converse with my new acquaintance.

A small smile crossed her lips. "I knew this morning that you work regularly with horses—that much was clear from the state of your apparel and hands. Since you admitted to being a regular visitor to the opium den but your extreme good health precludes your own imbibing, I concluded that you must use the narcotic as animal medication and therefore must work in the veterinary profession. And finally, just a short while ago you said that the police released Mr. Wu into your custody, a highly unlikely occurrence unless they knew you well and had confidence in you. You verified my hypotheses when you admitted that you work at the police stable."

"But how did you know to send the cabbie to the Leman Street station?"

She shrugged. "The Leman Street headquarters is the closest station to the opium den, and as the lead station the one most likely to house the veterinary services."

The cab stopped. Letty released a snuffling snore, which relieved my mind; the woman was not dead nor even comatose. "There is one thing I don't know," Miss Holmes said as the cabbie assisted her to alight.

I assisted Mr. Wu. "What's that?"

Ignoring her sleeping companion, Miss Holmes gave the cabbie instructions to wait then turned to look up at me. "I still do not know your name."

I blushed, but it was dark so that was all right. I'd been blushing ever since she had referenced the persistent manure line under my fingernails. I'd always known I was gawky, but no one ever made me as aware of that as Miss Holmes. "I'm Miss Madeleine Barquist," I said.

"Miss Barquist, I am glad to make your acquaintance," Miss Holmes said. She did not hold out her hand since both of mine were full of Mr. Wu, now struggling again. He was not happy to return to the police station.

We walked around the back to the stable, Mr. Wu settling more at ease the farther we removed from the front doors of the station house. He actually smiled a bit as we entered my little office in the stable. "I like horses," he said.

"I'm glad to hear that, Mr. Wu," I said. "You'll be sleeping with them tonight."

He shrugged. "I have slept with worse," he said, yawning.

"I don't have much in here for food," I confessed. "All I can offer you is gingerbread and tea." I noticed that Mr. Wu's nose was running, and I looked around for a semi-clean rag.

Miss Holmes withdrew a pristine lace handkerchief from her reticule and handed it to the man. "If you have sufficient provisions for both of you for this evening, I will stop by in the morning with additional comestibles," she said. "But I believe Mr. Wu is going to want something else even more. Are you an opium addict, sir?"

He sniffed. "What do you think?"

I turned from the stove, where I had just placed some of my last precious lumps of coal to heat water for tea. Juno was nowhere in sight; she tended to spend her nights chasing mice in the regular stable, where the sleeping horses kept the temperature warmer than here. "Well, I can't help Mr. Wu with his opium craving," I said. "I have a bit of morphine left but the horse needles are much too large to use on a human. He'll just have to wait until after he gives his testimony to the coroner's jury and is released to go home."

"He won't be able to wait," Miss Holmes said. "It's already been over twelve hours since his last dose, and his nose has begun to run and his eyes to water. Soon the nausea will begin, the diarrhoea and vomiting. The symptoms of an addict's drug abrogation are most unpleasant. Do you have any tobacco?"

"I believe so." I went to the dusty cabinet in the corner and dug through the drawers. "Papa smoked a pipe." He had been dead over a year now. To this day, the smell of pipe smoke made me nauseous.

"Excellent. Bring the pipe over as well."

A few minutes later Miss Holmes, Mr. Wu and I sat drinking tea at my small table. Mr. Wu and I nibbled the remainder of the gingerbread, including the pieces I had set aside for Juno's tea tomorrow. Miss Holmes declined since she and Letty planned to have a meal in her own home shortly. It all seemed most civilized except for the tobacco, pipe and morphine jar sitting prominently on the table in front of Miss Holmes in lieu of a plate.

Mr. Wu had far less interest in the food on his own plate than he had in the vile instruments of enslavement awaiting him in front of Miss Holmes.

"Please tell us, Mr. Wu—what precisely did you see last night?" Miss Holmes asked.

"Can't think now," he said. "My mind will work better after I've had a smoke."

"No, Mr. Wu," she said firmly. "You will *not* be allowed to smoke until after you've told us all that you know about last night's vicious murder."

He glared at her with a look of pure malevolence. "You're a tiny girly. I could just take it from you."

"No," I drawled. "You could not."

He glowered at me a moment then collapsed in his chair; his rebellion quelled. "I didn't see anything," he said sullenly.

"Then how did you know someone had been killed?"

"One of my customers saw something. He was leaving for the night but ran back in screaming. I went to go look, and saw Miss Sarah dead on the street, all bloody, her guts falling out of her." He shivered and took another sip of tea. "I'm cold," he complained, but it looked to me as though he was perspiring.

"You knew the victim?"

He shrugged. "She was a regular." His hand moved toward the morphine bottle, but I slapped it down and Miss Holmes continued her interrogation.

"Did you see anyone else? Anything suspicious?"

"No."

"How about the man, the customer who ran back into your shop. What did he see?"

"He said he saw a snake."

"A snake? He screamed and ran back in because he saw a snake?"

"A snake as big as three lions." He sighed. "This is not unusual. Many of my customers see snakes."

"Why did you go out to investigate?"

"They usually see their snakes while they are smoking or while they have the craving. Not minutes after they've left to go home."

"Did you tell the police about this customer?"

"No."

"Why not?"

He shrugged again. "They didn't ask."

"And you don't want to lose a customer by turning him in to the police."

"Losing one customer wouldn't matter. Whitechapel is a dangerous place. I lose customers every day. There are always more to take their place."

"Didn't it occur to you that he might have been the killer?"

Mr. Wu shook his head. "No. He had only just left—he didn't have time to kill anyone. And he was too scared. And he didn't have any blood splashed on him."

I finally spoke. "You know the police will want to question him. You'll have to tell them about him."

He scowled at me. "I don't know his name anyway. He is not a regular customer."

Miss Holmes spoke again. "Mr. Wu, what caused those gouges cut into the brick wall by your door?"

He blanched. "I don't know," he said.

"What do you think caused them?"

"I don't know. A knife maybe."

"What do you fear caused them?"

As Mr. Wu looked at Miss Holmes, I saw a glimmer of respect in his eyes. "What do I fear?"

"Yes."

Several moments passed, then he spoke. "When I looked at the wall and thought about the bloody body of poor Miss Sarah, I remembered a story my grandmother used to tell us, a terrible, frightening story, when I was very young."

"Yes?"

"I don't even remember the story anymore, but I remember how it ended, and how very scared I was."

"How did it end, Mr. Wu?"

"It ended with bodies all over the ground, bloody bodies, everyone dead, and three long cuts in the wall of the house."

"Three cuts?"

"Just like the three you saw on my wall. The three cuts on my wall looked exactly like the three cuts my grandmother described in her story."

"Do you remember what caused the gouges in the wall in your grandmother's story?"

"A claw. They were claw marks, Miss Holmes. The claw marks of a great monster." He began shuddering and could not seem to stop. I helped the little man to stand.

"I do not believe he has anything else to tell us," I said.

"No," she agreed thoughtfully. "Or at any rate, nothing else he would be willing to tell us. Do you have a room where he can ingest his poison? You can't contain him in a horse stall lest he set fire to the straw."

I nodded and led them to the empty, fairly clean room where I performed small animal surgeries. I gave Mr. Wu a horse blanket and a lucifer; Miss Holmes gave him the accoutrements of his vice; and we ladies watched as Mr. Wu prepared his vile decoction. When we left, taking the almost-empty morphine bottle with us, he lay curled up in the blanket, loathsome smoke trailing up from his pipe to pollute the room.

"You'd best close the door," Miss Holmes said. "You don't want that miasma to permeate the remainder of your surgery."

"He's going to freeze in there," I said, though I did close the door. I did not think the vapours from the pipe would be any detriment to my horse patients but if the cat came hunting on this side of the stable tonight, I did not want her breathing the cursed fumes.

"He won't notice the cold. You should try to stay awake for another hour or so and then go look in on him, give him another blanket perhaps. He will probably be deep in his sleep by then, which will most likely last a number of hours. You might even be able to go home to rest yourself."

"I don't think I dare," I said. "But I might go home to clean up a bit." I lived across the street. Once Mr. Wu fell asleep, I could doze here for a while and then go home to perform my ablutions and change clothes. "I'll purchase some breakfast and tea items from the bakery on my way back. You needn't stop in the morning."

She nodded. "Fine. I'll leave you then."

"Shall I walk you out? It's getting late. Are you certain the cabbie is still waiting for you?"

"Yes. He will wait as long as necessary, as will Letty. And I admit it is late, but this is a police station. You don't need to walk me out." She gathered up her things. "Claw marks. You know, those engravings in the wall could be described as claw marks, couldn't they?"

"I suppose. If there were a three-taloned creature with claws strong enough to cut through brick," I replied.

She nodded and held out her hand. "Goodnight, Miss Barquist."

I shook her hand. "Goodnight, Miss Holmes."

Not more than twenty minutes after she left, a great shriek pierced the sky and I froze, remembering other terrible screams from another terrible time. I shook off the horrific memory and ran back through the stable to look in on my newest patient. But Mr. Wu was quite asleep. The sound had erupted from yet another sad and fated denizen of this dark city. Whether the origin of the cry was man or woman, I never knew.

Chapter Two

Following a fitful and haunted sleep I left the stable in the early morning hours to go to my home and clean up, eyeing my poor bed with longing but resolutely putting the yearning for more sleep behind me. When I knocked on the bakery door the first loaves of the day had not yet been removed from the Feinmans' oven, but they had a few breads and cakes left over from the day before which they were pleased to give me.

The office was quite chilly when I arrived, and I fed the stove like a miser. If I didn't receive the quarter's income or Frank didn't come through with a bucket of coal in the next day or so I would indeed need to move my office in with old Toby.

Mr. Wu still slept, snoring deeply, content with his makeshift bed.

I received visits from several police constables that morning, curious about my prisoner. I hated thinking of Mr. Wu that way—but of course that's what he was, and it was all his own fault. If I had confidence that he would report to the coroner's jury on his own I would have left him at his own doorstep, but Miss Holmes had been quite right about that; the man could not be trusted. I comforted myself with the thought that my dog surgery prison was more comfortable than the jail would have been. Here he'd had privacy and two thick blankets—and I doubted the police would have allowed him the comfort of his pipe dreams.

The constables who visited that morning made this clear enough.

"Gawd, Maddie—it smells like an opium den in here," Police Constable Garlick said. "Don't say you've taken up the oriental curse?"

"On the plus side, keeping an opium den in the police horse stable would make our jobs much easier," PC Melman observed. "Consider the convenience when it came time to round up the usual miscreants."

I knew the proper manner in which to take this jocularity. "Boys, you know you can always depend on me to aid you in any way I can," I said. "Why, now I'm even housing your prisoners, just to lighten your load."

"And we do appreciate your taking on that burden," PC Garlick said. Mr. Wu's cacophonous snores filled the air with their steady pulse, accompanied now by old Toby's early morning "I'm ready for breakfast" snort, rising above the snores like an aria descant over the chorus.

"You might have considered the horses' comfort before you decided to expand your business functions," Constable Melman said. "It's a wonder they obtained any sleep at all, with that hideous noise blasting through the place all night."

Forget the horses—it was a wonder I had managed any sleep at all, but I wasn't going to mention that subject. I knew that what Constables Garlick and Melman really wanted to know was: where had I slept last night? They hadn't quite the nerve to ask me such a presumptuous and indelicate question but would have no qualms about thoroughly parsing the topic if I raised it myself. I was determined to avoid the crude teasing that would ensue if they knew the truth.

Fortunately, the coroner's jury announced they were ready for Mr. Wu that morning. I had fed my two horse patients and prepared a simple breakfast for my human prisoner when Frank Froest appeared and obliged me by providing Mr. Wu with wash water and escorting him out to the facilities. As they were about to leave, I saw Mr. Wu dig determinedly through his pockets. He finally managed to remove a tiny ball of filth, blithely using a fingernail to mash it onto a piece of bread-and-jam. He shoved the nasty bite into his mouth, winked at me, and followed Frank out the door to perform his duty as a citizen.

I sputtered with anger. I hadn't needed to waste my precious morphine on Mr. Wu after all. He'd brought his own drug supply with him, jumbled in the detritus of his clothing.

The morning chill receded with three pieces of the precious black bitumen Frank had delivered in a large coal bucket. I would return to my parsimony tomorrow; today I would allow myself warmth in exchange for my lack of sleep. The day proceeded as usual, and I only twice fell into a dozen at my desk.

*****

Because of those brief naps, I felt alert enough to attend a highly-anticipated public lecture that evening sponsored by the Fabian Society, the socialist debating group and offspring of the Fellowship of the New Life, a pacifist organization of which I am a member.

Now, I do not regularly attend meetings of the Fellowship, although certainly I support the majority of their tenets. Improving our society by living a life of unselfishness, love and wisdom seems to me a most marvellous ideal. But some of the Fellowship of the New Life's concepts are naive. They believe that the road to a social Eden is through the development of one's own intelligence. I do not believe that pure intelligence will lead to an improved society. My own father, the most brilliant man I ever knew, was also the evillest.

I'm also somewhat hesitant with the Fellowship's focus on enlightened sexual expression. I always find myself discomfited to be one of the few women in a room full of men conversing about radical sexual endeavours. Consequently, my attendance at such meetings had fallen of late.

However, I do usually attend the public lectures organized by the Fellowship's sister group, the Fabian Society. The scheduled event this night was a public lecture by a guest speaker, the Chinese Minister to Britain, Guo Jiegang, on Britain's moral responsibility to end the coercive opium trade, the grossest imaginable example of capitalism's exploitation of the common man. I had anticipated this event all month but felt more than a bit hypocritical now, given my activities of the previous thirty-six hours.

An omnibus carried me most of the way to the lecture hall where I was discomfited to be embraced at the door by Mr. Havelock Ellis, one of the Fellowship members who could always be depended upon to bring up the sex topic at meetings.

"My dearest Maddie, how are you?" he said, wrapping his arms around me. He stood taller even than me, a large man, and his embrace thrust me into a memory of when I was small, and my Papa took me into his arms. Fighting off the nausea, I suffered the man's attentions for a polite moment then pushed him firmly away. I could hardly take true offense at his notice, since his manner toward all of his friends was similarly affectionate, whether women or men.

"I am looking forward to the lecture, Mr. Ellis," I said, forcing a weak smile to my lips and moving past him to join the small queue entering the lecture hall. I confess I have more than once been chastised for excessive prudery.

"Miss Barquist, how good to see you here!" I turned from my place on the stairs to see my new acquaintance Miss Holmes in the vestibule. This nonplussed me; I would not have expected such a respectable and fashionable young lady to be a friend to the socialist movement—although now that I thought about it, only a social reformer would choose to work in the East End as she did. Miss Holmes was accompanied by a familiar fellow Fabian, Ramsay MacDonald, private secretary to a Liberal politician and vocal proponent of Scottish home rule. I remained unconvinced by Mr. MacDonald's frequently expressed arguments that the anglicisation of Scotland was harmful to its people and culture but do admit I always enjoyed listening to his passionate entreaties on his homeland's behalf.

Miss Holmes took my arm and led me up the rest of the stairs to the meeting room. Mr. MacDonald nodded hurriedly to Mr. Ellis and to another society member, Mr. George Bernard Shaw, before catching us up.

"Astraia, how do you know our Miss Barquist?" Mr. MacDonald asked politely, his eyes searching the room to find a place where we could sit together near the speaker. Perhaps two dozen people milled around, sitting and confabulating, with chairs set out for about thrice that many.

"We met yesterday at the library," Miss Holmes said sweetly, making full use of her girlish voice and long lashes. Mr. MacDonald momentarily paused from his search to stare at her, entranced.

"There are three seats in the second row, near that fern," I said. I was taller than Mr. MacDonald so better equipped to scout out the room. He nodded and rushed off to claim our places.

Miss Holmes and I sauntered more slowly, as befitted ladies.

"Has Mr. Wu been called to testify to the coroner's jury yet?" she asked. We did not discuss the white lie she told to Mr. MacDonald. Clearly, she intended to keep her adventure secret from her admirer.

I said that he had, adding that constables had gone looking for him later at his place of business to follow up on some information but had been unable to track him down.

"He's scarpered," Miss Holmes said.

"I believe so, yes," I said as we reached our chairs.

"Who's scarpered?" Mr. MacDonald asked, amused at Miss Holmes's use of street can't.

"Drunk Willie," Miss Holmes said, and proceeded to tell us an amusing and possibly entirely fallacious story about one of her library customers, bringing the tall tale to a close when our host for the evening moved to the front of the room to introduce the event's guest speakers.

"My dear friends, the Fabian Society welcomes you all to tonight's public lecture and debate on the topic '*British Imperialism, the Opium Trade and the Native Races of India and China: The Contrasting Interests of the Financial and the Moral Good*'. I am Frank Podmore, tonight's debate facilitator. We will begin this evening with a lecture by the distinguished Chinese Envoy, Guo Jiegang. Mr. Guo will speak on the despair of the native people of China, and the horror behind the two wars they fought with Mother Britain in their attempt to end the opium trade to their country. Following Mr. Guo's remarks will be a debate between Sir Joseph Pease, president of the Anglo-Oriental Society for the Suppression of the Opium Trade, and Sir William Forrester Clydon, retired Lieutenant Governor of the Punjab and current board member of the British East India Company. Sir William will represent the pro-trade side and Sir Joseph the anti-trade. But first we'll hear from Mr. Guo, the Chinese envoy."

The audience applauded as Mr. Podmore walked back to his seat and two Chinese gentlemen moved toward the podium at the front of the room.

The older fellow, a man dressed in the ornate long silk robe and trouser garb traditional to his culture, his feet in silk slippers and a long grey pigtail flowing down his back, a tiny silk cap on his head, walked in a slow, distinguished manner to stand at the raised podium. His companion, dressed in sombre British clothing with close-cropped hair and mutton chops, stood a foot or so to the older man's side, his head bowed. The gentleman at the podium began to speak. In Chinese.

After a few minutes of this the audience began to grow restless. The British are a very polite people, but even we are strained to sit quietly through a lecture in a foreign tongue.

Fortunately, the older gentleman eventually halted his incomprehensible words and the younger man took his turn.

"Ladies and Gentlemen, the Honourable Ambassador Guo is very grateful for the honour of addressing you this evening. I am his aide, Mr. Hong, and I am pleased to be permitted to translate the gracious ambassador's words into English for you. First, he wishes to express his gratitude to the Fabian Society for sponsoring this distinguished evening, and for inviting him to express his opinion about the coercive, greedy and despicable opium trade destroying our country. Further, he passes on his good will toward the two debaters, both Sir William and Sir Joseph, and his confidence that by the end of the evening all here will be convinced of the rightness of our feelings on this matter."

Mr. Hong went on translating similar polite nothings for a while, but eventually the Chinese envoy provided a few instructive comments on the evening's topic. To encapsulate: British India's major crop is opium, which Europe does not want. China produces many things that Europe desires, especially tea, silk and porcelain, but the only thing Europe possesses that China wants in return is payment in silver for its goods. And rather than pay in good silver for these marvellous things, England floods China with India's opium—because China's people, to its government's horror, are quite addicted to the monstrous poison. And whenever China objects, England sends out war ships to protect the opium traders of the British East India Company.

Mr. Guo and Mr. Hong spoke of these atrocities for almost two hours, followed by the debate between Sir William and Sir Joseph. Happily, Mr. Podmore, the debate facilitator, recognized that everyone in the audience was emotionally enervated after hearing the envoy's tragic tale of a half-century of opium wars, so he kept the following lively discussion between the two Englishmen blessedly short.

Sir Joseph Pease of the anti-trade side did not address the extraordinary economics driving the thing, which Minister Guo had emphasized. But this was a room full of socialists, and one thing we socialists all knew: whenever there are powerful people trying to foist their will upon weaker persons, you don't need to look very deep to find the capitalistic motivation. Instead, Sir Joseph emphasized the immorality of China's opium bondage by England. He brought several members of the audience to tears with his argument that Britain's brutal subjugation of the Chinese people into drug slavery was ignoble and unchristian.

Sir William Forrester Clydon, the representative from the East India Company, twisted the moral argument on its ear. He said that as a Christian nation it was Britain's duty to insist upon trade with China for the good of Chinese souls, since it was only due to the presence of armed European trade delegations that Christian missionaries had been able to enter the country to spread the Gospel to ignorant heathen desperate to hear the Word of the Lord. Expecting British ships to kowtow to the will of the emperor of China was a slap to the sovereignty of the British Crown. And similar such arguments intended to arouse the nationalistic pride that roosts within every Briton's breast.

Mr. Podmore allowed Sir William the closing statement. Sir William spoke earnestly to the audience: "Ladies and Gentlemen, I know you are all good Christian people, and I know the sad stories you've heard tonight from Minister Guo and from my friend Sir Joseph about families suffering the burden of drug addiction and children running naked and hungry through the streets of Hong Kong and so forth have stirred your compassion, which is only right. But let us look at the issue from the other side—what about the children of India? The Indian economy depends upon the opium trade— Indian children would starve without it. Opium use is a decision each Chinese man makes of his own free will—and if he sometimes chooses to ingest too much, is that the fault of the honest opium trader? Is the captain of a trading vessel any more responsible for an opium addict's excesses than a farmer is for the glutton who consumes too much of the food he grows, or a vintner is for the person who develops gout from drinking too much of the wine he produces?"

As Sir William spoke, the Chinese envoy Mr. Guo became increasingly agitated, his face purpling with rage. Clearly, he did not really need Mr. Hong to translate the English language into Chinese in order for him to understand.

Sir William continued to expound his argument. "Forbidding the Chinese man access to opium is not the way to stop him from overindulgence. If you wish him to moderate his habits you should instead give him access to Bibles and missionaries and teach him Christian values. It is not the honest opium trader who's to blame for the opium problem in China. The true fault lies with heathen Chinese decadence."

Sir William pounded his walking stick on the ground to emphasize his words. I had just a moment to admire the gold dragon handle on his black lacquered cane before the venerable Chinese Minister to Britain stood up from his seat with a growl and lunged at the retired Lieutenant Governor of the Punjab.

The surprisingly spry Mr. Guo began the attack with a forceful and exciting kick to Sir William's abdomen. It seemed unlikely Sir William experienced much pain, since the envoy wore cloth slippers and Sir William's girth provided an excess of padding, but the East India Company board member began defending himself forcefully anyway by striking at the Chinese gentleman's shoulder with his cane. I was grateful we had found seats near the front of the room as I had never before had opportunity to witness two elderly gentlemen engaging in fisticuffs.

But the affray terminated before any significant blows found their target. Ramsay MacDonald leaped up from his seat beside Miss Holmes to rush toward the two men. Mr. Hong and Sir Joseph Pease held the Chinese Minister in a firm but respectful grip as Mr. MacDonald and Mr. Podmore pulled Sir William and his frantic cane away from the Chinese man's angry feet.

Being separated did not end the fight, however. Mr. Guo began yelling at Sir William in harsh-sounding Chinese and Sir William responded by screaming back at him in the same language. Mr. Hong tried to intercede, but the two older gentlemen both ignored him and continued their incomprehensible vociferations.

"I wonder how many years they've known each other," Miss Holmes said calmly.

A voice rose from the back of the room. "This fracas is not at all an appropriate sight for the gentler sex. Ladies, I urge you to wait in the vestibule while we work to resolve this unfortunate contretemps."

"What? You think they're previously acquainted?" I responded to Miss Holmes, ignoring Mr. Ellis's imprecations to the ladies to leave the lecture hall. However, the women sitting in front of us obediently left, which much improved our view of the proceedings. Honestly, the way men decide what is appropriate for women and what is not quite boggles the mind. Havelock Ellis was perfectly comfortable discussing the Kama Sutra in mixed company but seemed terrified tonight that the ladies might witness a little spilt blood.

"I'm convinced they're quite well acquainted," Miss Holmes said. "Mr. Guo's response seems excessive for a stranger. I expect he's argued with Sir William on this subject many times and finally decided he's had enough."

"Perhaps," I said. I couldn't understand a word the two men were shouting at each other but had to admit the intensity of their communication did seem unusual for noble gentlemen who had previously been unacquainted.

"And Sir William has obviously spent many years in China. Mandarin is not an easy language in which to gain fluency. Did you see the cane he carries, with the gold dragon handle? It's most certainly from China."

"Well, he is a trader," I said.

"He never said so," she said. "He admits to having spent considerable time in India of course, and he sits on the board of the East India Company, but he did not say one word this evening to indicate he had ever personally travelled to China or even held Chinese trade investments."

I had to admit the truth of this. "You think they knew each other back in China?"

"I expect so. Mr. Guo must have at least a modicum of familiarity with British ways in order to have been selected by his government to represent them as envoy. And Sir William must be speaking in a Mandarin dialect the Minister can easily understand, since they seem to be having no difficulty whatsoever in communicating their thoughts to one another."

I observed the two wildly screaming men for a few moments. "I concur. I detect no language constraints at all."

A man's tweed-covered breast suddenly obstructed my view of the altercation. Mr. George Bernard Shaw loomed over us to add his entreaties to those of Mr. Ellis that we leave the room lest we witness something unseemly. "The test of a man or woman's breeding is how they behave in a quarrel," he said.

Mr. Shaw can be a delightful man, quite droll in fact, when he's not being a pompous busybody such as now.

"I do hope you are not expressing criticism of Miss Barquist or myself, Mr. Shaw," Miss Holmes said, wielding her long eyelashes like a duelling saber. "We are not quarrelling. We are simply waiting for our friend Mr. MacDonald to escort us home. He would not like us to leave without his protection." She followed her eyelash thrust with a dazzling smile riposte.

"No, of course I intended no criticism of you ladies," Mr. Shaw said, gazing soulfully into Miss Holmes's eyes, disabled by a fencer so masterful he was unaware of having been bested.

"Indeed, we must wait right here for Mr. MacDonald," I said, attempting my own eyelash manoeuvres, but I was the merest amateur and the man did not seem pierced in the slightest by my blunt blades.

The three of us glanced over at the elderly combatants, now limp and gasping for air. Unaccustomed as they were at their age to such violent exertions, each was now quiescent in response to the imprecations of the men holding them back and the insistent urgings of their own bodies for respiration.

Now able to relax a bit, Mr. MacDonald looked into the audience and nodded to us, his primary attention focused on simply holding the gasping Sir William erect.

"You needn't worry about us anymore, Mr. Shaw," Miss Holmes said to the tall man leaning solicitously over her chair. "As you can see, the altercation has abated, and Mr. MacDonald will return to us directly. But it was dear of you to be concerned about our welfare."

She fluttered her eyelashes so outrageously I thought for certain Mr. Shaw would realize she was pulling a jape, but no such thing—this man, one of the most astute men I've ever met, gave her a smile of such ignorant adoring condescension it appeared for a moment as though he might deign to pat her on the head like a trained puppy or beloved child. And then, to my astonishment, she held her hand up to him to bid him farewell—and he kissed the back of it before strolling away!

I re-evaluated my previous opinion of her. Miss Holmes was no flighty society miss.

Astraia Holmes was a very dangerous woman.

"I would like to discuss this matter with you further," Miss Holmes said to me. "I am not scheduled at the library tomorrow. Are you able to get away from work for a short while, perhaps for luncheon or tea?"

I was not enamoured with the idea of pursuing an acquaintance with this bold young lady but found myself agreeing out of sheer curiosity. "If there are no urgent surgeries, I can usually take a meal break. What time would you prefer?"

Ramsay MacDonald returned to us, solicitous and apologetic for having inflicted such an unconscionable sight upon us as two old men flailing at one other.

"My dear Astraia, I am so very sorry to have deserted you at such a time," he said attentively, taking her hands in his. "Oh, and you too, Miss Barquist."

"Do not concern yourself," I said absently, watching Mr. Hong and Sir Joseph escort Mr. Guo out of the room while the exhausted Sir William sat collapsed on a chair, sipping at a flask Mr. Podmore held to his lips. Now that the affray had ended, numerous members of the audience approached both groups of men, presumably interested in acquiring details about the recent contretemps. Mr. Hong and Sir Joseph waved curious persons away from conversation with the envoy and soon escaped through a side door, but Sir William welcomed one and all to heed him declaim on the base brutality inherent in the Chinese temperament.

"No apologies needed, James. I must confess I found it most exciting!" Miss Holmes said with a girlish giggle, then looked down at her lap, abashed.

I stared at her in awe. Even Mr. MacDonald's closest friends never called him by his Christian name, choosing instead the less familiar "Ramsay".

"Well, even still I am sorry you had to experience it," Mr. MacDonald said, and he actually patted her hand. "I can only assure you that most Fabian lectures do not include demonstrations of fisticuffs. Don't you agree, Miss Barquist?"

"Oh, most assuredly," I said. "The debates can sometimes get loud, but this is the first true brawl I've been witness to."

"I found the disputation most enlightening," Miss Holmes said. "In fact, Miss Barquist and I just made arrangements to meet at the St. Sabrina Tea Shop tomorrow at three o'clock, to further discuss the matter." She looked at me with an insipid smile, a perfect illustration of the old chestnut regarding oral butter melting.

"Um, yes, I'm looking forward to it," I said, running through my head the changes I'd need to make in my schedule in order to attend an afternoon appointment at an establishment at least two miles from the police station. I'd have to cancel my standing tea date in the police stable with PC Froest, for one. Well, he'd cancelled on me on more than one occasion; in fact, come to think of it, he missed more days than he attended. Perhaps it would be a good thing for him if for once I was the one to provide the rebuff.

Of course, I would have rethought that decision if I'd known it would result in my encountering my nemesis, not to mention being run over by a horse.

Chapter Three

"Please sit, my dear Miss Barquist," Miss Holmes said when we met the next day, waving me to the seat in front of her and pouring me a cup of tea. "You must be quite unnerved after your mad rush to get here and the unfortunate accident you had with a vegetable dray."

Her perspicacity stunned. "Yes, but how do you know about all that?"

Miss Holmes shrugged. "I can tell you've been rushing because although you've changed from your work attire to a modest dress and styled your hair in a manner similar to last night, your coiffeur is terribly mussed, you appear to have lost the hat I'm confident you must have been wearing at the beginning of your journey, and you're puffing as though you've been hurrying for an extensive time. Really, you seem most distracted; almost, one could say, distressed. Please, do take a sip of tea and calm yourself."

Miss Holmes had selected a corner table of the St. Sabrina Tea Shop. She drank daintily at a cup of oolong, a plate of buttered teacakes in front of her. A lovely lavender day dress skimmed her slim form, topped by a matching hat enhanced with swirling ostrich feathers. Her Titian hair and porcelain skin glowed almost ethereal against the lavender hue of her costume. Her very white gloves remained pristine even as they held a cup of tea—a talent I must confess I've never attained, being unhappily inclined to regular spillage.

I'm not sure I've ever owned a pair of gloves quite that clean, even freshly purchased. I placed my handbag—much plainer and larger than her dainty lavender embroidered reticule—on the third seat of our table and obediently sipped at the brew she had poured for me, forcing myself to concentrate on the immediate task and not spill any tea on my person or trembling hands. The oolong odour had tempted me from the moment of my entrance into the establishment, even though now I knew the horror of its antecedents; I was both refreshed and repelled as the delicious evil liquid slid down my throat. She'd added just a touch of milk and sugar, exactly as I like it. Her own was so adulterated with milk the colour almost matched her pristine gloves.

She continued. "I can tell by the state of your frock that you had an accident with a load of vegetables. Fresh tomato and turnip residue fleck your skirt."

"Oh, no!" I set my cup with care down on its saucer before examining the skirt of my dress, my best day dress. Leaving work, I had first run from the stable to my lodgings to change, having no desire to appear in a respectable lady's tea establishment in my customary feculent work clothing. I wanted to look decent. Last night I had even soaked my fingernails in vinegar.

"Do not fret yourself," she said. "It's only spattered in a few places, and I'm sure you'll be able to brush the worst of it out. The red of the tomato is hardly noticeable against that...brown shade you're wearing." She paused as though she'd tried and utterly failed to find a pleasant descriptor for the colour of my dress. I would have said "drab" or "mud" best characterized the hue. Or perhaps "pale manure".

40

"But how do you know it was a cart I ran into, rather than a vegetable stand?" I asked, my voice hardly quavering at all despite the shock I'd had on the street which had caused my inattentiveness to such things as vegetable carts and the horses that pulled them.

"The fact is made clear in two ways. First, there are no vegetable stands between here and the police station. However, many drays use this road, and this is the time of day when the old produce left unsold in the morning market is transported for sale to animal feed lots. And second, your left shoe bears a distinct horseshoe imprint across the top, as though a horse has trodden upon it, an enhancement which I'm quite certain was lacking in those same shoes when you wore them last night. Also, you are limping." She sipped delicately at her tea. "Are you sure you're quite fit? You have probably broken some toes."

I shrugged. I had other troubles to think about. This was not the first time a horse had stepped on me. It would not be the last. Though this one hurt more than usual. "Probably," I agreed. "But I must confess I am quite impressed by the strength of your perspicacity." I hoped her perceptiveness was limited to the horse cart.

"It's a habit, honed from years of playing a silly parlour game at home when I was a child," she said dismissively. "My brothers and I called it Observation and Deduction."

"Oh, you have brothers?"

"Yes, two—Mykie and Sherlie. They both live here in London."

"How wonderful for you!" I said. I have no family.

"In some ways, perhaps. But they're both the worst sort of nosey Parkers; I do my best to avoid them as much as possible. I might encounter Mykie this afternoon if I am not careful to avoid doing so."

41

I allowed myself a bite of current teacake as Miss Holmes refilled my cup with the immoral brew. Now that I was able to relax, now that the pounding of my heart in my ears had waned, I could clearly feel an insistent throb in my foot. I'd have to wrap it up tightly tonight or I would no doubt be unable to squeeze a shoe upon it on the morrow. I lifted a hand to my mussed hair and sighed. So vexatious. Now I must needs buy another hat. I'd given mine to an urchin on the street after the accident, deeming it unwearable in respectable society once the dray horse had taken a sizeable bite out of it.

Hats. I must be feeling better if I could now worry about hats. Thank God for tea.

"Have you seen today's papers?" Miss Holmes asked.

"No, not yet." Usually PC Froest brought the newspapers over for my perusal and fire stove at the end of his shift, but I would miss him today.

She handed me a copy of one of the local rags, folded to display a particular article. I read obediently.

"Oh, my goodness," I said, much struck.

"Indeed."

A witness had come forward in the matter of the prostitute's murder. He claimed to have seen an enormous snake-like creature in the vicinity during the time of the tragedy. The police dismissed his story as nonsense, and assured the public there was nothing of which to be frightened. An illustration of a huge snake looming over a terrified woman accompanied the news item.

"What do you make of it?" I asked. My mind was spinning with horrific possibilities.

"Nothing, yet," she said. "There is as yet not enough information even to invite speculation. But it is interesting, is it not?"

I nodded. 'Interesting' wasn't the half of it. "Mr. Wu must be greatly agitated. He will surely remain in seclusion after this." Tomorrow I would walk down to the docks and ask Little Joey for introduction to another morphine supplier. After I looked into a few other things. Most particularly, the unwelcome return of Bert Cranston, Papa's henchman in evil, whom much to my horror I had seen on the street today after months of decampment. It was my shock at seeing him that had caused me to flounder directly in front of a vegetable cart and the surly horse pulling it.

We consumed our tea in silence for a few moments, each deep in our own thoughts. I noticed her gloves remained free of butter stains, even though she ate quite as many of the teacakes as I did myself.

"What did you think of the debate?" she asked.

It took me a moment, but then I remembered. The debate. Last night. Before I knew the monster's partner was back. "I've decided to join the Anglo-Oriental Society for the Suppression of the Opium Trade," I said, recalling my outrage from the night before. "I'm quite horrified that Britain should participate in the sort of vile, wicked things we heard tell of last night." I took another sip of vile, wicked ambrosia. But at least I felt guilty about it.

"I agree," she said. "I joined myself, this morning. There's a meeting later in the month; perhaps we could attend together?"

I nodded absently, and we discussed the event locale and possible transportation options.

"I must say I admire Mr. Guo," she said. "So impassioned, so determined to do everything in his power to cleanse his country of that dreadful poison."

"Indeed. And I was also impressed by Mr. Hong. Such a respectable-looking gentleman in his attire and bearing."

"Quite British in his appearance, in fact," she agreed. "And handsome too, do you not think?"

I nodded. I have always preferred men of short stature.

"Well, I must leave now," Miss Holmes said. "I'm obliged to deliver some books on natural theology to my brother at his club. Would you like a ride home?"

I shook my head in the negative. "No, I—" I stood, and then quickly fell back into my seat. My foot was quite uncooperative, refusing entirely to support my effort to stand.

I revised my response to her query. "Yes, thank you; I would appreciate a ride, as there are no omnibuses along my route. It's quite a distance back to the stable, and I confess my foot has begun to throb a bit," I said, huffing as I heaved myself back up, balancing most of my weight on my right foot and the back of my chair.

Miss Holmes nodded and waved to a patron sitting in the farthest corner of the room. The woman scuttled over and I recognized Miss Holmes's companion Letty, an average-sized woman of middle years and unremarkable appearance.

"Letty, can you please tell John I am ready to leave and ask him to come in to assist Miss Barquist into the carriage? She has hurt her foot."

Letty bustled out to do Miss Holmes's bidding, returning a few minutes later with a man I recognized as Miss Holmes's cabbie friend from the other night. Together the three of them assisted me and we managed to heave my person into an old carriage parked nearby. I would normally have eschewed such dramatics, but in this particular instance I believe I would have passed out had the option not been offered.

I was severely disappointed with my foot. It had successfully conveyed me from the accident to the tearoom, a good three streets away, with minimal outrage; but evidently had now decided to be recalcitrant regarding my mobility requirements.

Miss Holmes sat beside me in the carriage, very kindly suggesting that I rest my churlish foot on the opposite seat beside Letty. The seating accommodations in the old carriage were more expansive than those of the cab the other night, for which I was quite grateful. I asked Miss Holmes how it came about that her coachman was also her occasional cabbie.

"John's family has been with us for many years, and when I moved into our family home here in town after our parents died, he and his sister Letty accompanied me. My brothers insisted upon it, just as they insist that Letty attend me everywhere I go even though I'm now six-and-twenty, gainfully employed and quite able to make do on my own. But they can compel me because they own the house and control my meagre inheritance and refuse to allow me access to either if I don't acquiesce to their wishes. Standing guard over me is hardly a taxing occupation. John was pining from boredom, so Mykie bought him an old hansom so that he can augment his income if he wishes while I'm at work. I'm not entirely satisfied with this, because sometimes when I particularly desire John to take me somewhere I'll find that he and his cab are off running errands for Sherlie, which can be quite aggravating. I had to tell John last night to be prepared to drive me today, otherwise he'd no doubt be gadding about collecting fares or traipsing around for Sherlie even now."

"John and Letty are your family retainers?"

"Some would call them so. I prefer to think of them as my jailers."

Letty rolled her eyes, the first spark of human expression I ever saw in her, but she made no comment.

I smiled at Miss Holmes's grumpy words. Now she sounded like the flighty society miss I had assumed her to be at our first meeting.

"We're going to drop some books off for Mykie at his club first, and then we will determine what to do with you," Miss Holmes said.

"What sort of books?" I asked, feigning polite interest. I really could not have cared less, my foot now pounding at me for full attention.

"He sent his man over to the library yesterday morning for some books on natural theology. I had no time to look them up for him then-and-there, as he seemed to expect me to do, as though I would put all of the rest of my work aside just to do him a favour, but I did agree to deliver the requested volumes to his club this afternoon."

"Your brother is a theologian?"

"No, my brother is a notoriously indolent bastard who more or less directs the British government from his club. He's agnostic but can argue any side required in any debate. No doubt he wants the books to substantiate his chosen argument in some philosophical discussion."

Letty sniffed in disapprobation at Miss Holmes's use of the derogatory term "bastard" in reference to her own brother, but Miss Holmes ignored her.

My new friend spent the rest of the trip to her brother Mykie's club railing against the ignominies pelted upon her by her troublous siblings, but I confess I heard little of it, my attention instead focused on my own worries and the increasing discomfort of my extremity. I wanted nothing more out of life than to remove my shoe, down some whisky, go to sleep and wake up tomorrow healthy and healed—and living again in a world empty of my nemesis, Hubert "Jolly Bert" Cranston.

But I doubted such a pleasant outcome to this adventure. As it was, I knew I'd need to slice the shoe off my foot, due to extreme swelling. Which would hurt. And my father's scalpels and other surgical tools were at the veterinary stable. I did not know if Papa's razor, which I did have at home, was sufficiently sharp to slice through my leather shoe, nor was I confident that in my current state I could wield the implement with sufficient finesse so as not to further injure myself. Furthermore, besides being obliged to buy a new hat to replace the one the horse ate, once my shoe was destroyed, I would need to buy new foot apparel as well, which I could ill-afford.

And the most significant worry of all: now I knew for a fact that Bert Cranston had returned to town, despite the anonymous notes I had sent to him threatening to disclose his heinous connection to Jack the Ripper. For a year he had acquiesced to my unnamed insistence that he remove himself from London, but now he had returned. I would have to take more forceful action.

But how could I, with this blasted foot—no doubt broken, so painful as it was. To add to my misery, this carriage was old and the interminable ride over the cobblestoned streets bumpy. The seat cushion upon which my foot reposed was not well padded.

Now my head hurt too. My eyes felt moist, but I blinked the annoyance away.

The carriage finally stopped in front of a nondescript building a long way from my home and my bed. Miss Holmes spoke for a few moments to John; I could see through the small window the burden of books held in his arms as he listened to his mistress's instructions. He entered the place, returning several minutes later carrying two new items: a large, soft pillow, which Letty placed with care and solicitude beneath my foot; and a glass of golden liquid, which Miss Holmes handed to me.

"Drink this," she said.

I sipped and almost sputtered, so surprised was I to be imbibing that about which I had yearned this last hour: strong whisky, of a much higher quality than I had ever before tasted. Even Papa in the good years had never had such excellent stuff.

"Oh, thank you," I murmured, the tears I had prohibited from appearing for the last hour now filling my eyes. I sniffed, sipped, and then felt a cloth shoved into my hand, a clean, simple handkerchief—no embroidery, no lace, just good strong linen. I glanced up and saw Letty closing her reticule.

"Thank you," I murmured again, then loudly utilized the borrowed accoutrement in its intended purpose. She nodded, saying not a word.

"You cannot stay in your own home tonight," Miss Holmes decided.

I took another sip. Strong spirits truly did help. "I beg your pardon?"

"You will not be able to climb the steps to your flat. We could help you do so this evening of course, but what if you need to procure food, or—forgive my indelicacy—use the convenience? I am correct that you have no servants to attend to your needs, am I not?"

I couldn't muster the strength to ask how she knew I lived in a room all alone rather than in a lodging house with many others. "No, there's no one to help me," I admitted. The whisky glass was halfway empty now. I mourned its coming demise, and committed myself to smaller, slower sips.

"You are falling asleep. Do you have a dog or bird or any other animal or human dependent upon whom you must attend tonight?"

Juno was a stable cat, responsible for her own needs though she might be annoyed if I missed teatime. "No," I said. "I have no one." Used to, but then I killed him.

"Fine. Finish up your drink and try to sleep. I instructed a couple of drops of laudanum be added to your whisky, so you should experience no difficulty in that regard."

She had drugged me? I stirred in foggy indignation, but really, I was just too tired and tormented to advance much agitation. I obediently downed the rest of the decoction and settled into a restless sleep, one filled with terrible nightmares, true, but I was more than familiar with those. A part of me knew I was in great pain, but in my drug-induced hallucinations I confused the agony in my foot with the ever-present pain in my heart, so all-in-all I do not complain about Miss Holmes's imperious decision to kidnap me.

I was only vaguely aware of the trip up strange stairs, supported by an abundance of hands and arms draped about my person. The bed into which they placed me was soft as a cloud and as sweet smelling as an angel's breath, so if I had awoken in heaven I would not have been surprised; however I was awakened instead by hellish agony when some vicious person began wrenching my poor foot into untenable positions.

I screamed, and my torturer ceased her perverse exertions.

"Letty, when John returns with the doctor, please tell him we need him to bring a variety of sharp cutting implements. I tried my gentlest to remove the shoe intact but unfortunately we'll have to cut it off instead."

I groaned. My head was lifted and after more ambrosial liquid passed my lips I fell back to sleep.

*****

Many hours later sharp, stabbing sunlight pierced my retinas. My head throbbed with an ache as great as the pain pounding in my heavy foot.

Sunlight? Heavy foot? I flipped the lacy coverlet off my person and stared down the length of my lower limb to the gypsum-plaster-encased appendage attached to my left ankle like a lumpy white rock stocking.

I looked around the room, a wholly alien place, too clean and too frilly. Too pink. The only familiar item in the room was my old handbag, sitting atop the chest of drawers by the doorway. On the table next to the bed rested a single periodical: *Beeton's Christmas Annual* of a couple of years past with the cover story *A Study in Scarlet* by A. Conan Doyle; also, a tumbler and pitcher of clear liquid. I realized I was thirsty but couldn't assume the drink to be unadulterated. My pounding head made it very clear I had imbibed sufficient alcohol and narcotics for the nonce.

"Halloo!" I tried to yell, but a hoarse whisper was all that I emitted. What was wrong with my voice?

Letty came in, carrying a breakfast tray covered with serving dishes. She helped me sit up, placed the tray over me and poured me a cup of hot chocolate as I enjoyed the wonderful smell of a good English breakfast. My throbbing head derided the idea of eating, but my empty stomach insisted upon it and as usual the stomach got its way.

The fork half-way to my mouth, sausage impaled upon the tines, I paused. "This food has not been drugged, has it?" I asked Letty suspiciously.

"Probably not," she said, the first words I ever heard the woman speak. I wasn't overly comforted by this response but ate up anyway.

Between bites I asked her about the new accessory surmounting my lower left extremity. She seemed surprised I didn't remember the doctor, the procedure, and most significantly the horrific minutes when they removed the shoe from my swollen foot.

"You screamed," she said. "A lot. The police came."

Hence the hoarse voice. I wouldn't be singing arias to the horses any time soon. "The police?"

"Friends of yours, apparently." She sniffed, evidently having no high opinion of persons who committed the sin of friendship with law enforcement professionals.

"How did they know I was here?"

"Your screams bothered the neighbours. The constables didn't know it was you until they saw you. But they helped us hold you down, which was useful. You were quite out of your mind."

Wonderful. Now the whole station would gossip about how my colleagues had encountered me drunk, doped up and screaming like a mad woman.

"They said to tell you they would be back to see you today, if you are up to visitors."

Now that my appetite had been appeased and my headache somewhat tamed, the throbbing in my limb gained predominance again. "Why is there a gypsum plaster cast on my foot?" I asked in my hoarse whisper. "When I've broken toes in the past, I just bound them up and wore my Papa's old work boots."

"Apparently you've not just broken toes," Letty said. "The doctor will return this morning to examine you, but he said you fractured your midfoot. He said it had to be casted;

otherwise you would have had to spend the next six weeks in bed, which Miss Astraia felt sure you wouldn't like."

No. I certainly could not spend six weeks away from work. Six days would be too long away. If no emergencies occurred one of the stable boys could come over to feed the animals and administer simple medications and bandages, as they did on my day off, but if I stayed away for more than a day or two my superiors might decide to find a permanent replacement for me. When my police friends returned today, I must convince them that I was wholly on the mend and would return to work shortly.

"Where is Miss Holmes?" I asked Letty.

"She had work to do at the library," Letty sniffed. "John will stay there with her today."

After breakfast Letty aided my efforts to perform my ablutions and other private matters which I shan't discuss here in detail but which I found most challenging and distressing under the present circumstances.

But afterwards, clean and refreshed, wearing a spotless nightshirt which probably belonged to John the coachman since it had no lace and actually fit my large frame, I felt much more the thing and thought I might be able to tolerate a visit or two, perhaps after a filling lunch. Letty spent a glorious five minutes brushing my hair and then braided it for me. I hadn't had my hair brushed by another person since I was a small child and had not realized how wonderfully luxurious such a kind service felt.

"She's a servant," Miss Holmes said dismissively when I mentioned my gratitude toward Letty that evening over a light tea. "That's what servants do."

"But she's not my servant," I said. "She didn't need to do it for me. She could have just handed me the brush to manage for myself, and I wouldn't have thought twice about it."

Miss Holmes and I were consuming our tea in my bedroom, which I now knew had been her bedroom when she was a girl and her parents still alive. I sat up in bed, my back supported by downy pillows, the same location where I had held court numerous times today visited by a physician and an assortment of colleagues from the police force including my friend PC Froest. All gentleman visits scrupulously chaperoned by Letty, of course.

"I got the name of the witness who saw a big snake creature at the murder site, from one of the police constables who visited me today," I said.

She looked at me, a thoughtful expression on her face. "Why did you do that?"

I shrugged. "I thought you might be interested," I said, taking a small bite of muffin, better even than those made by the Feinmans. My clothes had started to hang on me over the last year, but a few more days of the good food I was now receiving should begin to fill them in again. Which reminded me...

"I need some of my things," I said. "Do you think John could take Letty to my home to collect them for me?"

"Already done," she said, nodding toward a suitcase sitting on a chair near the door, which I now recognized as one which had belonged to my Mummy. It reminded me of the innocent early years of my life, when Mummy would sometimes take me out on a Sunday afternoon for ices and a magic lantern show. I kept it stored under my bed now, out of sight.

"Oh. Well, thank you," I said.

"I packed up undergarments and a couple of dresses, plus your books and a few other things I thought you might want." Her moue of distaste illustrated her opinion of my wardrobe and possessions.

"Oh. Well. Thank you," I repeated, my tone a bit frostier than before.

She walked over to the ancient shabby case and opened it, then brought a small chipped china shepherdess over to me, placing it on the nightstand doily. "You had this sitting next to your bed," she said. "I assume it belonged to your mother and thought that having it here might make you feel more at home."

I stared at my beloved little Grace, the only feminine knick-knack I owned, tears filling my eyes. After Mummy died, Papa had sold every item she and I had loved, starting with the piano and all of the china statuary that had been displayed upon it. Grace had been saved only because I hid her. "It did indeed belong to my mother," I whispered. "Thank you, Miss Holmes."

"When you go through your things, if you think of anything I missed let me know. Frankly, it was hard for me to decide what articles you might particularly prize since almost everything you own was tossed onto the floor. It's hardly onerous to at least hang your dresses on wall pegs, which you seem to have in sufficient quantity for your few garments."

I stared at her. "What are you talking about? I am not a messy person." I am very careful with my meagre possessions, keeping everything folded and in their proper drawers or hanging on their specific pegs, and always putting my laundered clothes away the moment all dampness was abated. My little room had been immaculate when I left home yesterday, other than my work clothes of that morning which I may have left tossed onto the floor for later laundering though even that was unlikely, as I have a basket I keep for that purpose.

"We all have different standards of cleanliness and so on," she continued, "but I don't know why you bother to waste your minimal floor space with that large chest of drawers when you clearly don't bother to use it."

She finally noticed my shocked face. "Or wait—are you telling me you're not the person who left all of your clothing and dishes and other personal items scattered all over?"

"No," I said, numb. There was only one person who would have torn apart my room: Hubert Cranston. And there was only one reason for it.

He must have realized I had to be the anonymous person who had sent him the threatening letters instructing him to leave town. Those letters made it clear Papa had documented his hideous butcheries. Bert was looking for Papa's journal. And who but I would have it?

She sat down next to the bed and looked into my eyes. "What is going on, Miss Barquist?"

How to tell the story without revealing the real truth?

"It was probably a thief looking for something," I hedged. "Although any thief who would think he could find anything valuable among my possessions is a poorly informed criminal."

"I concur. Not only do you not possess any fencible goods—a deduction I make by the fact that you show no concern that thieves may have absconded with priceless treasure—you're also an employee of the Metropolitan Police," she said. "Somehow I don't think any of our local miscreants would be that ill-advised."

I decided to tell part of the truth. "I don't know for a fact what happened, but I can guess," I said. "My father died a year ago. He had a drinking chum, a man who owned a local pub named Hubert Cranston. Very jolly fellow—in fact he's known in the neighbourhood as Jolly Bert."

"*Jolly Bert.*" She looked thoughtful.

"Yes. After my father died, Bert began to badger me about some journal he said Papa kept. I believe he feared my father may have documented some unsavoury things about him. I told him I knew nothing about it. But he wouldn't let up, until one day he just vanished from town. I haven't heard from him in over nine months. I did notice him on the street yesterday, so it appears he's returned. He's the only person who has ever expressed any interest in anything I might possibly possess."

"A man named Bert was in your veterinary surgery today," Miss Holmes said. "He looked the jolly type, though he wasn't smiling at the time."

"Really?"

"Hmm. A bobby escorted me in there to see if there might be items that you would wish to have brought to you here. We found a man already there, clawing through that old cabinet where you keep your Papa's pipe. PC Froest took umbrage at first, but when the man turned around the constable addressed him as Bert and seemed to think it perfectly normal that he be there."

"When Papa was the police horse doctor, Bert was there all the time. Frank probably didn't think anything about it, seeing him there, an old family friend."

"Do you think your Papa's journal might be in that cabinet?"

"Perhaps," I said. "But I went through all of Papa's things most carefully when he died."

She didn't respond, just continued to look at me.

"If it was there, I hope Jolly Bert found it," I said. "Anything to keep him away from me. As I said, he's not a nice man."

"I don't believe he found it," she said. "He was frowning when he left. But he seemed to know you wouldn't be working in your surgery today."

56

"Well, he has a lot of friends on the force," I said. "They patronize his pub. My accident has no doubt been a topic of conversation in the yard." Probably the main topic since last night, when police constables had to hold me down while I screamed. "Did you go to the surgery before you visited my room, or afterwards?"

"Before. That is how I found out where you live—PC Froest told me. And we will assume Jolly Bert searched your home for the journal before trying your office, since your room was torn apart when I got there, and I left the police premises soon after he did."

"Hmm."

"Well... are you going to report your break-in to your friends at H Division?" she asked.

I sighed. "Probably not," I said. I was causing them enough trouble just by missing work. "Nothing of import could have been stolen since, as you noted, I have nothing valuable to steal. And they probably wouldn't believe me anyway about the intruder being Hubert Cranston." I didn't want policemen investigating the relationship between me, my father and Jolly Bert.

"What are you going to do about Jolly Bert's excessive interest in your possessions?"

"I'll have to think about that for a while," I said. "By the way, how did you get into my room? I always lock the door."

"The door was open," she said. "I expect Mr. Cranston picked the lock. But I wasn't to know that in advance, of course. I forgot to check your bag for a key but always carry my own lockpicks with me; I was glad to not have to use them though, since PC Froest was with me and might have disapproved. He used a skeleton key to lock up when we left."

Bert knew where I lived. He was able to pick the lock to my room. He had put his nasty hands on my unmentionables.

I looked at the suitcase and wondered how I could bring myself to wear those items of apparel again.

"Please, tell me about the witness who saw the giant serpent thing near where the prostitute was murdered," she said.

I shared the information my friends from the force had given me today. We discussed visiting the witness—Mr. Gerard Harris, a West End banking agent who said he had gone for a walk and got lost in the winding alleys of Whitechapel. It's fascinating how often respectable people become lost far from their home neighbourhoods, near gin dives and opium dens.

But his very respectability caused the bobby he contacted to pay attention to his statement, at least enough to write down his name. Evidently several other people had also seen a large serpent of some kind and told various constables, but in each instance the witness was a disreputable denizen and each constable had failed to make notes or keep names, due to the blatant absurdity of the statements and unreliability of the witnesses. Eventually the detectives from CID got together to discuss the case and realized this absurd serpent creature was a common theme.

"So, it seems evident that something that looked like a large serpent was present near the alley where Miss Prentiss was killed," Miss Holmes said. "What colour was it? How large was it, exactly? How did it move? Did it make any noise? Did it have scales like a snake or was it smooth? Did it move fast, or slow? How close was it to the murder scene? What time did the witness see the thing?"

"I do not have any of that information," I said. "I don't believe the police do either."

"Then we'll want to visit Mr. Harris as soon as you're able to leave the house," Miss Holmes said decisively. "What did the doctor say about that?"

I sighed. "He doesn't want me to put any weight on my foot for a couple of weeks," I said. "But that just isn't possible. If I don't go back to work in a day or two, I'll lose my job."

"I'll talk to John," Miss Holmes said. "He's very clever with mechanical constructions; perhaps he can contrive some sort of conveyance for your foot."

"That would be wonderful," I said. "But how are you going to convince Mr. Harris to speak with us? We don't have official status to question him." I accepted the role she had assigned to me in her investigatory scheme. This was exciting; I too was curious about Mr. Harris and the serpent, though admittedly I felt a few qualms about becoming involved in a police criminal investigation, being a person with secrets of her own to hide.

"I have some ideas," she said. "The fact that he came forth at all shows that he wants to talk about it. That is quite admirable of him. Most people are cowards, afraid to speak up to the authorities when they witness even the most abominable acts."

She said goodnight. Letty came in to clear away the tea tray and help me with my evening ablutions.

But I didn't fall asleep easily, and when exhaustion finally pulled me down my sleep was sporadic and filled with nightmares, terrible dreams in which I relived the most horrific night of my life: the night I followed my father and his best chum Bert Cranston to a hovel in Spitalfields and peeked through a window to see Jolly Bert pound lasciviously into a woman on the bed while Papa, standing nearby, opened his medical bag, took out a scalpel, and waited patiently for Bert to finish; then with Bert still inside her, his hands firm on her chest to hold her down, my father slashed the woman's throat, almost decapitating her; and then my dear Papa gutted the poor woman while his jolly friend cackled with laughter, made jokes and accepted organ samples to include in the next day's pub pies.

Chapter Four

Three days later I was back at work, less ambulatory than before but in good spirits because the fourth quarter funds had appeared miraculously in the veterinary account and buckets of coal had magically filled the coal bin.

Mr. Wu's whereabouts remained unknown.

Under Miss Holmes's direction and with the Chief Inspector's approval, Letty and John constructed a bedroom for me in my small animal surgery room since I couldn't climb the stairs to my room above the bakery and I insisted on returning to work. They even brought my furniture, after I told them the bed, chest, chair and side tables were the only pieces I had kept after I sold my Mummy's house upon my father's death. They bedecked the bed with froufrou white pillows and a frilly, lacy, bow-laden white coverlet that had probably been too fussy even for Miss Holmes. Juno the cat, who apparently loved lace, immediately took possession and soon the white coverlet was sprinkled with black cat hairs.

John said he would move my furniture back to my apartment when I became more mobile, but I just smiled at that offer. Now that Bert knew my address, I knew I could never again live in that room, convenient though it was. I intended to contact the landlord at the first opportunity to tell him I had moved out.

I also planned to replace my apparel. I would have to breach my savings—money from the sale of my mother's house that I had squirreled away for my old age—but only my promise to myself that I would have new things to wear very soon made me able to dress each day in clothing and undergarments I knew Bert had touched.

Plus, I must still buy a new hat and shoes. Not that I would need a left shoe anytime soon. The doctor assured me I would be wearing the plaster protuberance for at least two months.

Chief Inspector West's approval of my new living arrangements surprised me greatly; but when he came over to visit, to look in on me, I was almost moved to tears by his concern and—may I dare say—his paternal affection. We had had few exchanges over the years. I had once cared for his dog, and I suppose he had heard stories about my work from the constables from time to time which had given him a positive impression. And of course, there was the loyalty he felt toward Papa's memory.

"Your father was one of the finest large animal surgeons the City of London has ever seen," he said. "The hernia work he performed on that bay gelding was top notch. I believe the old horse is still in service today."

Poor old Toby. He was indeed still in service, the dear thing. But he certainly wouldn't be if I had ever let my father touch him. Papa had been unable to wield a scalpel with steady hands for several years before his demise.

Miss Holmes had taken it upon herself to inform Chief Inspector West that my home had been burgled while I was away, but at least she hadn't presumed to mention my fear of Hubert Cranston to him. And maybe I could think of some way to plant clues to lead the investigation toward Bert's direction. The Chief Inspector took it personally that a crime had been committed against one of his people right across the street from division headquarters. Since nothing had been stolen, he theorized that the miscreant was a sexual deviant who had been hoping to attack me in my home and simply tossed my things around in frustration over my absence.

"It was actually a blessing that you broke your foot," he assured me, patting my hand, "because that's the only reason you weren't at home when the devil broke in. You should be very grateful to your friend Miss Holmes for providing you with a place to mend for those first few days. We will try to be as good a friend to you now, while you stay here. You be sure to let us know if there's anything else we can do for you."

"Thank you, sir," I said. I wanted him to arrest Hubert Cranston but did not know how to tell him that without revealing the whole story of what I knew and what I had done.

I had been a coward last year and now felt the burden of it, because how could I confess everything now—tell my colleagues that a year ago I killed my father who, by the way, was Jack the Ripper with Bert Cranston as his assistant? I agreed with Miss Holmes—witnesses to crimes should come forward, should tell the police what they saw. I had not done so. Instead I had taken matters into my own hands, poisoning my Papa and frightening his collaborator into leaving town. There were numerous reasons for my cowardice: fear of facing my father in court; fear of the authorities not believing my tales about their colleague; fear of being left destitute if Papa was arrested and our possessions sold to pay his court expenses; fear of losing my job and my friends here at the police station, the only security in my life since Mummy's death. And also, I suppose, basic personal fear of my father and his friend, an overwhelming fear that kept me shaking and tongue-tied whenever I was in their presence and even now when I thought about them.

But now Hubert Cranston was back and another brutal killing had occurred. Were these facts connected? Even though I had not thought the torn furrows in the wall of Mr. Wu's building to be the act of a normal man, I now began to question my earlier opinion. What if I were wrong, and Jolly Bert had decided to transcend his murderous mentor in violence? Not for the first time I railed at myself for my failure to run to the police on that fateful night. My father had spent an hour or more mutilating Miss Kelly's poor corpse, and I had watched each terrible moment of butchery in shock, not taking any action to stop him. Of course, I had not imagined the horror would last so long—every moment I thought he must be finished now, surely to God no additional violation could be possible. And truthfully, I worried that if I ran to the police Papa and Bert might leave during my absence to commit abominations against some other poor woman.

But I should have screamed, should have shouted for help that first terrible moment when I saw him slash her throat or during any of the hundreds of dreadful moments that followed. Why had I not screamed? Perhaps my own years of torture explained my silence. I had learned, in lessons most methodical, to never scream, never make a sound. Perhaps that was the reason.

But standing there, watching my Papa mutilate that poor dead woman's flesh, I made this vow to myself: I will never allow that monster out of my sight again until he is dead and his evil is ended.

At least I kept that promise.

Or so I thought. Other than the sexual act, for which he paid threepence to Miss Kelly, I did not see Bert commit violence against the woman's body that night. He did not kill her, although he made it easier for my father to do so. He was Papa's willing, jolly audience, urging him on to greater and more horrific acts of butchery—but he held no knife himself, which is the reason I sent him threatening anonymous letters to scare him away instead of killing him too.

Had that charitable decision been a deadly error?

And frankly, it would have been more difficult to kill Bert. I made all of my Papa's meals; adding strychnine to the sweetbreads was a simple thing. Upon finding him dead the next day I simply told the police doctor that he had been complaining of chest pains. There wasn't a single question. But I didn't have that sort of access to Bert's food.

Maybe I could send anonymous letters to the press...

I escorted the Chief Inspector to the door leading to the regular stable, my movements clumsy since I was still unused to manipulating the crutches and the boxy rolling contraption that John had constructed out of roller skates for manoeuvring my plastered appendage.

"I've instructed Harry the stableman to make his boys available to you any time day or night, to assist you with anything you might need," Chief Inspector West said, patting my shoulder as he left.

"Thank you, sir." Harry and I got along all right, but his stable boys would be furious to be at my beck and call. They were always disrespectful of me, treating me as the most menial employee in the stable hierarchy even though I was the doctor and they were the ones who slopped out the muck. I would enlist their assistance as seldom as necessary.

I worked in peace through the morning, softly singing my favourite contralto airs from Handel's Messiah oratorio as I tended an overworked horse suffering from bleeding. This was the poor horse's third visit to the horse doctor with this affliction in as many months, and again my recommendation to the department, upon returning it to duty after a few days' rest, would be to stop using this horse to pull the Black Maria, since hauling a heavy wagon full of prisoners for twelve hours a day put too much stress on this animal's lungs. *He was despised and rejected of men*, I sang, sadness in my voice as I thought of the horse's life. No doubt the authorities would again ignore my medical advice and put poor Molly back on the harsh schedule.

This was the type of injury that could have been handled in the regular stable—my services were not necessary as no cutting, sewing, bandaging or medicating would be done; all the horse needed was rest, clean food and oversight—but since Harry preferred to send all ailing animals to me and I didn't trust his stable boys to provide adequate care to ill and defenceless creatures anyway, I was happy to keep the old chestnut in the empty stall where Toby had been whickering a few days ago (and would no doubt be resident again very soon).

It is a great shame that most of the horses in the Metropolitan Police stable are nags, derelicts and has-beens. These are animals in the last years of their lives, bought on the cheap because there's never enough money in the police budget to replace a dead horse with a young, healthy one.

But despite my compassion toward our overworked equine companions, my mind only half focused on poor Molly's plight. I sang and tended her needs by rote, my mind plotting various ideas to trap and eliminate Hubert Cranston, an action I now acknowledged I should have undertaken long ago.

*****

Shortly after two o'clock an enraged Miss Holmes flounced into my office. "Miss Barquist, I need your help," she said angrily.

"Of course, anything," I said. I meant it; I was aware that I was in her debt for her household's care of me after my injury.

"Another woman was murdered," she said. "Early this morning, just down the street from my library."

"How terrible," I whispered, collapsing on a chair, my stomach clenched. I wanted to vomit. Was this death my fault, because I hadn't told the police about Jolly Bert?

"I intend to investigate the murder site, but the Whitechapel Vigilance Committee won't let me anywhere near," she said, her delicate doll's face tense and purpling with rage. "Mr. Aarons told me to return home to my husband and my dressmaker."

Mr. Aarons was a local publican, treasurer of the volunteer Whitechapel Vigilance Committee, excessively vocal in casting aspersions against the Metropolitan Police for their unsuccessful attempts to uncover the Ripper's identity.

He had been a drinking chum of Papa and Jolly Bert, one of those persons who would have attacked me as a liar if I had confessed the truth about my father.

"Do you want me to ask Mr. Aarons to stay out of your way?" I asked. I doubted my word would carry much weight with the man.

She frowned at me, disappointed at my denseness. "No, Miss Barquist. I want you to ask the police if I can have access to the scene."

I thought about this. My friends were all uniformed constables. I had no pull whatsoever with the detectives from the Criminal Investigation Department responsible for investigating the murders. But one of my friends had managed to involve himself in numerous CID investigations and had even worked with Scotland Yard a time or two.

"PC Froest usually comes by most mornings or early afternoons to join me for tea," I said. "I believe you met him the other day. He might be able to allow us access to the crime scene." I said 'us' because broken foot or not, I needed to be involved in this. If there were any clues connecting this crime to Bert Cranston, I must be there to see them.

In full agreement with this plan, Miss Holmes sent her servants out to procure sandwiches and cakes and collect a dainty tea service from her home. A short time later a happy tea party scene was set, and after Frank arrived he, Miss Holmes and I sat down to a resplendent meal. Four scarred and splinter-laden chairs and stools were pulled up to the lace-festooned table, one for each of us to sit upon plus one for resting my foot. We ate on plates painted with gambolling bunnies as we dallied and joked, each contributing to the jollity in our own way; one of us with a gay trilling giggle, one with a deep and hearty laugh, and one of us with an occasional hoarse snort of amusement. Miss Holmes regaled us with stories about her childhood, ludicrous stories involving her brothers Sherlie and Mykie, which Frank particularly enjoyed. Evidently, he had some experience with her brother Sherlie and didn't think very highly of him.

Until that day I had not realized Miss Holmes's brother Sherlie was the famous Sherlock Holmes from *A Study in Scarlet*. This discovery deeply troubled me. As a person possessing more than her share of secrets, I was grateful to learn that my new friend made a point of avoiding her detective sibling whenever possible.

By the end of the meal Miss Holmes—now known to us all as Astraia—and Frank were bosom friends, and she felt he might be inclined to respect her deductive ability.

"I wish there was photographic evidence of these things," he said after she told him about the claw-like gouges and the pictograph we'd found at the earlier crime scene.

She took two photographs of the claw marks out of her reticule, handing them to him.

He studied them for a few moments, his brow furrowed. "No one said anything about these," he said. "You say these marks were fresh?"

"The brick dust lay atop the alleyway filth," she said. "Of course, I doubt that remains the case. But Maddie will verify that the marks were not there a week before." I nodded.

Astraia let Frank think for a moment about all the police had missed, then asked: "Frank, do you think I could see police photographs of both crime scenes, to determine if by some chance the little blood etching was captured by accident on film? And I would also like to examine photographs of the murder victims, to compare the two crimes side-by-side."

Frank winced at the word 'accident' with respect to police evidence-gathering. He put Astraia's photographs in his pocket but bluntly refused to bring her any pictures of either of the murder victims to examine.

"Such brutal images are not for a lady's eyes," he said, unbending.

It occurred to me that since Frank had never been prone to show such gallantry to me, perhaps he would let me see the photographs later, after Astraia went home.

Then Astraia brought up the real reason we sat together here at this table.

"Frank, I'd like to view the crime scene from last night's murder," she said. "I want to see if there are similar clues present there."

"The blood has already been washed away," he said.

She shrugged. "We'll look for claw marks then."

"Very well," he said after just a moment's consideration, and to my great astonishment that was that.

John woke up and drove the three of us to the latest crime scene, my crutches and foot contraption taking up most of the space in the cab. When we stopped near the crowd still milling at the corner, Astraia instructed John to go to the library to close up and retrieve Letty—whom she'd evidently left in charge of the book business when she'd run out to investigate the murder down the street.

"You have very cooperative employers," I commented. "Most businessmen would not allow their staff to assign their own substitute."

"The library board of directors owed Mykie a favour," she said. "They're stuck with me and must tolerate *my shenanigans.*" She said the last with a snarl in her voice, so I knew she was repeating something she had been told by another, probably more than once.

Under Frank's escort we moved through the crowd and approached the Whitechapel Vigilance Committee phalanx.

Several dozen people milled closely together, filling a space better suited to four or five individuals. I do not like crowds. People kept touching me. I do not like being touched.

I noticed Jolly Bert standing to the right of his dear chum Joseph Aarons, the treasurer of the motley group. My breath caught but I remained closely behind Astraia as she followed Frank, who carried her photography equipment.

Unfortunately, I almost fell on my rear as one of my crutches slipped and the skate below my left foot continued its momentum forward. Strong hands grabbed at me, holding me steady.

"Hello Maddie," said a sinister voice well-remembered from my youth.

"Hello, Mr. Cranston," I said, hating myself for the meekness I heard in my own response and the fear that ran through my body the moment he touched me.

"Why, you don't need to call me Mr. Cranston anymore, Maddie," he said with a jovial laugh. "Not now that you're all grown up." His eyes roamed my body, with particular focus on my torso, and a familiar nausea began to claw up from my gut.

I felt frozen, until a small warm hand grabbed mine. "Come along, Madeleine," Astraia said, pulling at me. Jolly Bert released my shoulders and I continued my ungainly way through the people until we reached the presumed crime scene. Frank shuffled the photography equipment in his arms as he stopped to speak with the single constable still present.

As Frank had said, the blood had already been washed away. Only a wet rust-coloured residue in the pock-marked paving stones remained. A few mud puddles here and there might have seemed to hold a particularly reddish hue, but perhaps that was my imagination. I wasn't sure why there was even a crowd still standing around, since there was nothing left for them to see. What were they waiting for?

"There it is," Astraia said in triumph a few minutes later, pointing to a spot about five feet up the alley wall. Indeed, there were the three incisions, just as we'd seen on Mr. Wu's building.

She took her magnifying lens out of her reticule and held it up to the image. Luckily her kid boots added an inch to her height—otherwise she would have had to stand on tiptoe to see the markings.

"Hmm," she said, staring at the cuts, Frank's and the other constable's faces just inches from her own as they performed their own examination. Feeling the curious eyes of the onlookers I turned my back on my two friends and held my crutches out at my sides, a barrier to hold off the crowd as it pressed in on us.

"Stay back everyone," I ordered, using my best voice of authority while trying to avoid Bert's eye.

"What is it—what do you see there?" Joseph Aarons asked, leaning over my upraised crutch.

Frank turned from the wall to address him. "Mr. Aarons, it was my understanding that the Whitechapel Vigilance Committee is supposed to be keeping bystanders away from this site while the police mount their investigation," Frank said.

"What's there?" Aarons insisted.

"The police are still investigating. Hold back that crowd, or go home," Frank said. His eyes held Aarons's for a few moments, then Aarons backed off and instructed the crowd to leave. None did that I could see, but they did move back.

"Maddie, while I'm taking pictures of the incisions would you please look around the ground to see if there's anything interesting left to photograph?" Astraia asked me briskly. I obediently began to study the ground but try as I might I could see no Chinese pictographs etched in blood, which I presumed was what she meant.

Intent on studying the claw-like marks, Astraia spoke softly to Frank. "Even without seeing photographs of the victim, I know this murder was different from the other one," she said.

"What's that?" Frank asked.

"This killing wasn't as brutal as the last one," she stated. "The slashes to the body weren't as deep."

I looked up from my perusal of the ground to stare at her. How could she know something like that?

Frank also stared at her, a moment of suspicion on his face that quickly faded. "It was brutal enough," he said. "Let's take pictures of the cuts in the wall."

He set up the tripod, Astraia took a few photographs, and then Astraia and I pushed our way back through the crowd to the street.

"I'll be coming by to visit you soon, Maddie," Bert whispered to me as I wedged past him to heft myself back into the old cab, into the seat next to Letty. Frank stayed on the roadway to assist the Whitechapel Vigilance Committee in dispersing the crowd while the rest of us rode away. We were a silent assembly, Astraia deep in thought, Letty maintaining her usual reticence, and me just trying to hold in my panic while reminding myself to breathe.

*****

I would soon be alone for the first time in several days, as Astraia had a dinner engagement with one of her brothers that evening. A warm fire kept the chill away and sandwiches left over from the afternoon's tea waited temptingly in the bread box, safe from Juno's clutches, so I assured my new friend I would be quite cosy. And really, what was there to fear—several stable boys were near enough that I could hear their snores, not to mention the building full of policemen situated just a few hundred yards away. I could hardly be safer or more comfortable.

"Hmph," she sniffed. "I'll come by in the morning."

"Wait until after work," I said. "In the morning I'll try to get Frank to show me photos of the two victims."

"Take good notes," she said. "Also, get names of any witnesses." She left, the ribbons on her small bustle flouncing annoyance and worry behind her.

Though my bed tempted me I found myself too anxious to exchange my clothes for nightwear, too aware of my vulnerability to relax in the arms of Orpheus. Juno was off hunting; Molly with the bleeding lung was sleeping; I was all alone. I set the sandwiches on the table near the fire, made a fresh pot of tea (glad to see the oolong was almost gone, ensuring I would be forced soon to seek a new less-evil supply) and opened the paper-wrapped bundle that Letty had silently shoved into my hand as I left the carriage.

I smiled when I unwrapped the parcel. Letty had used her time as Astraia's librarian substitute to select two books for me: *She* and *King Solomon's Mines*. During my afternoons of indolence at Astraia's house this week Letty had read to me from these and other novels and stories by H. Rider Haggard, her favourite author. Although a great reader of Jules Verne and Robert Louis Stevenson in my youth, I had had little time to discover new melodrama authors over the last few years and was deeply grateful to be introduced to these thrilling and romantic tales of adventure.

Nothing could have pulled me more thoroughly out of my personal malaise than immersion in Allan Quartermain's exploits in Africa. It is no wonder that an hour after I opened the book, physically exhausted, warm and full from my late meal, I fell into a deep sleep, my head lolling on the old table.

But I was thrust horridly awake by the heat of fetid breath and wet tongue and teeth on the back of my neck. A meaty hand clasped my shoulder. Although the room was dark, the stove fire dead and the kerosene long-since sputtered out of the reading lamp, I knew the culprit. I stopped hyperventilating long enough to do what I should have done last year when I had seen this man and my father in Mary Kelly's room.

I screamed.

Chapter Five

I had never intentionally screamed before, or even sang to the fullest extent of my voice and found it a most exhilarating sensation. I screamed again, louder and longer; eventually hitting, I believe, an ear-bursting high A, a note I had never hit before; and it felt so good that even after I heard his footsteps running away I just kept pounding that A through my throat until strong hands shook my shoulders and the night sergeant's voice shouted in my ear, "Stop that caterwauling Maddie—it's all right. We're here now."

The room now illuminated by the light of a half-dozen lanterns, I saw that I was surrounded by six or eight night watch constables and police officials, faces concerned, plus two angry, sleepy stable hands who stood near the door, glaring at me.

"Your fucking singing has wrecked my fucking sleep, you fucking moron!" Little Teddy snarled.

A plain clothes officer—probably a member of the CID, not someone I knew—spun around to face the boy and back-handed him in a slap hard enough to fling the young rapscallion to the ground. "Never use that kind of language toward a lady again," he ordered.

The boy rushed from the room, tears of confused anger seeping from his eyes, his pal Jamie following in his wake.

I understood Little Teddy's confusion. He and his fellows had regularly heard much worse abuse heaped on me, in the years before my father's death. Unlike Papa's careful pretence of respectability around his colleagues, he had never bothered to hide his real character around mere stable boys. Little Teddy's obscene words to me had been mild in comparison to what the young fellow had regularly heard said to me by my own parent.

As I looked around the room at the men staring at me, I thanked God I hadn't changed into my night clothes. I wondered: had it just been a nightmare?

Evidently not. Someone had actually seen the man run from my office and had given chase.

PC Perkins, the newest officer in the yard, popped his head in the door, breathing heavily. "Sorry, Sergeant. I lost the damn bastard on Whitechapel."

The unknown detective gave him an admonishing look but elected not to chastise him for his language—presumably because Perkins's obscenities weren't directed at me.

"Well, go out and pound the streets, lad—all of you, go on and find him," Sergeant Wilson ordered. "I'll be damned if that bastard gets away with assaulting one of our own in our own building."

But instead of following this order all officers turned to stare at me again, presumably trying to ascertain the extent of the assault on my person.

Thank God, thank God I hadn't changed into night clothes.

"Maddie, did you see who it was?" PC Perkins asked.

"He seemed familiar," I hedged. "But it was dark." How much could I tell them? It truly had been too dark to see the man; how could I tell them that even in my worst nightmare I could never mistake the feel of his tongue on my skin for the touch of someone else.

"What did he do to you, Miss Maddie?" the strange detective asked, his voice gentle.

I took a deep breath, looking down at the table. I would do this. For once, in a room full of men, I would tell the truth.

Thank God I hadn't changed my clothes.

Thank God I hadn't gone to bed.

"He touched my neck," I said in a quivering whisper. My throat hurt. "With his mouth. And he grabbed my arm."

And then I made myself look up into their faces, my stomach churning, dreading what I would see. Disdain? Disbelief? Pity?

This is what I saw, to a man: anger. Anger at him, not at me.

I wanted to cry, my relief was so great. They believed me. And they were angry at him, at the man who had come here to hurt me.

"He was a big man," PC Perkins said, "tall, with a belly on him. But real fast," he said defensively to colleagues derisive that Perkins hadn't been able to catch a fat pervert.

I was sympathetic. Bert was fast, very fast. And strong. Not fat so much as heavily muscled.

"What was he wearing, Perkins? What colour was his hair? How old was he? Is there anything else you can tell us about him other than he runs faster than you do?" an exasperated Sergeant Wilson asked.

PC Perkins shook his head in frustration. "He wore a long coat and a cap; I don't know what colour his hair was; he might have been bald for all I could see. It's dark out there."

His frustration was nothing to mine. How could I help them without giving myself away? It was unfortunate Perkins was the officer who saw him running away—Perkins wouldn't know Bert, who had left town before Perkins joined the force.

"There was a smell," I said suddenly. Actually, there hadn't been, or at least I hadn't noticed it tonight in my panic, but it had always been there in the past. "I've smelled it before, I think. A friend of my Papa's smelled like that, an oily, meaty smell." I could feel my voice box, unused to the abuse of vocalizing so long and so hard, knotting up in my throat.

"A friend of your Papa's, you say? Was this friend also a big man?" the unknown detective asked in his gentle voice.

"Yes," I said.

"Well who is it then, Maddie? What is this man's name?" the sergeant asked.

This was it. This was my moment to set things right. "Hubert Cranston," I said.

Several of the men, including the sergeant, burst into laughter. "Jolly Bert? Your attacker smelled like Jolly Bert?" I saw constables shaking their heads, incredulous that this foolish woman should have said something so ridiculous.

I looked down at the table, my hands shaking. I felt gulping sobs straining for release and forced them back down my burning throat.

But the unknown detective wasn't laughing. He pulled up a chair to sit beside me, his demeanour serious. "Hello, Miss Maddie; I don't think we've met before. I'm Detective Inspector Rankin, on temporary assignment to H Division."

I nodded.

"I understand your home was broken into recently and the miscreant remains at large."

"Yes, sir."

"Now think carefully, Miss Maddie. Do you have any reason to believe Hubert Cranston could have been involved in that break-in?"

I thought furiously. Was there any proof I could fabricate to implicate Bert for that mess in my room? Was there a way to tell him that Bert had said he would be paying me a visit, without going into detail about what Bert wanted from me?

"I was away from home at the time and still haven't been back to see it," I said slowly. I had to strain to get my voice out. "I broke my foot, you see."

He didn't even glance at the enormous plaster-wood-and-wheel contraption resting on a chair between us. "Yes, that must be very painful," he said.

"But there is something that troubles me," I said slowly, my voice sore and hoarse from screaming that high A, thinking my way cautiously through this trap-laden maze. "My friend Miss Holmes came over here the day after my accident, to see if there were any personal things she should procure for me, and she encountered Hubert Cranston here in this office, rummaging through my Papa's things. And then she and PC Froest went over to my room to gather some clothes—and they found the place torn up."

"Do you know why Cranston was here?" DI Rankin asked.

"No, I don't," I said quickly, but from the intent way he looked at me I felt he knew I was lying.

"Do you know if Cranston has been questioned about any of this?"

I shook my head. The Inspector stood up to address the policemen. "Do any of you know if Cranston was questioned about the break-in at Miss Maddie's room, or if anyone has asked him what he was doing in here that day?"

"Not that I've heard," Sergeant Wilson said.

"But it's just Jolly Bert!" PC Granger protested. "Everyone knows Jolly Bert. Why, his pub provides most of the meals here at the station."

"Then it shouldn't be hard to find him and question him, should it, Constable?" The detective inspector walked to the door, and for the first time I noticed how handsome he was, with dark hair and a strong chin. A tall man, unfortunately. "No doubt you can show me where he lives."

Detective Inspector Rankin and PC Granger left, followed by most of the other policemen, leaving me alone with Sergeant Wilson and PC Mitchell, another new man.

"Well Maddie, needless to say I think it's a big waste of time pulling Jolly Bert out of his bed tonight but that's not my call," Sergeant Wilson said.

"I understand, sir," I whispered. I felt my vocal cords constrict more and more with each word I spoke.

"Which means there's still a villain out there who had the gall to come in here tonight, onto police property, and attack you, an employee of this police station."

"Yes, sir."

"We cannot have that."

"No, sir."

"It shows blatant disrespect for police authority."

"Yes, sir."

"And for the rest of the night, PC Mitchell here is going to stand guard outside your door."

I studied PC Mitchell's face at this pronouncement. Happily, he wore a heavy coat and didn't seem annoyed by the idea of standing around in the cold.

"Yes, sir," I said in my hoarse whisper.

"And tomorrow we'll send a locksmith out here to install some strong bolts for you, so that you can feel secure when you're here alone at night. Plus a dog—we'll provide you with a watchdog."

I knew the correct response, although I also knew what Juno the stable cat would have to say about that. She did not like dogs. "Oh, thank you, sir," I gushed as best as I could with little voice or genuine pleasure.

He heard the tears in my voice and patted my shoulder. "Now, now, don't you worry child. Your father was a friend of mine. I owe it to his memory to ensure your safety."

He waited long enough for me to light my lantern, then he and PC Mitchell left the room, closing the door behind them.

I now noticed the chill in the room and rebuilt the fire. After a moment I put the kettle on and set the last few sandwiches out on the table.

I glanced up at the old wall clock. Almost four in the morning. Chances were I wouldn't fall back to sleep until the new locks were installed. I picked up the copy of *King Solomon's Mines* but found myself unable to concentrate on the thrilling adventure because my mind kept slipping back to my own near escape with doom.

I didn't believe Bert would be arrested—didn't even expect him to be questioned very much—but at least there was a chance now he might leave me alone, if he thought the police were paying attention to him. At the very least, he would think twice before he stepped foot in my stable again.

As I realized that, for the first time in days my anxiety eased. Despite all expectations, I fell asleep before finishing a single page.

*****

"Maddie, can I come in?"

I raised my head from the table to gaze blearily toward the door. Grey light oozed in with the chill through the small windows and a few open slits between old timbers of the building, the narrow openings in the wall that allowed the cat to enter and exit the building at will. I felt her purring on my lap; evidently she had joined me during the night.

The voice yelled again. "Hey, Maddie, are you all right? Can I come in?"

Frank's voice. I frowned. Frank had never asked permission to enter the police veterinary stable before.

No one ever asked permission to enter the police veterinary stable.

"Of course, Frank; let me make some tea," I tried to say. But all that came out was a soft, strange, painful croak, and then I remembered last night.

My voice had been hoarse when I woke in Astraia's home, after my foot had been tended. But this was much worse; now I made no intelligible sound at all. I had damaged my voice, the one joy in my life, from singing too loud. But what a glorious A it had been.

I set Juno down and tried to stand up, to go open the door, but my foot crashed down and I slipped to the floor on unsteady wheels.

Frank heard the crash and rushed in. "Maddie, are you hurt?" he asked, leaning down to help me stand.

He had to speak loudly so that I would hear him over the sounds of a barking dog and a hissing cat. I shook my head, though I felt tender spots on my back and hip and knew I would feel bruised there for weeks. Juno ran off but the dog continued to bark. The barking exacerbated my headache.

"You remember Old Vic, don't you Maddie? Sergeant Wilson said to bring him over this morning."

Yes, I remembered the dog—Old Vicious, I used to call him. A particularly good sniffer, often used by police to find lost children or miscreants on the lam; I had treated him once for mange or mites or something—what I remembered most about him was the way he would bark, snap and growl every time he saw me. Maybe it was my fault. My natural affection is directed toward the noble horse. And cats, of course. I have always been one of those people who prefer cats to dogs. Although I treat canines and may provide an occasional friendly pat or gentle ear tug, I confess I don't quite understand the allure of dogs. Particularly this one, who exhibited the hostility of a wolf and the venality of a rat.

"You look awful," Frank said. "Go wash your face and do something with your hair, and I'll light the fire and make some tea."

I patted my snarled and tumbled hair. I was aware that I wasn't particularly distressed because Frank saw me like this yet horrified that I had no doubt looked equally awful when I'd met Detective Inspector Rankin after my screaming fit.

Foolish, foolish girl.

I accepted the crutches my friend handed me and hobbled off to my new bedroom to perform my ablutions, the barking dog following my every movement. Juno was on the bed, back arched, hissing, and I closed the door on Old Vic, petting the cat reassuringly before I washed my face and hands with water from the pitcher, then brushed my hair and changed my clothes.

I closed the bedroom door behind me when I left, hoping Juno would be able to soon settle into her morning nap. She would certainly miss her teatime treat today; perhaps I could bring her something later.

Old Vic hadn't moved from his position barking at the bedroom door and now he followed me as I went back to the office. I quickly discovered that as much as the dog hated me, he hated my rolling cast even more, trying several times to bite it, or maybe bite me through it. Happily, his attempts were fruitless—even Old Vic's jaws weren't strong enough to do more than dent that concrete-like plaster—but his gambols around my feet further strained my mobility.

Old Vic rushed past me as we re-entered the front room, again almost tripping me to the floor. Frank had placed a bowl of water and another of chopped horse offal on the floor by the stove, next to a folded horse blanket bed—evidently Old Vic was moving in, not just making a social call. Dogs weren't like cats, who could manage their own hygiene. Who would clean up after him? I feared I knew and tried to think how to do such work under the current circumstances. How could I clean up after a dog when I could hardly clean up after myself?

Frank had prepared a human meal as well. Not only had he filled the teapot, he had also laid a plate of the Feinmans' fresh baked goods out on the table, including two pieces of their splendid gingerbread. Mortified, I realized Frank knew my baking secret—had probably always known it—but this was such a minor humiliation compared to everything else I'd gone through lately I just gave him a sheepish grin and sat down to join him.

I noticed he had not closed the outside door. The cold wind blew harshly against my still-damp face.

He saw my puzzlement and shook his head. "Sorry, Maddie. But now that your bedchamber is down the hall, it's just not proper for us to be alone in here anymore with the door closed. You'll need to keep it open throughout the workday, whenever you have visitors or when people bring you animals to work on. Otherwise, it just wouldn't look right. Your reputation, you know."

I gaped at him, aghast at the ramifications of this statement. Convenient as it was for me to remain here while my foot recovered, my reputation would suffer if I were closeted with a man because now a bed throbbed in proximity, convenient for all my hot passions.

A solution must be found. I refused to be a mute cripple with chilblains, like some pathetic orphaned creature from a Dickens novel.

I saw only two alternatives. I could find a different place to live, or I could hire my own Letty. And since I certainly couldn't afford to pay someone to just sit in here and knit or whatever while I treated colicky horses, I supposed I'd have to move.

I sighed. I'd deal with that later.

"Frank, I—" I pushed breath out through my throat, but no sound emerged.

He handed me a pencil and a few pieces of paper snatched up from the desk. I nodded my appreciation and stared down at the paper.

I am not an epistolarian. I had never before tried to have a written conversation with someone. Should I start by saying hello? Ask who would be paying for the dog food? Instead, I looked up at Frank, smiled and gave a little wave.

He laughed. "Good morning, Maddie. Have you recovered from your scare last night?"

I nodded and took a sip of tea. The warm liquid gave a strange comforting pain to the raw flesh of my throat. I smiled my appreciation—Frank made a particularly good cup of tea—and took a bite of gingerbread while I considered my response.

'Did they question Bert Cranston?' I wrote, and damned if my hand didn't shake just writing the name.

He nodded. "Yes. He denied attacking you, but DI Rankin has him locked up while they further their investigations. Evidently his name was mentioned during the earlier Ripper killings and the DI considers him a suspicious character."

Relief blossomed in me. I fought to keep a smile from my face.

"DI Rankin read me the riot act," Frank continued, "because I hadn't questioned Bert's presence in here the other day."

He looked at me ruefully. I shrugged, a forgiving smile on my face.

I remembered there was some reason I had wanted to see Frank this morning. After a moment I recalled what it was.

'Can I see the crime scene photographs from the murders?' I wrote. Old Vic, tummy full, walked over to the centre of his bed, circled a few times, and collapsed down for a nap, indicating his satisfaction over the entire business by expelling a few bursts of odiferous gas before starting to snore. My immediate thought was that dog's owner needs to take him to a vet. Then I remembered that I now held both roles in his life. I sighed.

Frank frowned. "Why?"

I looked down at the paper and remembered my query. *'So, I can report what I see to Astraia.'*

He shook his head. "Oh, I don't think so, Maddie."

I wrote furiously. *'Didn't she tell you about the incisions on the wall, in both murders? That the police hadn't even noticed? And didn't she notice that the cuts on the newest victim were shallower than the first victim's—without ever seeing the body or even a photograph?'* I still had no idea how she'd done that.

He sighed. "We are grateful that she pointed out the cuts on the wall. And if there are more murders we're going to watch out for those little Chinese picture things, even though there are no photographs or any witnesses to verify them beside the two of you—that's how much we respect her insight. And yes, she was right about the cuts on the last victim. But she's not a member of the police, Maddie. At least her brother is a consulting detective to Scotland Yard—she's just a librarian, for God's sakes."

'*I work for the police, Frank. Can I see the pictures?*' I wrote.

"God damn it, Maddie," he said in annoyance, and I realized it wasn't just his failure to question Bert's presence here that had got him into trouble. He had probably also been ragged about letting a couple of ladies visit the crime scene, no matter how much "*insight*" one of them possessed.

I showed him pleading eyes. I may even have let my lip quiver.

"God damn it," he said again, but this time in resignation. He stood. "I'll bring them over this afternoon, for ten minutes only," he said.

He walked over to the still-open door. "You keep this open when people come visit you," he ordered, closing the door tightly behind him as he left.

I wished he'd thought to feed the stove again first. I hefted the crutches and hobbled over to give the thing more coal, careful not to disturb the sleeping dog, then took a piece of fresh—not day-old—gingerbread to the bedroom for Juno as an apology for this newest upset to her life. I'd realized yesterday she was expecting a litter again and wondered how kittens would fit into this quarrelsome menagerie.

For the rest of the day, every time it seemed like the place had gained a modicum of warmth, some man would stop by with an injured animal or a locksmith would come by to secure the latches and I'd have to leave the door wide open, trading comfort for respectability.

Unfortunately, despite my secret yearnings, Old Vic never took advantage of the open door to run away.

*****

Astraia—whom I now thought of as my guardian angel—paid a call at teatime, Letty and John following behind her, laden with provisions.

"Ooh, what a sweet little doggy!" Astraia gushed, and of course he licked her hand and rolled over so she could rub his tummy and performed all those other servile dog tricks that I find even more annoying than the barking Old Vic usually reserved for me. She then prepared our meal while John filled the stove with coal, restarted the fire and filled my empty water containers. Letty cleaned up my various messes, bless her, never saying a word about the black cat hair now speckling the white bedclothes. Letty was another cat person.

Hours earlier I had written up an account of my evening's fright and the reason for my inability to speak. I handed this to Astraia to read while I guiltily enjoyed a nice cup of regrettably-delicious-Chinese tea in my warm, clean stable office, redolent of horses, soap, lavender toilet water and dog flatulence.

"Is Bert still incarcerated?" Astraia asked.

I shrugged. I wondered this myself.

"You can't stay here if he is at large," she said. "John can't watch him every hour of the day and night. He has other duties."

I nodded. Old Vic slept on Astraia's ankle, slobbering over her hem. Letty glared at him and I knew she shared my sentiments over the pooch.

"Has Frank brought the murder photographs by yet?" my friend asked.

I shook my head. *'He'll probably bring them when he comes over for tea,'* I wrote. She nodded, and I realized she had anticipated this and had timed her visit accordingly. This was perfectly acceptable to me, as it meant I would not be required to take notes on what I saw in the images.

Frank arrived, also carrying provisions, including a stinky bucket of glop for the dog which I knew would not smell any better once ingested. But I curtailed my annoyance once I saw the quantity of human food Frank set on the shelf. I had never had such a surfeit of foodstuffs in my home before, not since I was a child and Mummy still alive.

Frank didn't want to let Astraia see the ghastly photographs but of course she managed to do so anyway, and I examined them after she did. There were photographs taken at the crime scenes and a few photographs taken by the mortician. Due to my personal history, I suppose, I was particularly fascinated by the images of the corpses on the mortuary table after the blood had been cleansed from them. The naked torsos looked almost identical—just the three cuts, identically spaced and terribly deep, particularly in the first instance in which the chest had been slashed almost to the spine, the cut continuing on to the victim's arm. In both cases, the ribs had been cleanly split.

My father would have never been able to make such deep and perfect furrows in living flesh and bone. I could not conceive of Bert being able to do so either.

Two images held Astraia's particular attention and she was bent over them, frowning through her magnifying glass, when DI Rankin walked in.

"Damnation," Frank said softly.

Astraia looked up. "Detective Inspector Rankin, what a nice surprise." She gave him a pretty smile and spoke with her man-soothing girlish voice, but I knew her well enough by now to know her normal approach around men was strained in this instance. She did not feel comfortable around this man. Old Vic knew it too and growled. "I don't believe we've met since your promotion."

"Miss Holmes. I had heard you were involving yourself in police matters again," DI Rankin said mildly, leaning down to scratch the dog under the chin, an endeavor which succeeded in soothing the animal and which I vowed to emulate in future. He pushed my purse off its stool to set a covered basket down in its place and came over to the table, helping himself to a fish paste sandwich. "Good afternoon, Miss Maddie," he said, smiling at me. "How are you feeling?"

I pointed to my throat. *'I can't talk,'* I told him, moving my lips without sound.

He nodded. "Does your throat hurt?"

I shrugged. It did hurt, but with all my other aches and pains I hardly noticed this one additional irritant.

"I hope you have Hubert Cranston locked up," Astraia said.

"We had to release him," DI Rankin said. "Three of his chums swore he was drinking with them last night when Miss Maddie was attacked. All three are dubious characters, but since Miss Maddie couldn't see who her attacker was, we had to let him go. Just smelling bad isn't sufficient reason to keep someone in jail."

I wrote furiously, for once not thinking first about my words. *'Do we know where he was when the two women were killed?'*

"We know where he was during the most recent murder," Astraia said with a sigh. "John was watching him that night. Cranston never left the pub."

DI Rankin looked at her thoughtfully. "John?" he enquired.

"My coachman John," Astraia said. "You know him. He's outside waiting for me. You should go question him."

"Later, perhaps. Why was he watching Hubert Cranston?"

"Because we believe Cranston was the person who broke into Maddie's room the other day," Astraia said, annoyed, then glanced sheepishly at me.

"You two never told me that!" Frank said, looking accusingly at both of us. The dog raised his head and growled.

Astraia leaned down to scratch Old Vic's neck in the preferred manner and he settled down again. She brought out her best disarming smile to try to sweep aside her rash words. "Frank, you're so busy, and we had no proof he was the blackguard. We just thought Maddie would be safer if someone kept an eye on the man."

"Too bad no one was watching him last night," DI Rankin said.

"John has to sleep sometime," Astraia snapped between clenched smiling teeth.

"That's why you should always report suspicious persons to the police," Frank said. "We have a night watch." But he smiled when he said it, forgiving her for her lack of foresight.

DI Rankin looked at me. "You know better," he scolded.

I just pointed to my throat and shrugged. This lack of voice might have some benefits.

Astraia decided there had been enough chastisement of the womenfolk for one day. "I doubt Hubert Cranston writes Chinese anyway," she said, pointing to the grisly photographs that lay on the table between the sandwich and tea cake plates.

DI Rankin glanced down at the two pictures, separated out from a small pile of photographs on the table, none of which were supposed to be available for public view. He looked steadily at Frank for a moment before responding to Astraia. "What are you talking about?"

Astraia handed him her magnifying glass. "This is from the first murder. You can see the pictograph there, that squarish blood patch on the ground just beside her shoulder. Quite clear—it's not even smudged as it was when Maddie and I saw it, after the police had tromped through the crime scene. Compare that to the bloody smudge just above the shoulder of the second victim in the other photograph."

He took the glass and bent over the two pictures, a copy of Astraia's earlier posture. Then he carried the pictures over to a lamp, to examine them in better light.

"Good God," he breathed.

"Can I see them, sir?" Frank asked.

DI Rankin handed him the photographs and magnifying glass and he walked back to the table. He lifted the stack of pictures and flipped through them. "There are a number of prints missing from this collection," he said, looking at Frank.

I had never seen Frank look nervous before today and felt bad for him. "I pulled the grislier photographs, sir. Some of the images from the murder scenes were just too frightful for a lady's eyes."

"I would have thought all of the images too frightful for a lady's eyes, Police Constable," DI Rankin said, slipping the photographs into his coat. "But I can understand your dilemma. Some ladies refuse to keep their noses out of things that are none of their business, no matter how many times you instruct them to do so."

"Now, that's just not fair, Samuel," Astraia said angrily, dislodging the dog as she stood and stamped her foot. "I'm the one who pointed out the incisions in the wall, and who noticed the blood pictographs. Dozens of your detectives and constables poured over those crime scenes, and not one of them noticed either of those clues. At either location."

Old Vic started barking but everyone ignored him.

"We would have noticed the incisions in the wall eventually," DI Rankin said. "I admit we probably would have missed the little blood pictures, and I'm grateful to you for bringing them to our attention." He bowed to me. "I hope you feel well soon, Miss Maddie. I brought you some foodstuffs, though I think perhaps you already have more provisions than your larder can hold. If any items go stale, I suppose you can feed them to your dog. I'll stop by again in a day or two." He nodded at Astraia. "Miss Holmes, your servant as always," he said, then looked over at Frank. "I'm going to interview Miss Holmes's coachman now, PC Froest. You may join me if you wish."

Frank looked like the last thing in the world he wanted to do was join DI Rankin. He sighed and followed him out, remembering at the last minute to give us a wink goodbye before he closed the door.

The dog continued to bark. Astraia sat down and he joined her, soon falling asleep again at her feet.

Astraia and I sat in silence for a few minutes, enjoying the food we had only picked at while there were men around to watch us eat. But eventually I felt sated enough to scratch a word on paper.

'*Samuel?*'

She blushed. "We grew up together. Same village, same church, same friends—you know the thing."

I nodded. I thought there must be more to the story but wouldn't pry.

But I wouldn't have had time to pry then even had I wanted to, because Detective Inspector Rankin burst back into the room, followed quickly by Frank. My mouth was full of cake, my cheeks no doubt puffed up like a chipmunk's, and

I quickly swallowed the unchewed morsel. I was lucky not to choke in the act, which scratched my tender throat.

Astraia stood, annoyed, not bothering with her usual girlish demeanour. "Well, what do you want now?" she asked. I would later learn that she had no patience with interruptions to her meals.

"PC Froest just informed me that the two of you became friends when Miss Maddie imprudently offered to vouch for a notorious opium dealer, which gives me great alarm. The Chinese pictographs found at the murder sites add an ominous new complexion to this case. Surely both of you are aware of the white slavery trade—the newspapers have been full of stories about London women being kidnapped and forcibly sent to the Orient as slaves and worse."

Astraia curled her lip in disdain at his misgivings. "I don't see how that applies to us. The poor unfortunates being kidnapped are prostitutes, not respectable women."

"The poor unfortunates being kidnapped are women who haunt unsavoury locales—places such as opium dens and Whitechapel neighbourhoods. I've been very clear about my disapprobation over your new work site, Miss Holmes, and these Chinese pictographs only add to my uneasiness. This case might be tied to the white slavery trade, and I insist that both of you stay out of it! No more friendships with opium purveyors! No more spending time on your own—either of you—in disreputable areas of town!"

As angry as he was, his anger was as nothing compared to Astraia's.

"I remind you, sir, that I hold employment in a disreputable area of town!"

"Well do I know it! You can be sure I'll be expressing my concern about that to your brother Mycroft!" The dog started barking again, upset that someone was threatening his goddess. I hoped he wouldn't bite the detective inspector.

"Mycroft has already foisted John and Letty on me," Astraia said, "to watch and tell tales of my every move—do you really believe he's going to make me leave my post after all the work he went through to arrange it for me?"

DI Rankin fumed but recognized the futility of arguing with her further, so turned to yell orders at me instead. Old Vic settled down, evidently experiencing no outrage over my being abused.

"Stay out of opium dens! And stay out of this case!" He stormed out, Frank following on his heels.

We both stared at the door for a moment, then Astraia turned to me, an overly bright smile on her lips. "Well, that certainly was exciting! Did you get any new witness names from Frank?"

I shook my head.

"That's unfortunate, but at least we have an appointment tonight to meet the witness from the first case, the one who saw the large snake."

I looked at her in enquiry.

"John made the arrangements. You do want to go with me, don't you?"

I nodded cautiously.

"Good. I should probably mention—we're meeting him in an opium den."

Chapter Six

We did not actually meet Mr. Harris in an opium den. We met him in a disreputable tavern next door to an opium den, which from DI Rankin's perspective would no doubt be just as bad.

John elected not to escort us into the place, a fact I viewed with surprise and Astraia with suspicion.

"I'm not leaving Letty out here by herself," John said from the door of his cab. "But don't worry. You won't be alone."

Astraia stared at him from under her mouldering bonnet, the final touch she'd added to her rags-and-soot disguise. I wore one of my usual work gowns but had daubed ashes from the stove onto my face and hands.

"You bastard, John," she said. "He's in there, isn't he?" She leaped from the cab and pushed angrily past the servant, waiting for neither answer nor assistance.

I was not so agile and held onto John's arm as he helped me down, grateful that he provided an anchor of stability as I steadied my crutches and wheeled foot on the ground between two inebriates collapsed on the cobblestones. Letty, not moving from inside the cab, agreed to guard my bag along with Astraia's reticule.

"Come along, Maddie," Astraia growled, her usual dulcet tones disguised in the local patois, the ratty fringes of her filthy shawl trailing in the grime as she pushed her way through the crowd of barely-garbed trollops and licentious men and through the door of the dive where we were to meet our quarry. I stumbled behind her, my crutches used more as a weapon than as a means of support.

Upon entry, it seemed as though we'd stepped into a painting by Hieronymus Bosch. I have not spent much time in taverns and had certainly never entered a place as dark, smoky, loud and crowded as this prototype of hell's saloon. Upon review, I believe the smell was the worst part of the experience. Happily, my stomach held little sustenance, our wretched tea being some hours past. But I struggled to keep even that small amount remaining where it belonged. I wondered how Astraia managed it, since she did not have my years of shovelling horse manure to precondition her to the stench.

I also wondered how she planned to find one specific stranger in this bacchanal of slatterns and reprobates.

She studied the room, then stalked over to a pile of elderly skin and rags sitting at a corner table beside another figure. A grungy cap covered most of the creature's head and eyes. A loathsome-smelling pipe poked out of ancient folds of filthy beard-flecked skin.

Astraia bent down, almost touching the pitiful thing's face with her lips. I barely heard her harsh whisper. "All right, where is he?"

The creature removed his pipe from his drooling lips with a palsied hand and waved the thing at the sorry fellow sprawled on the table beside him.

"Damn it," she muttered. "Is he awake?"

The old man poked the other man's arm with his pipe stem. The fellow stirred. Raising his head, I saw he wasn't much older than me, and much better dressed. Astraia moved around the table to squeeze beside him.

"Mr. Harris. Tell me about the serpent, Mr. Harris," she said, her voice smoother now but still of the underclass.

He looked into her face and smiled. "You're pretty," he said. "But unfortunately, I have no money left for a shag."

"Mr. Harris, we want to hear about the serpent," she said again. "The one you saw the other night. When that girl was killed."

"The girl. Oh God, the girl." He started sobbing.

"Maddie, perhaps Mr. Harris would like another cup of gin," Astraia said. "Could you go get him one, please?"

I stared at her. She wanted me to go to the bar, leaving her alone here with this inebriate and his friend the ancient pile of rags? I touched my throat, reminding her that I was incapable of giving an order to the barman.

"Just make signs to show you want something to drink," she said. "I'm sure Mr. Harris won't care whether it's gin or not." She settled his beaker into a basket Letty had attached to one of my crutches.

I stood impotently for a moment then turned in frustration and left, making my slow way to the bar. People kept touching me, and more than one felt a crutch slam down into his foot, sometimes by accident. Once I reached my goal, I stood watching customer-barman transactions for a time. When I felt confident I understood the way of things I pulled a few farthings out of my pocket, slapped them onto the bar along with Mr. Harris's cup loudly enough for the barman to notice, pointed at my neighbour's drink and then at my own lips, and before very long I was making my ponderous way back to the table, careful not to spill any more of the unlovely intoxicant than I could avoid. Unfortunately, my wheeled appendage did not glide smoothly across the rutted wood-plank floor and much sloshing occurred, mostly over my dress. I would need to wash the old gown before wearing it to

98

work again, because if there's anything a copper's nose is trained to smell it's a person soaked in gin.

Astraia took the half-spilled beaker of gin from my hand and placed it on the table just out of Mr. Harris's reach.

"Tell me about the snake, Mr. Harris. You said you would tell me about the snake."

He raised his head and I saw swollen red eyes under thick dark brows. "It was big, as big as a horse," he said, "and it makes me sick just to think about it. Give me the drink, and I'll tell you my story."

Astraia glanced at the moss-backed fossil sharing the table. The vile old geezer gave a slight shake of his head, and Astraia moved the cup further away from her interviewee.

"Talk first, Mr. Harris," Astraia said. "Gin later."

He glared at her, then began his tale. "As I told the police, I was on my way home from my club and got lost in the wrong part of town," he said.

Astraia and I both glanced around at the debauchery surrounding us. Mr. Harris made a habit of getting so lost, it seemed.

"Go on," Astraia instructed.

"A woman on the street smiled at me, and, um, I thought I would ask her for directions home, since she seemed to be familiar with the locale. She motioned me to follow her around a corner, and I did so."

He stopped, and Astraia had to urge him on again.

"Can I have that drink now?" he asked.

"No. Tell me what happened when you followed the woman around the corner to receive, um, directions home."

"I didn't see the attack," he said. "It happened very fast, because I was just a few steps behind her. I turned the corner, and I saw it."

She had to prod him again. "Saw what?"

"Give me the drink."

"No. Saw what?"

"As I came around the corner I stepped into a huge cloud of smoke, sickly-sweet, overwhelming my senses. I saw a giant snake looming over the woman, its claws raking through her body. It turned when I came around, and it saw me, its huge green eyes alit with fire. I turned and ran, leaving that poor girl bleeding to death on the ground. I will never forgive myself for that. She was bleeding, and I ran." He began sobbing again, great wrenching, sucking, slobbery tears.

"Oh, for God's sake," Astraia said in disgust. "Stop snivelling for moment, if you please; I have questions. How could a snake have claws? Was there anyone else there? What else can you tell me about its clawed hands—did you see it write anything on the gr—"

But Astraia didn't get the chance to finish her questions, because a large, hairy and very drunken man grabbed her by the waist, pulled her into his arms and began to kiss her. I braced myself against the table and lifted a crutch to whack at the importunate fellow, but before I could make contact the disgusting old codger sharing our table set his noxious pipe down and stood, back straight and face tensed in anger, and punched the man hard in the head. The man fell, Astraia fell, my crutch hit the shoulder of a different dipsomaniac, and very quickly a crowd of arms and legs flailed in blows and pokes as the orgy mutated into a melee.

Mr. Harris took the opportunity to stretch over the table to grab his well-earned cup of gin.

The old geezer, whom I now realized was a young and vigorous man in disguise, pulled Astraia up from her accoster's belly—and did so quite roughly, I thought, unnecessarily so—and with her in his arms began pushing through the fighting bodies toward the tavern exit. I didn't need his rough "Hurry up, Miss Barquist!" to follow as quickly as I could but was astonished that he knew my name.

My crutches came in quite handy as I made my way through the crowd, and I promised myself that once my foot healed I would always carry a cane with me, because there's nothing so satisfying as the "thwack" a piece of wood makes when used as a defensive weapon.

We made our way to the cab, the erstwhile geezer almost throwing Astraia in beside Letty before assisting me up with a rough push to my nether region. He chucked my crutches in and leaped inside himself, hitting the side of the cab hard with his hand before pulling the door shut.

"Make tracks, John!" he yelled.

"Yes sir, Mr. Sherlock," John responded, and set the whip to the horse. We jerked ahead and soon the disreputable tavern and its repellent habitués were far behind us.

Once I was able to catch my breath, I looked across at the fuming Astraia, then pointed to the man squeezed tightly against my side.

"Oh, I'm sorry, Maddie," Astraia said. "That is my brother, Mr. Sherlock Holmes."

I turned my head to look into piercing eyes just inches from my own. He doffed his filthy cap and I saw nasty straw-like hair which I later learned was also part of his disguise.

"How do you do, Miss Barquist," he said in a deep, cultured intonation.

I nodded.

"Maddie lost her voice," Astraia said in explanation.

"Oh? How did that come about?" he asked politely, but I could tell by his expression that he expected my malady was his sister's fault.

"I wasn't even there," she said huffily. "Maddie was attacked last night," (had it only been last night?) "and she screamed until her voice broke."

"She was attacked last night, so you thought you'd entertain her tonight by putting her again in harm's way?" Astraia's brother asked softly.

"She wanted to come," Astraia said with a pout, settling back into her seat. Letty rolled her eyes, but otherwise ignored us all.

"I apologize for my sister's negligence with regard to your safety, Miss Barquist," Mr. Holmes said.

"Don't be ridiculous, Sherlie," Astraia scoffed. "Maddie can take care of herself. Did you see her knock that ruffian down with her crutch? Good job, Maddie!"

Her accolade embarrassed me, but I couldn't help smiling. It is hard for me to take compliments, but I must admit I was proud of that one myself.

"I thought you said she was attacked last night?" Mr. Holmes said. "I'm sorry if this topic is painful for you, Miss Barquist, but my sister can't have it both ways—either you can take care of yourself or you can't."

"Last night's villain attacked her from behind while she slept," Astraia said in my defence. "I expect even you would have been inconvenienced by such a circumstance."

"I expect I would," Mr. Holmes said. "I beg your pardon, Miss Barquist. Very well, Astraia, we have determined that Miss Barquist can take care of herself. What about you?"

"Me?"

"Yes, you. When did you become such an imbecile as to think you could safely traipse into one of the most disreputable gin dives in London?"

"John made the arrangements to meet Mr. Harris there, not me."

"Because you told him that if he didn't devise an interview with Mr. Harris, you'd make the appointment yourself, behind everyone's back! John thought that if he arranged for the assignation to take place in a gin dive, you'd have the good sense not to go!" Her brother's voice, which had been calm all this time, started to rise.

"Well, John was wrong then, wasn't he?" Astraia said. "Anyway, I was perfectly safe."

"Safe? *Safe*? A drunkard grabbed you and kissed you! What would you have done if I hadn't been there to rescue you?"

"If you hadn't rescued me, Maddie would have done so," Astraia said calmly. "She would have hit him with her crutch."

I stared at her, as incredulous as her brother.

"You were trusting Miss Barquist to take care of both you and she?"

"I was."

He turned to me. "Miss Barquist, I salute you," he said with a drawl. "My sister trusts you to keep her safe—a confidence neither my father, my brother nor I have ever been able to garner. You must be quite the Amazon."

"Stop it, Sherlie," Astraia snapped. "Maddie doesn't deserve your impertinence. If you must be angry, take it out on me, not her."

He sighed. "Again, I must apologize, Miss Barquist—for what, the third time? This may be a record for me. I do not fault you for my sister's madcap scrapes. I know whose fault this debacle was. It was mine, because I allowed the infamous meeting to occur at all."

"You couldn't have stopped me, Sherlie, so hush that nonsense now," Astraia snapped. "If John hadn't agreed to arrange the meeting, I would have secured the appointment myself."

Letty snorted. "No one doubts that," she said, her first and penultimate contribution to the conversation.

"I just wish I had been able to get answers to my questions," Astraia said. "It will be a great deal of bother to establish another rendezvous with Mr. Harris."

I heard that by-now-familiar tone in her voice and looked at her in suspicion. Was she trying to manipulate her brother?

She was, and it worked. "There's no need for you to meet Mr. Harris again, Astraia," Mr. Holmes said. "I questioned him quite thoroughly before you arrived."

"Oh?"

He sighed. "I don't want you to have anything more to do with this case," he growled. "I believe it may be tied to a case I'm investigating, involving a dangerous Chinese secret society operating in London. I'm concerned you may be intruding yourself in the gang's business."

"You may as well tell me what you learned from Mr. Harris, Sherlie," she said. I couldn't see her face clearly in the dark, but we all heard the smile in her voice. Did she want to involve herself in a dangerous gang's business? Or did she simply believe her brother was only trying to frighten her off?

Wishing to avoid further fruitless debate on the matter, Mr. Holmes capitulated. "I will tell you the facts as Mr. Harris recalls them. I do not put any faith in his memory, however; no doubt he was in an opium stupor at the time, as well as suffering both shock and guilt after witnessing the poor woman's slaughter.

"He had spent the evening in an opium den, an activity in which he apparently regularly indulges. He has a respectable position in the City and a trust fund, but I suspect he will lose the first and deplete the second before much longer. At any rate, on the night in question he left the opium den at some point in the early morning hours to go home—he cannot remember the exact time nor give even an approximate time, due to his inebriated state—but before he had gone even a short distance he decided to return for another dosage instead of continuing home. He followed Miss Prentiss into the alley, witnessing the scene he described to you this evening. He did not see anyone else. He did not see anyone inscribe pictograms in blood. He does not remember if the snake had scales or smooth skin or fur or feathers. He does not remember what colour it was, except for the green fire colour of its eyes. He has no idea if it had feet or wheels or slithered across the ground. He smelled a sickly-sweet odour in the vicinity, but that is not surprising as the vicinity included an opium den. I will add that the police found nothing in the blood pattern on the ground to give any explanation of the killer's ambulation—and I presume you saw no clues about that either."

"If there had been any such clues at the site, they were completely trampled under police boot prints by the time I observed the scene," Astraia said.

"Ah yes, and certainly that brings me great brotherly pride, thinking about my sweet little sister venturing alone into an opium alley to kneel in the blood of a slaughtered prostitute, engaged in a search for murder clues."

"I wasn't alone. Maddie was with me."

"Not when you first ventured in, she wasn't. You were lucky indeed that she was the person who joined you. What if it had been one of the opium den habitués whom you encountered instead? Or a scoundrel such as the man who accosted you tonight?"

"If John had seen any such person entering the alley after me he would have followed, despite his annoyance with me," she defended.

"John is not to leave your side again in such circumstances, even to teach you a lesson, a matter I have stressed most strongly to him," Astraia's brother said.

"He didn't accompany me tonight," she commented.

"He didn't need to. I was there."

"You didn't need to be. Maddie was there," she snapped.

They both slumped back into their seats, rage radiating from the pair of them. I resented being used as tinder in Astraia's fight with her brother, but unfortunately, I could not speak.

Or perhaps it was fortunate after all, since I lacked the articulation of the two siblings and would never have been able to hold my own in a debate with either of them.

Mr. Holmes broke the silence. "How did you recognize me so quickly?" he asked in a reasonable and enquiring voice, no trace of anger remaining in his tone.

Astraia gave a merry laugh. "There are traces of theatre face paint on your scarf," she said. "Quite out of character for the frail old geezer of your pose."

He frowned but did not say anything for several minutes. I was horrified when he did choose to speak again, because this time the focus of his attention was myself.

"I understand your father died last year, Miss Barquist," he said.

I nodded, grateful again for the loss of my voice.

"I never met him but it's clear he was an unpleasant fellow and an abysmal father. My felicitations on his demise. Certainly you—and indeed the entire community—are much better off without him."

I stared at the man in awe and dread. How much did he know?

Astraia gave an unladylike snort. "Don't be impressed by his words, Maddie. He's always showing off like that but it's the commonest thing, a mere parlour trick. Not to mention a very rude thing to say about your father, even if it is true."

Mr. Holmes glared at his sister.

"Anyone could do it," she continued. "Evidently he knows that your father trained and practiced as a physician, and the fact that the man left you in such penury, not to mention exposed you to the basest sorts of elements by allowing you to work with him in the police stable, indicates that not only was your father a wastrel of some kind—either through drink or gambling or incompetence in his field, but also that he had no care for your delicacy and reputation as a female or for your future economic and marital prospects. Clearly he was both a poor father and the sort whose absence would improve the quality of any community."

Now I stared at her. How had she known these things about my Papa?

She responded to my consternation by rolling her eyes in frustration. "Now I have to do it, this showing-off thing that Sherlie so revels in but which I consider a display of very poor manners. It's simple, Maddie—the rusting accoutrements of your father's former profession remain displayed in abundance in your stable office. The surgeons' tools. The jars of chemicals. The medical tomes in the bookshelf. The medical bag itself. These are not the appliances of a mere horse doctor. Clearly the man was once a skilled professional, brought low before his death with no compunction about dragging his family down with him.

"Now, how did my brother—who to my knowledge has never seen the inside of the police stable—know these things about your father? Several possibilities come to mind. John—a fairly astute observer himself—has been in your office numerous times. He feels driven to tattle every little thing about my life to my brothers and no doubt has shared each observation he's made about you with both of them. Or my brother here might have done his own investigating—after all, you're spending time with me and he can't bear not to hover over every crumb on my plate, so as a man with contacts in the police force he may have spoken with your colleagues about you and your father. I'm sorry our friendship should become a burden to you, Maddie, but this is the fact: you can possess no secrets now. Sherlock Holmes has taken an interest in you."

I began hyperventilating.

"That's enough, both of you!" Letty said harshly. She reached across the space to comfort me as best as she could, patting my knee in solicitude.

"It's just as well we've arrived at your home, Miss Barquist," Mr. Holmes said, subdued by the reproach from an old family retainer. "I'll escort you in while John drives my sister home."

"You're not riding the rest of the way with me?" Astraia asked.

"No. I have some business in this neighbourhood."

"Well then, you can just get on to your business. Letty and I will escort Maddie in. I won't have you interrogating her—she's had a long day, what with the attack last night and all."

"I can hardly interrogate someone who can't respond, now can I?" her brother said mildly, hopping out of the door.

She rolled her eyes but allowed him to assist her down from the carriage. "That's a specious argument if I ever heard one. Imagine Sherlock Holmes allowing someone's lack of voice to keep them from answering questions."

"You do know you're the only person I allow to speak to me in such a manner," he said, watching as John helped me down, not choosing to assist me himself.

"And Mykie," Astraia said.

"No," he said. "Even Mycroft has learned to respect my acumen."

She shook her head but allowed him to lean down to kiss her cheek. She put her arm through mine and we headed toward the police gate, but after a moment she turned back, knowing he still stood there, watching us. "Oh, in future, Sherlie, if you sincerely wish to disguise yourself from me..."

"Yes?"

"Don't wear Papa's old gardening jacket. Did you really think I wouldn't recognize it?"

He gave a shout of laughter and headed off down the street, leaving Astraia and Letty to ensure that the fire in my stove was lit, the dog fed and walked, a small tea was set out for later, a warming pan had removed any touch of damp from my sheets and the strong new door bolts had been engaged behind them before they left me to my uneasy dreams.

Sherlock Holmes had taken an interest in me. Could things get any worse?

Chapter Seven

After a quick examination of a new patient in the second stall I donned my nightclothes and slept in my bed because, why not? If Mr. Holmes was about to unveil my misdeeds to the world, I would at least be well rested, or at least as well rested as I could expect to be, sharing my bed with a snoring, flatulent bed mate (I couldn't force Old Vic to sleep in his own bed without shutting him out of my room—which would also shut out the few wisps of warm air that occasionally trickled down the hall from the stove). Happily, Juno was a creature of the night, and the two had quickly settled into a bedroom rapprochement in which Juno held the bed territory by day and Old Vic claimed it during the nighttime hours.

I woke up very early to check on the injured donkey which had been brought to the stable last night during my absence. The brief examination I'd made before I went to bed showed I would need to operate on its flank, very soon, to remove several shallow shotgun pellets fired by some unknown person either by accident or malice. I could not do this to the poor fellow without morphine to ease its pain. Unfortunately, I had used the last dregs of my morphine on poor bleeding Molly. I needed a new source of the drug, but I'd heard that Little Joey, who'd introduced me to Mr. Wu, was in the dock and therefore unavailable to assist me in my pursuit. I would have gone to the opium den next door to last night's tavern brawl—but unfortunately, I had not paid attention to the direction.

Perhaps I was feeling especially prideful after the plaudits Astraia had showered upon me the night before; the woman seemed to think even crippled I could hold my own in a bare-knuckle match. Perhaps it was wishful thinking that all the walking I had been doing of late meant my foot was healed enough to easily make an hour's jaunt through the streets, never considering that it would also be an hour back. At any rate, well before dawn I was hobbling toward Limehouse, the Chinese district, which seemed the likeliest place for finding a replacement for Mr. Wu's establishment.

I won't go into detail about my physical response to rolling my broken foot over lumpy cobblestones and brick and broken sidewalks and curbs covered with muck and the occasional bits of slippery ice. It is no exaggeration to state that my discomfort from my foot and the cold weather was extreme. But by the time I admitted to myself that I was not in fact healed enough to take on this errand I had almost reached the Limehouse district, so I kept on with the business.

I knew from Mr. Wu that most of the Chinese immigrants to London lived in the Limehouse area. I did not consider the fact that I couldn't speak Chinese, nor that if I was fortunate enough to find someone who spoke English and who would consent to steer me in the direction of an opium house, the hoarse whisper which was as much voice as I could muster today would hardly encourage conversation.

But in the end, it didn't matter anyway because the only Chinese person I encountered close-up was too dead to provide any answers to my queries.

Other than the pain and chill I had a fairly uneventful trek, only twice needing to fend off street menacers with my crutch. Eventually I entered an area where I noticed more and more signs written in Chinese, and ever more people wearing Chinese garb and speaking their unfamiliar language, and I used the increase in these as guides toward the most favourable direction.

There were some people about—not many, as it was just barely dawn—when I saw a person exit an alleyway nearby, and as he passed me I smelled the unmistakable whiff of opium. So, I turned into the alley from which he had emerged.

I had not gone very many steps when I heard a terrible scream. Without thought, I hurried toward the sound.

Suddenly two huge, bright green eyes moved toward me. As they got closer, I realized I was staring into the face of some sort of large illuminated mask, made of wood or perhaps papier-mâché. The image presented was of some sort of bearded monster, with a face of gold and with green, glowing, lighted eyes that illuminated the face and spikes of hair or feathers. As it reached me the face turned to stare at me, its egress almost stopping as we stared at one another.

If my life were a romance, this is the point where I would have fainted, or where perhaps the hero would have ridden to my rescue. But I have had few such moments in my life, so instead I lifted a crutch with threatening intent, for in truth I was not particularly afraid of the glowing monstrous thing, perhaps because it was so ludicrous in appearance not to mention shorter than I. I imagined I heard it snarl as it ran on, the alley darkening behind it as the illumination provided by the lamp-lit eyes became lost. Whatever body or bodies carried the mask were hidden under long flowing sheets of material that I could not identify in the dark.

When the thing exited the alley I heard screams from the inhabitants of the street behind me, but I paid no mind to them. I smelled blood and knew there was no time available to waste. I lit the lantern I'd fortuitously placed in my crutch bag and began to search the alley floor. Very quickly, I found the source of the blood smell.

The victim was a Chinese man, dressed in raggedy Chinese garb, perhaps in his early twenties. I knelt down to examine him, but he was quite dead. His throat had been slashed, as had his chest and belly. Three slashes—but these were nothing like the three deep and evenly-spaced cuts that had killed the two earlier victims. For one thing, these cuts, though quite lethal, were shallow in comparison. And for another, there was no symmetry to the wounds.

Although I was confident this was the victim of another murderer altogether, I nevertheless looked carefully around the body, examining especially the area next the shoulder, to see if a Chinese pictograph had been painted on the ground. There was none. There was a splintered area in a nearby wall where perhaps someone had tried to scratch the wood with a sharp implement, but it was nothing like the deep and precise incisions at the earlier crime scenes despite the fact that the wall incisions at the previous murders had been made into brick, while this was simple wood, a much more pliant surface for carving.

I had plenty of time to look, because no one entered the alley during my tenure. I tried to scream for help but could produce no more than a harsh whisper. So eventually I just left the poor man there, his dead body deserted in the filthy—and now bloody—alleyway muck.

The street was empty of people when I reached it. The market stalls which had just opened when I arrived were now tightly shut. All was still, the only sounds the cries of the sea birds that feasted on the refuse of the harbour.

I headed back toward the direction of the station, eventually finding a bobby some distance away from the unfortunate occurrence. The officer listened carefully to my frantic, barely intelligible whispers, and soon we were hurrying back toward the alley where I had left the dead man. A few people had ventured back into the streets, though most of the market stalls and businesses remained closed. The body of the Chinese man was gone, only the blood pooled in the cobblestones a confirmation of my story.

"We'll send someone over to question these people, but I don't expect we'll ever know what happened to the murder victim," PC Thomason said. "We are not welcome in this neighbourhood. These people take care of their own."

By this time, after all this movement, I could barely remain standing upright. I knew I would not be able to roll myself back to the stables without assistance. PC Thomason recognized my plight and obtained a cab for me, instructing the cabbie to escort me into the Leman Street precinct to receive his payment, and instructing me to tell my entire story to the desk officer.

Happily the desk officer turned me over to Frank Froest to be interrogated in my own facility, so that wasn't so bad except for the repeated chastisements I heard from my friend for venturing out to find an opium purveyor in the first place, plus the icy wind which blew continually in through the open door during his visit.

"With no body, no identification and no witness other than yourself, Maddie, there's not much we can do," Frank said before he left. "But if someone in that neighbourhood reports a missing person we'll follow up."

One good thing came from it all: before noon Police Constables Melman and Garlick tracked down a goodly quantity of morphine for me, and since no debit appeared in my account for what equated to six months' worth of supply I did not enquire into the horse medication's antecedents. The donkey hardly complained at all as I cut buckshot from his flank, then covered it with salve before sticking an ungainly bandage over it. Happily, it was dead winter—no flies would settle into the animal's open wound.

I wrote a letter to Astraia, telling her of my adventures and of my certainty that despite a superficial similarity this murder had not been committed by the same hand that killed the two women.

*****

The next night I had agreed to accompany my friend and Mr. Ramsay MacDonald to the latest Gilbert and Sullivan opera, *The Gondoliers*, at the Savoy Theatre. I say "latest" as though this were a regular thing for me, but in fact this would be the first time I had attended the opera since my mother's death, so I was quite excited. I was familiar with many Gilbert and Sullivan songs, of course; no music hall concert was complete without at least one performance of *Modern Major General* or *When I Was a Lad*. I found them all quite droll; an opinion Letty, who had originally been intended as the chaperone for Astraia's night out, did not share. Although my foot continued to ache, I was excited about the opportunity and told myself I could rest my appendage as easily sitting in a theatre seat as I could sitting home alone with my animals.

Of course, I did not own apparel appropriate for an evening at the theatre. But in this dilemma too, Letty would provide. John appeared at the door of the stable early in the afternoon to whisk me away to Astraia's house, where Letty would work her magic on me. Hoarsely singing *I'm Called*

Little Buttercup from **H.M.S. Pinafore**, I quickly settled my latest patient—an old mule with a lame foot—into a comfortable stall with food, water and clean bedding. As usual with my patients, what this animal needed most was rest and a few good meals. John walked the dog while I set out food and clean water for him, and then I let the surly stable boys know I would be out for the rest of the day and rolled/hobbled myself out to John's carriage.

For the convenience of the boys I did not lock the stable office door.

During the few days I had spent in Astraia's home the previous week it had occurred to me that Letty might possess an affinity toward dressmaking. Today I realized hers were the skills of a sophisticated modiste. I had never owned and seldom seen anything as beautiful as the emerald green taffeta evening gown in which she decked me, the prominent bones of my shoulders and hips concealed in flounces that simulated an elegance I lacked in actuality. My knobby elbows, strong forearms and rough hands hid under long white gloves; my good foot looked almost dainty in a French kid opera toe slipper of perfect fit; my waist was a tiny thing in the corset I commonly abjured; my thin brown hair gleamed luxuriant in a bun ornamented with green ribbons and peacock feather tips. Letty finished her composition with a few skilful swipes of the curling tongs against my hair fringe then led me to a full-length looking glass, a rare prideful smile on her face and no wonder: I looked regal, an impression substantiated by Astraia when she entered the room and joined me to examine our paired reflection.

"Maddie, you have often impressed me as Amazonian, but today you are Queen Hippolyta herself," she said, giving me an affectionate squeeze. "Clearly your unfortunate experience yesterday did you no lasting harm."

She of course looked like a tiny goddess, all lavender swirls and glorious red hair, but I wasn't a bit envious of her beauty. Not tonight. Tonight, I was a queen.

And then I turned from the mirror too fast and almost tripped on my casted foot. Which was a lesson to me in hubris, but still—I felt beautiful.

We were to meet Mr. MacDonald at the theatre. En route, Astraia and I talked about the murder I had witnessed the day before.

"I agree this could not be the same perpetrator," Astraia said, "for the reasons you mentioned—the shallow cuts, lack of symmetry, etcetera. What seems likely—especially when we consider the scratches made on the wall—is that the murderer or murderers are trying to mimic the other deaths by making it look like the killer of the two women is also at work in the Limehouse district."

"For what purpose?" I croaked in inquiry.

"The most likely reason is that they wish to sow fear among the Chinese community. You witnessed the market sellers flee the scene after that absurd masked creature ran out of the alley. And remember Mr. Wu's grandmother, the horrific tale she told him? And how scared he was to see the incisions in the wall of his building? Clearly there is some type of dread serpent creature in China who kills or is purported to kill in this manner."

By the time we reached the theatre we had thoroughly parsed yesterday's horror, changing the topic only when Mr. MacDonald opened the door to the carriage to assist us to alight. Mr. MacDonald—who soon insisted I call him by the familiar "Ramsay" though not the even more familiar "James" used by Astraia—looked dapper and handsome as he accompanied us into the Savoy Theatre. I felt pride to be in his party even if only as chaperone. I was not sorry to be leaving the sordid topic of murder. I wanted to enjoy tonight—enjoy the music, my beautiful dress and the company of friends.

There was hardly a moment of that evening that was not magical—much of it unexpected, which is the best sort of magic. I had expected to be enthralled by the music, the actors and the story. It had not occurred to me that the Savoy Theatre itself would be a source of extraordinary enchantment, but so it proved. The building was entirely lit by electric lights, even the stage where the performance was held. Although I was not of course ignorant of electricity, which had been installed in more and more buildings over the last ten years, the use of electricity at the Savoy was unmatched in my experience: I had not known there were so many electric lights at one place in all of London. In fact, Ramsay told us that the Savoy had its own electric generator, built on land near the theatre. Some of our fellow theatregoers appeared to hold trepidation about the building, no doubt fearing to be surrounded by so much dangerous electricity; I saw one woman actually refuse to enter the place. But brave Astraia had no such qualms and strode confidently into the theatre lobby and up the stairs to our tier of seats. I followed her, my progress much slower due to my disability which required assistance from both Ramsay and a theatre assistant present at the steps inside to aid the elderly and infirm.

The grand and melodic score; the soaring beauty of the voices; the hilarity of Mr. Gilbert's libretto; the costumes, dancing, characters; the titillating, even sometimes shocking story; the twinkling electric lights sparkling in both sky and canals that made the Venice locale of the initial act even more magical—I could continue on and on in this vein, so enthralled was I by what was, for me, the most sublime evening of my life.

Anyway, that part of the outing was fun.

I had expected Astraia, like most ladies, would elect to remain seated during the interval, thus allowing me to avoid the difficult exercise of wheeling my bulky cast around the tender toes and draped skirts of those who chose to stay in their seats, but no such luck—her eagle eye targeted a particular gentleman exiting the auditorium and she determined to follow. She told me I might stay behind and Ramsay with me, but of course it was inconceivable that she be allowed to traipse away without escort and chaperone. Ramsay and I followed after her, neither of us overly happy about it. She was in quite the hurry and I blanched at the idea of wheeling myself down the steps to the lobby, clinging to the balustrade in my rush.

Happily, such exertion was not necessary. Astraia stopped in the narrow hallway outside the auditorium doors and spun around, presenting her back to a small party of gentlemen and ladies nearby. It was then I spotted the mark of her focus: Sir William Forrester Clydon, retired Lieutenant Governor of the Punjab, spokesman for the opium trade, was one of that group. My friend began to engage Ramsay in inconsequential conversation but her expressive eyebrows waggled at me, thus instructing me in my task: I was to listen in on the conversation of the other party. I gave a slight nod then shifted my position so as to bring myself closer into eavesdrop range.

Even I knew this was abominable behaviour but luckily, I have no pretensions to culture so didn't let bad manners preclude me from my assignment. I paid close attention to the other group, masking my attention by smiling whenever Astraia laughed and nodding whenever Ramsay appeared to speak. In truth I have no idea what topics my friends discussed.

The conversation behind us was dominated by the two ladies of the party, speaking with great excitement.

"Sir William and I were never so surprised," said the first, a lean woman just past middle age. "Maria came to us from Monroe's, you know, a very respectable employment firm."

"Yes, I engage them for all my servants," said the second, a more portly lady still breathing heavily from the walk out of the auditorium. "Although after this I may decide to transfer my custom to Madame Hollande's."

"Yes, I'm considering that too," said the first, presumably Lady Clydon. "Sir William will speak with Mr. and Mrs. Monroe tomorrow, to see if they have any explanation for Maria's outrageous behaviour. Why, we hadn't even known she'd left the house."

"If I were you, I'd count the silver. Who knows what else she was up to?"

"Our butler is doing that this evening," Lady Clydon said. "He's also interviewing the other servants."

"Good idea. If anyone in your household was aware of her shameful behaviour, they must be sent packing, immediately."

"Certainly."

Sir William spoke up. "Robert and I are going out to blow a cloud. Shall we fetch you ladies a glass of wine or some biscuits?"

"I'll have a lemonade please, Sir William," his wife said, and her friend concurred with this selection although I suspected she would have preferred the wine and biscuit option.

Sir William and his friend shifted through the crowded space. I saw just a flash of gold dragon handle before the

retired Lieutenant Governor's heavy black lacquered walking
cane came down hard on my casted foot. I lurched and rolled,
but Ramsay and Sir William's friend caught me and helped
me to stand upright. Many apologies ensued, and I assured
them that it was no bother at all although in fact it is a great
deal of bother to have a fat man's walking stick stabbed into
one's broken foot. But eventually Sir William and his friend
left to smoke their cigars while their good ladies continued to
rail against the unknown runaway slattern Maria and her
many unproven but no doubt illicit activities. I could still
overhear their conversation through my haze of pain and
realized that both women were involved in the Social Purity
Movement, which equates all crime and immoral behaviour
with the existence of prostitution—an industry whose
existence they blame solely on the women in the profession,
with no responsibility attached to the clients who encourage
the market by purchase of such services. After a couple of
minutes Astraia, recognizing my discomfort, said "James, I
find I'm quite parched. Could you be a dear and fetch Maddie
and me a drink? I can assist her to our seats, if we go quite
slow."

Ramsay left as bid. Astraia and I re-entered the
auditorium and began to make our way slowly to our tier.
Once we were seated, with most of my weight gratefully
shifted to my nether regions instead of my throbbing foot, I
gave her an inquiring look.

She glanced around, saw no one was paying attention to
us, and whispered "Did you hear Sir William speaking to his
party when we first arrived this evening?"

I shook my head in the negative.

"I thought not. I believe you were trying to disengage your
wheel cast from the carriage door when they walked past us,"
she said. "I just heard a bit of it before they were swept into

the crowd, but from what I could gather it appears that the latest slasher victim has now been identified—I do not mean the man you saw in Limehouse, dear Maddie; we agree he was not a victim of the same killer—I am referring instead to the second woman from the photographs. She was not one of the wretches usually found in the East End plying the tragic trade but rather had been a housemaid in Sir William's London residence, the unfortunate Maria so maligned a short while ago."

I stared at my friend, appalled. If I'd had better voice I would have expostulated, condemned the unfeeling overheard matrons or, at the very least, asked a few cogent questions. But my throat hurt from the little speaking I had done earlier and all I could do now was listen, horrified at Astraia's words.

"I'm not sure how Sir William found out," Astraia continued. "I presume the police told him. We have a lot of questions to put to your friends at the station tomorrow."

I nodded vigorously, then tried to relax in my seat as other theatregoers began moving back into our row in readiness for Act Two. Ramsay brought us each glasses of lemonade—a rare treat during the midst of winter.

The second act was as magical as the first. When the last curtain calls were made I was as sorry for its end and as enthusiastic in my applause as anyone else in the theatre.

As we began to make our way out of our row, I looked around the audience, trying to find the other party. Astraia noticed and whispered, "Don't bother—they did not return to their seats for the second act." I wondered if perhaps one of the ladies had taken ill; I could not imagine anything else that would keep ticketholders from missing such glorious entertainment.

Certainly, the gruesome death of someone in their household hadn't been enough to keep Sir William and his lady wife away tonight. But since the grisly murder I'd witnessed the day before had not kept me away either I could not feel too self-righteous about that.

Our exit from the Savoy lasted almost as long as the first act, since it appeared everyone knew everybody else and all wished to stand around visiting, blocking the aisles, staircase and lobby. But eventually we reached the street and found the faithful John waiting for us—tonight as a cabbie hired by Ramsay rather than as Astraia's family retainer.

"I must say, it's rather ridiculous for you to pay John to drive us when he would do so anyway if I so instructed him," Astraia said as Ramsay helped her into the cab.

Ramsay said nothing as he assisted me inside, waiting until we were on our way before responding.

"I appreciate that John is your family servant, Astraia—however, he is not mine," Ramsay said. "I only hired his cab tonight rather than another because I knew your brothers would take comfort in knowing he was with you as an extra chaperone and protector."

Astraia took note of his cross tone and, remembering her role, tried to jolly him back into good humour.

"Oh, I know, James; and I'm confident my brothers have the greatest respect for you and your care for me," she said, lightly touching his arm with her gloved fingers in an almost-caress. "I am sorry to be so churlish." She said this last sentence in a light, apologetic, girlish voice that I thought for certain he would see through.

But he laughed and caressed the fingers still resting on his coat sleeve. "Nonsense, Astraia; you could never be churlish. Put it out of your mind and tell me what you thought about the songs. I thought the story-line a bit fast, myself, but

I understand the Queen approves so perhaps I'm just betraying my callow Scottish prudery."

I listened with half-a-mind to Astraia joke Ramsay out of the sulks, my fuller concentration on Maria's sad history. I imagined her to have been a poor orphan, left alone to support herself as a skivvy in the household of people so callous they could not even mourn her brutal death, slashed to pieces in a filthy alley late at night, far from home.

Which begged the question: what was a servant from a respectable household doing in a filthy alley late at night in a bad part of town? No doubt Astraia also pondered that same question. Though he was a dear man, at that moment I wished Ramsay MacDonald to the devil so that I could hear Astraia's theories on the matter.

It seemed Ramsay wished me to the devil as well; when John finally stopped the carriage in front of the stable Ramsay seemed rushed to be rid of me, the inconvenient chaperone.

"Look around her office to make sure it's safe," Astraia instructed him from inside the carriage as he assisted me to the street before leading me to the stable door. He took my key and opened the new lock, lit a lantern, and then made a cursory inspection of the office and front rooms. He opened the room set up for my personal use, obtained a glimpse of my virginal bed looming in the darkness and quickly closed the door of my boudoir without entering.

"It all appears fine here," he said. He placed the lantern on the table and looked over at the little stove. "Would you like me to light that for you?" I noticed Juno beside it, back arched and hissing. Frowning, I shook my head no. The room felt chilly; I didn't want to get ashes on my beautiful gown; but I could tell he was in a hurry to leave. I would change, then light the stove myself.

I gave him a little wave, walking him to the door. As he stood in the open doorway, the moonlight shining behind him, I suddenly hesitated, not wanting him to go.

Something was wrong but I couldn't put a finger on it.

"Be sure to lock this behind me," he said. I nodded and he left.

What was wrong, what was wrong? I pondered the matter for another moment—and then I realized.

Why was Juno here hissing in the cold office when she should be out hunting? And where was Old Vic? We had heard no barks, no growls, no doggy snores or dog slumber farts. Just the normal chesty wheezes of old Toby, back in my stable again, his heavy breathing so familiar I hardly noticed it.

Old Vic. Old Toby. Old Maddie.

I remembered then that I had left the office door unlocked when I departed, for the convenience of the stable boys. But that door had been locked when we returned.

"Crap," I whispered to myself, grateful to hear a soft voice emit from my throat, hoarse yet coherent. Still far from high A calibre, unfortunately. I looked around for a weapon. A heavy mallet lay propped in a corner of the room—but I didn't see how I could carry it while one handheld the lantern and the other manipulated the crutch.

After a second's consideration I made my decision about which items to carry and headed down the hallway toward the make-do bedroom, my movements awkward but deliberate. I stopped at Toby's stall, holding up the lantern as I craned to see around him. Nothing there but sleeping, wheezing horse.

The second stall held the lame mule sleeping fitfully next to the injured donkey.

The next door, quite closed, was the entry to my new bedroom. I stared at it for a moment, trying to control my anxious breathing, and then I pushed it open. At my feet, Juno hissed.

Dark, a room with no windows, facing a hallway with no windows. All four corners of the room hunkered deep in shadow. I knew a large lamp sat on the side table abutting the inside right wall; usually just a few steps away it seemed miles distant now. Between me and it lay huge pools of darkness.

I heard a soft whimper and raised my lantern to peer farther into the room. The lacy white coverlet shone bright in the lantern light, making quite visible the shivering animal drenched in dark red blood puddled near the head of the bed. I felt a moment's gratitude to Letty for giving me the virginal white coverlet; if she had used my old dark serviceable spread I would not have seen the poor injured dog so clearly, so quickly.

My voice was broken; I could not scream. My foot was broken; I could not run.

But the rage that overwhelmed me when I saw that my dog had been sliced open and left hurt and bleeding on my bed is the thing that saved us both.

I don't know which happened first, if I heard the man breathe or felt his movements in the air. But suddenly he was there, and just as suddenly so was my arm, swinging the heavy mallet. It connected. Something crunched.

I am very strong. I handle sick horses for a living. The man flew back, his head hitting the wall, his knife clattering to the floor. He did not get back up.

I lurched down the hallway, out of the building and over to the bright lights of the police station. I have walked that path a thousand times but doubt I've ever done it as quickly as I did that night, even hampered as I was without a crutch to aid my ambulation.

The desk officer stared at the sight of a panting horse doctor in a green taffeta evening gown, peacock feathers drooping from her falling hair, a bloody mallet gripped tightly in her white gloved hand. Then he called to his fellows and they followed my staggering lead back to the veterinary stable.

The man in my bedroom hadn't moved. Unfortunately, he would never move again.

"Do you know this miscreant, Maddie?" PC Mitchell asked, holding his lantern close to the crumpled and bloody cranium.

I glanced at the pulped face and shook my head.

"Do you recognize the weapon?" he said, pointing to a bloody dagger on the floor.

"No," I breathed hoarsely, then moved to turn the focus of my attention on Old Vic. The room blazed with light now and I could see that although the animal had many cuts and had lost a lot of blood no arteries had been sliced. The most dangerous cut was one across his throat; I could not know if he would ever be able to bark again, even if I were able to save him. He had also taken a nasty bump to the head, which had probably knocked him out at the beginning of his interaction with the intruder. He had not bled anywhere but on my bed, which told me that the blackguard had lain the unconscious dog on my bed and then taken a knife to him, solely for the effect of covering my bed with my dog's blood. Juno now lay in the blood next to him, licking his poor cuts, and my eyes filled with tears I quickly shook off.

The first few frantic moments examining the poor animal ruined my beautiful long white gloves. I impatiently yanked them off, throwing them onto the floor. This room had been my small animal surgery just a week ago and I tried to remember where John and Letty had taken my small-animal surgical tools when they transformed the space into a bedroom. I thought I had seen my medical bag in the office. I instructed a bobby to lift the dog, bloody coverlet and all, and carry him into the front room. I handed Juno to an officer, who took her without complaint while the other officer gently carried Old Vic out of the room. I would have carried the dog myself but couldn't trust that I wouldn't fall down, walking as I was with a rolling cast and no crutch. It was amazing I had accomplished all I had over these last nightmare minutes without one.

I nodded in approval at the officer building a large fire in the stove and cleared off the table to set the dog and his bloody bedding on the space used just the day before for an impromptu tea party. The building was active with police officers, inspectors and medics—the entire night watch, in fact, was in my bedroom—but for the moment I was oblivious to them all. I did notice Juno settle into Old Vic's usual place by the fire, where she licked blood off her fur and watched me work.

I had an injured dog to save.

After a couple of hours of cleaning, shaving, stitching, anointing and bandaging Old Vic I let PC Mitchell, my de facto nurse, gently set the sleeping, drugged dog into a soft basket next to the stove. Juno promptly joined Old Vic, and after a few comforting licks on his head she fell asleep next to him. When Mitchell, smiling at a job well done, opened the door to leave the stable I realized the place had gone very quiet. All of the officers had left, long ago. I trusted that the corpse was gone from my bedroom as well.

Only then did I notice DI Rankin sitting patiently in a corner of the room, watching me.

"Would you like a cup of tea?" he asked.

I nodded my gratitude, suddenly feeling exhausted. I glanced over at the clock. It had wound down at 11, but I had heard it still ticking when I began Old Vic's surgery so thought it couldn't be much past midnight. "What time is it?" I rasped.

"Half one o'clock."

The detective inspector walked over to the stove to prepare a pot of tea while I removed the surgical apron, I had thrown over my green taffeta gown. Even with this protection I feared the beautiful dress was ruined. I knew Letty didn't care for the scruffy old dog but hoped she would understand why I hadn't taken the time to remove her wonderful gift before I began my work.

Before tonight I too had been unenthusiastic about Old Vic's intrusion into my life. But I have always been vulnerable to any animal in distress. I glanced down at the basket, glad to see the dog's sides still rising and falling with his respiration. It had been a near thing. It still was a near thing. But Juno was fast asleep beside him, evidently unworried, which I took as a good sign.

I sank down onto an old wooden chair. A ghost of a memory floated past, of my Papa collapsing into this very chair late one night, similarly blood drenched. He told me he had been operating on a horse, a private patient, but even then, I was doubtful. And later of course I realized what he had actually been doing that night which had resulted in him coming home covered in blood.

The deliciously divine smell of evil oolong woke me from a doze, and I saw DI Rankin sitting across from me at the table, a pot of tea and a few sandwiches on a plate, left from the day before, steamed soft and tempting in front of me.

"Eat," he said.

I nodded and obeyed. I hadn't eaten before going to the theatre, so excited had I been. I glanced down at my ruined dress again, sighing.

"I'm sorry I didn't see you earlier in the evening," DI Rankin said. "I'm sure you looked quite beautiful."

I reached up to my hair, touching reflexively. Spilled and messy. I saw that my hand holding the sandwich was covered with blood. I quickly set the sandwich back onto the plate. No doubt my face was smeared with the stuff as well.

I needed to wash up, but I was so tired. And where would I sleep tonight?

Oddly enough, he seemed to guess my thoughts. "The boys removed the bloody bedding and brought some clean blankets in for you," he said. "You can go to bed after you answer a few questions for me."

I nodded. Despite everything, I thought I might be able to sleep.

"Just a minute," he said. He got up to pour some water into a bowl, mixed it with hot water from the kettle, and brought the bowl and a clean rag over to the table. "Here," he said, handing me the rag and setting the bowl of warm water on the table.

I saw that fresh blood stains had permeated the worn wood of the table and made a quick mental note to bleach it down tomorrow. But for now, my attention was fully on my face and the cloth in my hand. Nothing feels better on a tired face than a warm, wet cloth. I luxuriated in the pleasure of it, gently cleansing my face with a relieved smile and then carefully cleaning my hands. DI Rankin waited for me to finish, then handed me a dry cloth to wipe the damp from my hands and face.

Only Letty and my Mummy had ever been this kind to me. I think I fell a little bit in love with him then, despite everything.

"Ready for a few questions now?" he asked.

"Yes," I said in my whispery voice.

"What in God's name did you think you were doing going into Limehouse yesterday morning?" he bellowed. It seemed that before he started questioning me about the events of tonight he felt obliged to vent his anger over my having blatantly ignored his orders to stay away from opium purveyors and out of disreputable areas of town.

I find I have little patience these days for men who yell at me, and after a few short minutes of his tirade I started glancing around the room for another mallet. Happily, the man soon wound down and began asking cogent questions regarding the events of the night.

Had I ever seen the intruder before? No.

Had I noticed that the man was a person from the Orient, probably Chinese? No.

Was I sure I had never seen him before? Yes.

Might he have been a part of the murder I'd witnessed in Limehouse yesterday? Perhaps, all I had seen was a mask, which tonight's rapscallion had not worn.

What was I doing in Limehouse? Did I often frequent opium dens? Where had I gone tonight? Who had been with me? Did I know the man would be waiting for me when I got home? How did I think the man got in? Why would the man butcher a defenceless dog and leave it on my bed? Why had I carried a mallet into my bedroom? Had the intruder said anything before he died? Had there been anybody else here with him? Anyone else here with me?

The questions went on and on like that; some sympathetic, some confused, some accusing. I felt bad for DI

Rankin's frustration and answered the questions as best as I could, but I was as muddled as he regarding any motivation for an unknown Chinese man to sneak into my room and cut up my dog.

"The most likely explanation is that this is connected in some way with the murder you witnessed in Limehouse," DI Rankin said finally. "Perhaps he was the killer—he thought you had seen his face and wanted to eliminate you."

"Perhaps," I croaked.

"The only other possibility is that this was the same man who attacked you the other night."

"No."

"Are you certain?"

"Yes, I'm certain," I insisted. I remembered that there had been another witness to the other assault. "PC Perkins also saw the man who attacked me," I reminded my interrogator. "He described him as a big man, and fat. The man tonight was neither."

"How about the man or men in the alley yesterday?"

"I don't know how thin or fat he or they were," I said in a frustrated whisper. "But the person wearing or carrying the mask was much shorter than me. PC Perkins said the man who assaulted me the other night was big." Bert was a very large man, tall and broad. I could not conceive of any connection between him and the alleyway murder from the day before, but tonight's attack? Who could say? I glanced over at the basket. Both animals still slept, though one of them had just passed wind.

DI Rankin shrugged. "PC Perkins is no longer certain of his original description."

"It wasn't the same man," I reiterated. "It is possible, however, that the man who attacked me the last time hired an underling for the task tonight." This thought filled me with dread—could Hubert Cranston have taken on his own apprentice in crime? It seemed unlikely, but I had to consider every possibility.

Finally, it was my turn to ask questions. I was curious about two things: how the intruder had become locked in, and why the stable boys hadn't investigated when the dog suddenly stopped barking (I assumed Old Vic had barked when he first saw the intruder—he barked every time he saw me, and he'd known me for years).

DI Rankin told me that the stable boys had entered the office around ten in the evening to bring Toby into his regular stall. Old Vic was barking all evening before they entered and continued barking the entire time they were there. When they left, they locked the door behind them, and shortly thereafter Old Vic stopped barking. They didn't question their good fortune at the sudden silence. The police suspected that the intruder snuck in first, hiding in my bedroom while the stable boys brought in Toby, and that he had knocked Old Vic out before carving him up on my bed. They were unsure about whether the man had planned to assault me but thought not; they believed that he probably intended to leave the dog as a warning and then sneak out before I returned. Unfortunately for him, he had been locked in by the stable boys and didn't have a key.

"He could have broken the lock, or climbed out of a window," I said.

"No doubt he would have, if you hadn't returned as soon as you did."

We sat there in silence for a few minutes, both ruminating on the events of the night. Finally, I got up to look in on Old Vic, and then on Toby, the mule and the quickly recovering donkey. Juno stretched and left through a crack in the wall, no doubt to hunt. But I thought all four of the others would sleep through until morning.

"Why don't you go to bed, Maddie? I'll set up a watch outside."

"Thank you."

DI Rankin stood. "We'll talk more tomorrow."

"Yes."

I managed to remove the green taffeta gown and corset before falling into bed, and even hung the dress up on a peg, hopeful that perhaps Letty could work one more miracle and make it wearable again.

True to his word, early the next morning the interrogation began again. But DI Rankin's morning harangue was interrupted when Astraia Holmes came to my rescue like a tiny white knight armoured in lilac chintz. I choked as I read this headline from the top newspaper on the stack she dropped in front of me:

Lady Horse Doctor Bravely Foils White Slaver in Her Bedroom!

Chapter Eight

"Don't be an idiot, Samuel," Astraia chided after Detective Inspector Rankin ordered her to leave. I flipped through the pile of papers. *Spinster Lady Horse Doctor Kills Intruder in Police Stable. Chinese Hooligan Attacks White Woman in Her Bedroom. Police Stand Impotently by As Woman Is Violated on Police Grounds.* I groaned. This was my first glimpse into the nightmare which was about to become my world. At least that first morning the stories were not yet illustrated by images of semi-clad damsels fighting off brutes. Those titillations would not appear until the afternoon editions.

DI Rankin glared at Astraia, annoyed at the interruption. "I am questioning Miss Maddie about the fact that she vouched for Mr. Wu just a few days before she was attacked by a Chinese man. It seems an unlikely coincidence."

Letty marched in behind my saviour, the knight's squire carrying provisions of boiled eggs, toast and preserves. Astraia's companion closed the stable door behind her, to my great relief. There was a terrible wind today and I had been freezing, all for the sake of respectability.

Astraia waved to Letty to set out breakfast and tidy up the place. Letty wrinkled her nose at the smell of bleach permeating the table but said nothing.

"This has nothing to do with you, Astraia—other than the fact that your gentleman friend did a profoundly inadequate job of looking inside the building before leaving Miss Maddie alone last night to fend for herself," DI Rankin snipped. I heard a weak growl emanate from the dog basket, which engendered great relief in my chest. Old Vic was on the mend. I glanced over and saw Juno, who had joined him after a few hours out on the prowl, again licking the dog's injuries. Happily, Old Vic didn't seem to mind the maternal attention from his erstwhile enemy.

"Sounds to me like she did quite a good job fending for herself," Astraia said with a smirk. But I knew DI Rankin wasn't really annoyed with Ramsay for his sloppy inspection of my rooms. He was annoyed with himself and all the other police officers who'd allowed a scoundrel to sneak onto the premises with villainous intent, not once but twice, without interception.

And perhaps he was also annoyed with me, for my contribution to making the police look foolish.

The food on the table made my mouth water, and I wondered how soon these two would stop arguing so we could get down to the important work of eating. I watched Letty walk to my room to clean up my messes. I shuddered to think of her reaction when she saw the green taffeta ruin.

"If you don't mind, Astraia, I'm questioning Miss Maddie on the events of last night," the inspector said again.

"It's good I'm here then," Astraia said. "This way she won't have to tell her story twice. Where's that nice Police Constable Froest?"

I had been wondering the same thing. It was long past our usual morning teatime.

DI Rankin answered her. "He's following some leads this morning in Limehouse, where most of the Chinese immigrants live and Miss Maddie witnessed that killing. If you come back when he returns, I'm sure Miss Maddie will be happy to tell her story to both of you then."

"Oh, Maddie won't need to tell anything to Frank," Astraia said. "I'm sure he's heard the full story already from the other policemen who were here last night. But I'm anxious to hear all about it. All I know is what I've read in the newspapers." She smiled brightly and sat down, placing a lacy serviette onto her lap, clearly intent on staying for breakfast.

DI Rankin gave in. He rubbed his face, then helped himself to a boiled egg.

"All right, Miss Maddie—to get back to the issue at hand. You were going to explain the Chinese connection to me," he said, exhaustion in his voice. I realized he probably had not slept at all yet.

"Is there any tea?" Astraia interrupted.

He glared at her but obediently poured boiling water into the teapot and brought it over, along with a packet of tea for her preparation.

I had not had tea—or any sort of nourishment at all—yet this morning, and for the first time it occurred to me this shortcoming might have been intentional. DI Rankin may have hoped to withhold sustenance from me as inducement to obtaining my confession to some criminal activity.

Astraia of course had deduced this fact the moment she walked in and saw no food or drink on the table.

Once again, I was grateful for her friendship—although I knew the attacker might not have appeared last night at all if I hadn't involved myself in her investigations in the first place.

"From your impertinent question when I entered, I conjecture you assume a connection between Maddie's association with Mr. Wu, her witnessing that killing in

Limehouse and the attack on her dog last night, is that correct?" Astraia asked the detective inspector. "Maddie, how is the dear little doggie doing? The papers said his prognosis was dire," Astraia said as she measured and stirred tea into the pot.

I nodded over to the basket by the stove. "He'll live." I wondered how the newspapers had learned of the dog's critical condition.

"Your voice is much better today, I'm glad to hear," Astraia said. "But it doesn't sound as though you're entirely comfortable with it yet, so I'll help you out. Question one: was Mr. Wu last night's evil doer?"

I shook my head no. She was right; I was not yet comfortable with my hoarse voice—it had always been deep, but now I thought I could probably sing bass. However, I thought it more likely she wanted to control the direction of the conversation, which she could more easily do if she asked me leading questions.

"Had you ever seen last night's villain before?"

Another head shake.

"Do you know any Chinese people at all other than Mr. Wu? Men or women?"

I shrugged. "Mr. Guo and Mr. Hong from the lecture the other night," I said.

She looked at me sharply. "You know, I'd almost forgotten about them. But you don't really know them, do you? You just heard them speak that one time?"

I nodded.

"You don't know any other Chinese people—any of the restaurant or laundry proprietors, for example?"

I shook my head in negation. I did not possess sufficient funds to eat in restaurants or to send my washing out to a Chinese laundry. Although perhaps I could make an arrangement with a respectable business such as I had with Feinmans' Bakery—free laundry service in exchange for taking care of their delivery horses. It was an idea worth considering.

Letty walked past us to the door, a long swath of green taffeta in limp folds covering her arm. She looked over at me sorrowfully, her shoulders slumped in disappointment as she left.

Astraia continued. "You would not recognize the murderer from the alley, and you can't identify the man from last night. Can you think of any Chinese person who could identify you?"

I thought. "Only Mr. Wu," I said.

She nodded. "You need to arrest Mr. Wu, Samuel."

I looked at her in inquiry.

"Dear Maddie, I don't wish to cause you pain, but your friend Mr. Wu must be responsible for that man being in your room last night. He is the only person from the Chinese community who would have recognized you in Limehouse and known where you lived. I suspect he might have been the person with the lamp-lit mask, since it was clear from your description of the incident that that person would have seen you quite clearly."

"And if Wu was the murderer you saw, then no doubt he's also responsible for the other two murders," DI Rankin said.

"I disagree," Astraia said. "Maddie said that although there were three cuts in each instance, the weapons and methods used were very different. Also there was no pictograph or deep claw marks left in the wall of any building in the Limehouse incident."

DI Rankin shrugged that off. "Wu was present at the first murder. Clearly, he's the link in all of this. And no doubt he's also the person who attacked Miss Maddie that first time, probably because you and she have been asking too many questions and he thought she knew too much about the case, or else in anger that she had not allowed him to escape her custody, thereby forcing him to testify to the coroner's jury. You may be unaware, but he's been missing ever since that day."

Astraia shook her head. "No," she said adamantly, then turned to me. "I'm going to have to ask you to use your voice a bit, dear Maddie, because I need you to explain something. How do you know last night's intruder wasn't the same man who attacked you the other night?"

I stared at her, trying to think how to explain it without confessing my history with Jolly Bert.

"The man who attacked me the other night was bigger than me," I rasped out. "The man I killed was smaller."

"Are you positive on this?" DI Rankin said.

"Quite positive," I said. "Also, the man who attacked me had that oily smell I mentioned the other night. I did not notice an oily smell on the man last night, although I only encountered him for a moment. You examined him, Detective Inspector. Did he have a strong oily smell?"

"No," DI Rankin said. "He had a strong opium smell."

"Then it's someone different."

"He might have bathed the oil off," Astraia suggested. "Did the man look to have bathed in the last few days, Samuel?"

DI Rankin glared at her. "He did not look to have bathed in the last few years, to tell you the truth."

"Then I do not know why you're bothering to pursue this line of questioning," Astraia said. "Clearly these are two different intruders."

DI Rankin finally gave his frustration rein. "You're telling me that you honestly think Miss Maddie has accumulated two different enemies, both determined to kill her or at least scare her quite badly, in just these last few days—after years of working here in the police precinct without difficulty? And that you believe there's no connection at all between these incidents and the fact that Miss Maddie has accompanied you in your hare-brained investigations into slaughtered prostitutes and Chinese pictographs?"

"The last woman killed wasn't a prostitute," Astraia said quickly.

"How do you know that? Did PC Froest tell you that?" he said angrily.

"No, I discovered that fact on my own. Through detection. And no, I'm not saying there's no connection between the incidents—no doubt there is some kind of connection—but what I'm saying is two things: first, Maddie was attacked by two different men—and since she only killed one of them perhaps the police might attempt to find the other. Who is not Mr. Wu. Just a suggestion. And two: whatever connection there might be between all these things, she doesn't know what it is, and you need to stop hectoring her."

After fuming at her for a few moments DI Rankin turned his intent blue gaze on me.

"Do you feel I've been hectoring you, Miss Maddie?"

I shrugged. My only real concern with these questions was the possibility that they might lead to other questions on a topic I definitely did not wish to discuss.

"Can't you see how aggrieved she is?" Astraia asked. "She killed a man, for God's sakes; don't you think that troubles her?"

I tried to look troubled; but really, once you have committed patricide, killing a man who has just carved up your dog hardly warrants a second thought.

But evidently, I carried it off. "Of course, you're right, Astraia," DI Rankin said. "I'm sorry, Miss Maddie. I'll leave you alone now, although I may come back to ask you one or two more things after your visitors leave."

He took a final long gulp of his tea, grabbed his hat and another hard-boiled egg, and walked to the door. "By the way Astraia, I know I don't have any more influence over your behaviour than your own brothers do. I know none of us can stop you from putting yourself and Miss Maddie into danger by meddling in these affairs. But one thing I can do: I can take measures to ensure you receive no additional assistance from the police. You will not be allowed at any more crime scenes and you will not obtain access to any more crime scene photographs. So don't even ask."

He turned his stare on me. "And Miss Maddie, it sorrows me to threaten you but you leave me no choice: if you wish to remain employed by the Metropolitan Police, I strongly suggest you expend your time performing animal care and refrain from involving yourself in police criminal matters." He slammed the door as he left, in emphasis.

"That's very unfortunate," Astraia said. "I had a lot of questions about what the police have discovered about our Maria."

"I can't lose this job," I said.

She reached a small, gloved hand across the table and patted my large calloused one. "Don't worry, Maddie. You are going to remain secluded here for a couple of days, which should satisfy your employers. I have some research to do."

This sounded ominous. "What kind of research?"

"Oh, this and that," she said airily. "First I have some library research to do... I suppose I had better go to work."

I wondered what it was like to be employed by people who did not seem particularly bothered by whether or not you actually came to work. What was the pay? And were they hiring?

"Thank you for bringing breakfast over," I said.

She bent down to run a light finger over Old Vic's ear. He opened his eyes to look at her but didn't move. "I'm so sorry you got hurt, little darling," she crooned to him. "You get well soon. You need to watch over our Maddie girl." I saw his tail lift a bit, as though he were trying to wag it without bringing too much hurt to the cuts on his rump. "You too, darling," she said to Juno. "You keep taking care of our dear little doggie." She stood, frowning as she picked black cat hair off her white gloves.

"Please tell Letty I'm sorry about getting blood on the beautiful green dress. Also on the gloves," I said. "The shoe and stocking are still in pretty good shape though, I think."

"Don't concern yourself about it," Astraia said airily.

"No, I mean it, I— "

"I said don't worry," she interrupted. "Letty thrives on having things to complain about. If she is complaining about the dress, that's less time she'll spend complaining about me. You did me a favour, letting the dress get soaked in blood."

I couldn't view the situation in quite the same way but kept silent as she gathered her things and left. I liked Letty and hated having disappointed her.

The next day John dropped off a new frothy white coverlet to replace the one the dog had been tortured on. The new one was even fancier than the first, which is how I discovered Letty was not just a generous woman but a very forgiving one as well. A true cat lover.

*****

For the next three days I did not see Astraia Holmes. I stayed in my office and stable, keeping my head down, resting my foot and voice, caring for old Toby and Old Vic and the buckshot mule and other sundry animal patients; and eating when hungry from the various baskets of food that had been heaped on me over the recent days, until the bread became too stale to consume and inquisitive mice too audacious to scare away even with Juno's assistance.

And I read the papers. *Lady Horse Doctor Fights Off Brute in Her Bedroom. Crippled Policewoman Defends Her Virtue Twice in One Week—And This Time She Kills Him!* The headlines became increasingly outrageous, even salacious, over the next few days, most articles accompanied by a lurid illustration of a beautiful young damsel in torn negligee fighting off an evil-grinning pigtailed man. There was even one dark and blurry photograph of me, reprinted over and over, which I realized must have been taken surreptitiously by some journalist who had snuck in while I was in the office working to save Old Vic's life, probably taken with one of the new box cameras that didn't require a tripod or set-up time. My weary face and messy hair, adorned with torn and drooping peacock feathers, certainly supported the story of a woman who'd barely survived a battle to the death to protect her virtue.

The reporters tried to get into the stable to interview me, but happily the police were so mortified about my having been attacked twice on police property their presence was suddenly everywhere, prepared to defend me from all potential enemies—and that included the fourth estate, who had made no friends on the force with their scurrilous coverage of police ineptitude last year during the Ripper investigation.

Occasionally little titbits of truth would pop into a story otherwise packed with conjecture and hyperbole—like the fact my father had been the police horse doctor before me, and the fact I had vouched for the Chinese man who was witness to the first "serpent slasher" death, as the tabloids were calling the latest murders. When the news came out that I had actually housed the opium purveyor in my stable one night instead of letting him rot in jail while waiting for the coroner's jury (and you can imagine the hints of impropriety alluded to in that story) I realized one of the stable boys, probably Little Teddy, must be selling information to the press. Luckily the police figured it out too, and that source of tattle quickly dried up.

I received repeated exhortations from the newspapers to grant them interviews—money was even offered, more than a simple bribe, which I was told was not their usual practice—but I of course stayed vehement and consistent in declining their invitations. I did not want any in-depth articles written about me or my history or my family. I wanted desperately to go back to those halcyon days of anonymity, when no one thought about me and I whetted no one's curiosity. The police, determined now to guard against all interlopers onto police property and no supporters of the press anyway, were happy to enforce my determination to avoid all journalists and photographers because it fit in with their own strategy. If I hadn't already wanted to steer clear of reporters for my own reasons, I am confident the police would have insisted upon it for theirs.

Frank Froest visited every day, bringing fresh bakery items for our tea and copies of the day's rags so that I could keep current on the lies being printed about me. He kept me apprised on the so-far-fruitless search to discover the identity of my intruders. He amused me with his stories about the ingenious but ultimately unsuccessful schemes reporters devised to get past my police sentries in order to gain access to me or at least to the infamous bedroom crime scene. But Frank remained steadfast in two things: he would not close the door when he visited no matter how cold it was, and he continued to refuse to talk about the investigation into the serpent slasher deaths.

Until tea three days after I killed the intruder, when I managed to harry Frank into letting an important detail slip.

"You'd at least tell me if there had been any more killings, wouldn't you, Frank?" I asked.

"I bring you the newspapers every day," Frank said. "You know as much as any other citizen about the case."

"There's been no more killings?"

"What do you think?"

"I think you can at least ease my mind on whether or not any poorer women have been mutilated!" I almost shouted at him. It was the first time I had ever raised my voice to Frank, and it thoroughly discomfited him.

"Sweet Jesus, Maddie, calm down! No more women have been killed!"

"You'll tell me if any more are?"

"Yes, I'll tell you if any more are!"

"You'll tell me if they're prostitutes or maids or fancy ladies...or horse doctors?"

"Fine! I'll tell you if they are prostitutes or maids or fancy ladies or horse doctors! Fine!" He got up from the table and reached for his policeman's helmet.

"How can I believe you about that? You never told me the second victim was a maid, not a prostitute!"

"And I never told you her name was Maria Murphy or that she was Irish or that she was twenty-five years old or that she was pregnant when she died!" he said. "The crime details are none of your affair! I'll tell you if any more women are killed and if they are, I'll let you know their social standing, but that's it! You are to stay out of this investigation!" Now he was shouting at me, something I would have never imagined could happen.

But the fight had gone out of me. I stood as he opened the door to leave.

"Thank you, Frank," I said. "I apologize for my temper. You'll forgive me?"

He smiled, his shoulders relaxing. "Of course, Maddie. I just don't want you to get in trouble."

"I know."

"Or to lose your job. That would be a terrible thing, if you no longer worked here. Well, what would I do for tea?"

I smiled because I knew he wished it. "I had better keep my job then." I thought of one more thing. "You'll tell me if you find Mr. Wu?"

He looked at me soberly. "You know we're doing everything we can to find the bastard, Maddie."

"I know, Frank. See you tomorrow?"

"Of course," he said. "And remember I never told you anything," he said, and winked at me before he left.

I hated putting my friend in the untenable situation of choosing between following orders and appeasing me, but what else could I do? The fact was, women were being killed and the police were off on a wild goose chase, focusing on Mr. Wu. Perhaps he was responsible for the last murder, the one I had practically witnessed in Limehouse—but I was confidant he had nothing to do with the deaths of the two women. I feared Jolly Bert might be responsible—but I couldn't tell everything I knew to the police. I also could not tell it to Astraia—but she at least deigned to take my concern about the man seriously. I also thought she was cleverer than the police and more likely to discover what was going on.

Maybe she would even figure out what Chinese people had to do with the thing, because I had no idea.

I remembered suddenly that Jolly Bert had been a sailor in his youth. Had he spent the year of his absence in China? I wondered again: had the man who almost killed Old Vic been working for Bert, rather than for Mr. Wu?

If so, I was doubly glad I had killed him.

As I realized this, I felt troubled in my mind about this new level of callousness I seemed to have developed. I was a singer and a healer—not a killer or someone who enjoyed causing pain. I would have never thought I would take pleasure in anyone's death by any means, and certainly not that I would ever feel joy over having killed someone myself. Plus, I had discovered a murder myself less than a week ago—and had spent hardly a moment grieving for that anonymous man and his unknown loved ones.

A horrid thought: was this the latent development of a taint of madness inherited from my father? Would I soon find myself traipsing through London eviscerating people?

Old Vic whimpered and I put aside my black thoughts to tend to the unhappy animal. He tried to bite me, which I took as a sign his naturally vicious temper was returning. He must be feeling better.

Astraia paid me a call that afternoon, accompanied by Letty who took charge of cleaning the place and replenishing the larder. As Letty scurried around, I also saw her bringing in clean laundry—evidently the last time I'd seen the woman, two days before, she had taken home all my dirty things to wash and I hadn't even noticed them gone. I knew I should demur, but frankly my life was too complicated right now to reject any offer of assistance. I had no pride and was glad to

148

have someone else worry about whether or not I had fresh water, food and clean undergarments.

As Astraia set the table with the dainty china bunny pieces I filled the tea pot with hot water and said, "I have interesting news about the maid who was killed."

"Excellent. I knew I could count on you to ferret out details of the case despite DI Rankin's injunction," she said, satisfaction in her voice. "And I have news for you too. I believe I have identified the Chinese element."

Chapter Nine

"The pictograph we found etched in blood at each of the first two murder scenes is the Chinese depiction for the Ya Zi dragon," she said. "One of the nine sons of the dragon god king, the warrior dragon, Ya Zi is the Chinese dragon variant of Mars in Roman mythology, or Ares in the Greek."

"How do you know all this?" I asked, thoroughly impressed by my friend's perspicacity.

"I am a librarian," she reminded me. "I researched it. The dragon has been the totem of the Chinese Emperor for thousands of years, and Ya Zi was the emblem for an arcane society of warriors who served as the emperor's private guards."

"Why would the Emperor of China want to kill women in England?" I asked.

"I don't imagine he would," she said. "But any secret organization thousands of years old would no doubt have expanded its interests beyond simply guarding one person. My brother Sherlie mentioned that he was investigating a dangerous Chinese secret society operating in London. I expect this is it."

Oh no, not him again, I thought. "Does that mean you plan to consult with your brother Sherlock on the matter?" I asked.

"I don't want to," she said. "We'll see what we can find out without him. What did you discover?"

"Maria Murphy, Sir William's maid, was Irish, 25-years old, and pregnant when she died," I said, sharing the information but not the source. I hoped she wouldn't ask how I had gained this knowledge, since I didn't want to betray Frank.

"Very interesting," she said, not asking how I had obtained the information. "Pregnant, eh? That adds several new possibilities to the thing, doesn't it?"

"Does it?"

"Certainly. I think it's vital we find out who the baby's father was, don't you?"

I shrugged. I could not see how discovering the identity of Maria's paramour would help us to understand why a Chinese secret society was killing British women in the East End. And what could it possibly have to do with the murder in Limehouse? Were all three killings connected after all, or was the Chinese factor only a coincidence? But I was relieved to hear she didn't plan for us to speak with her brother.

"I believe I need to speak with my brother," she said.

"What?"

"Not Sherlie," she said. "Mykie. I want to ask Mykie about Sir William Forrester Clydon, retired Lieutenant Governor of the Punjab, current board member of the British East India Company, and erstwhile employer of Maria Murphy."

This enquiry too seemed irrelevant to me, but I was not a detective so didn't gainsay her stratagem. We ate in silence while she further ruminated.

Finally, she stood, determination in her stance and the firm set of her shoulders. "Yes," she said, "I have several things to do today. And there's something you need to do as well."

I eyed her with foreboding. "What?"

"You need to find out if the prostitute who was murdered outside of Mr. Wu's shop was also pregnant," she said.

That I could probably do. "All right," I said.

"Letty! We're leaving!" she said, her voice raised in a most unladylike manner, clearly impatient to follow up with her allotted tasks. She walked over to the dog basket to gently caress the head of the injured animal, then strode to the door, slipping on her hat and inserting hat pins to secure the thing as she waited for her companion.

Letty perambulated out of my bedroom as though she had all the time in the world. I told her thank-you, though I had no idea what she had been doing in there; no doubt it had been something helpful like sweeping the floor or changing the sheets or painting the walls. Or maybe she had just spent the time petting Juno, who was probably in there anointing the new white bedspread with black cat hair.

Letty nodded to me, transferred the leftover food from the lovely bunny plates to my old chipped dishes, gathered together the breakfast china and linens, and exited the stable without any acknowledgement whatsoever of her employer's presence by the door.

"Is she angry with you?" I asked Astraia.

Astraia shrugged. "Who knows? Who cares?" She set her gloved hand on the doorknob. "Oh, by the way—I have some questions for Minister Guo of the Chinese legation. I think the most likely way to get an appointment to see him will be if you request one, therefore, I will send him a letter in your name, if you don't mind."

"Me? Why would he be willing to see me?"

"You are the woman who killed one of his compatriots, are you not? I shall say you wish to express your sorrow over the matter or some such thing. Don't worry; I'll come up with a convincing story."

"I expect you shall," I said, waving good-bye as she left.

Over tea with Frank the following day I easily accomplished the task Astraia had set to me. The prostitute had not been pregnant at the time of her death, although she had experienced that interesting condition several times during her short life.

Frank had just left when John arrived, carrying a note. I had an appointment at the Chinese legation for one o'clock the following day.

I wondered what on earth I would wear, then brightened to remember that Letty had cleansed the vegetable matter off my brown day dress. I thought I had also seen my one remaining good shoe in a corner of my bedroom, the leather revived and shined. I would need to buy a new pair before my cast was removed, but for now the one would do.

But my only decent hat had been eaten by that pernicious dray horse just after he crushed my foot. I would need to roll myself down the street to Jenny's rag store, to see if I could find a serviceable second-hand hat, something adequate for a visit to a legation.

This afternoon was not too far gone; Jenny's shop should still be open. I considered changing from my work attire, then opted against it. Wearing clean apparel would only encourage Jenny to increase her prices. I hoisted my handbag, looked inside to make sure everything was in place as it should be, grabbed my crutch for stability and undulated down the street for the first time since witnessing the killing in Limehouse. A police constable insisted on accompanying me for my own protection; I insisted that he remain at least ten feet behind, which he acquiesced to do.

*****

The next afternoon I considered my mirrored image as I waited for John to collect me. Green taffeta and peacock feathers had for a time lured me into aspirations above my station but now I was past all that. Mine might be a life of quiet desperation, as the American poet put it; so were most people's; there was no shame to that. My belly was full and I was moderately warm. My hair was neat, my unmentionables clean and mended, my face and fingernails had been scrubbed; I looked respectable and presentable—who could want more?

"That is the ugliest hat I've ever seen," Astraia remarked as John assisted me to enter the cab.

"Is it?" I said, trying to sound surprised. I wore the only respectable (i.e. not designed for a prostitute) lady's chapeau on display in Jenny's shop yesterday. It was a truly awful hat.

On the positive side, it perfectly matched my dress and coat.

She examined me critically. "You need to buy a new wardrobe."

"The clothes I own are adequate for my needs," I said, attempting both prudence and sanctimony, and hoping she wouldn't say anything about my worn, discoloured gloves. After Bert broke into my room and handled my clothes I had wanted to burn all of them, but now that Letty had laundered everything—in some cases more than once—I was able to think more practically about the matter.

The horse lurched forward. I remembered that this was the bumpier, less comfortable of John's conveyances. Then I flagellated myself for my discontentment at this minor discomfiture. At least we were not crowded today. Letty was not present, so I assumed she was substituting for Astraia at the library again.

And who was I to complain about being crowded, anyway—I who did not have to share my living quarters with anyone but a dog and cat and the occasional horse? Also, the intermittent housebreaker or two, but no real harm done there yet, right? Well yes, I was almost strangled, and one man did die, but—

"Sometimes in the course of our investigations you will need to conform to a more decorous appearance," Astraia remarked. "We will be associating with victims, witnesses and perpetrators at all social strata and you will need to fit in."

"I don't possess the funds to—what are you talking about? When will we be associating with victims and perpetrators at all social strata?"

"I have decided to follow a new vocation. Consulting detective. Like my brother." She twitched at her perfect white gloves, not looking at me.

"That should be interesting," I said. What I thought was: I wonder if she would give me a reference to replace her at the library?

"I should like you to assist me. Like John Watson assists Sherlie."

I had read Dr. Watson's account of his work with Sherlock Holmes in *A Study in Scarlet* while convalescing at Astraia's home. One important element was never mentioned in discussions of that relationship.

"Does Dr. Watson receive any remuneration for his work with Mr. Holmes?"

"Of course not!" she said, seeming shocked by the question. "Dr. Watson is a medical man. I presume his patients provide his income and support."

"My patients are not so well-off as his, I think." But one other possibility did occur to me.

Detectival exploits often appeared as stories in periodicals such as *Lippincott's* and *Murray's*. One assumed magazines paid for such things...

I eyed Astraia speculatively, then rejected that idea. As a lady she would no doubt disdain to have her name bantered about in the public press. And surely the last thing I wanted was to court cynosure, what with the patricide and all.

"I'll have to think on it," I said.

"I can't imagine what there is to think about," she said. "Surely you've enjoyed our adventures thus far?"

Well, let's see. Since meeting Astraia Holmes a horse had crushed my foot, the Ripper's associate had manhandled me, I'd been crippled and lost my voice, I'd experienced trespass at either my home or my workplace on four separate occasions, I'd witnessed a murder, killed a man and alienated most of my work colleagues, and my dog had been cut open.

"I enjoyed the opera," I said. And of course, I enjoyed our friendship.

She smiled and inclined her head, as though that settled the thing. We rode the rest of the way in silence. As the cab slowed in front of the Chinese legation, I remembered I hadn't told her what I'd discovered about the first victim, Sarah Prentiss.

"The prostitute who was killed on Mr. Wu's doorstep was not pregnant," I said.

She nodded in satisfaction. "If she had been, I might have had to rethink my hypothesis," she said, "or at least embarked on tedious research that would been fruitless to our inquiries. So that is good to know. Well done, Maddie."

I smiled in gratitude at her accolade until I remembered: wasn't that one of the things Sherlock Holmes was always saying to Dr. Watson, the man who accompanied Holmes everywhere without receiving any pay for his time?

I followed Astraia into a fine neoclassical building on Portland Place. There weren't as many steps as I'd had to traverse at the Savoy Theatre, but still—marble steps are a significant challenge when one of your extremities has wheels attached to it. I was grateful to finally enter the foyer, because getting stuck in carpeting nap is preferable by far to losing control of one of your appendages on a slick or waxed floor.

After just a few minutes wait Hong Guofan, the Chinese Minister's aide, entered to greet us. He glanced past me and reached to shake Astraia's hand. "Miss Barquist, I presume?" he said to my companion.

"No, this is Miss Barquist," Astraia said, reaching over to pull me beside her. "I am her friend, Miss Holmes."

"I apologize, Miss Barquist," he said, shaking my hand. "I assumed because of your incapacity you could not be the person who killed my countryman. Or were you injured in the contretemps?"

"No," I said, electing not to explain my affliction.

"As Miss Barquist said in her correspondence, we are here so that she can apologize to Minister Guo in person for the terrible outcome of that meeting," Miss Holmes said. "We both have the very highest regard for the Chinese people and for your culture and are despondent that events occurred as they did."

I tried to look despondent. But the man did carve up my dog. I hadn't been particularly fond of the creature at the time, but since his injury I had become quite attached to the scruffy little fellow.

Mr. Hong looked at me, no doubt waiting to hear my apology, and I tried to think of something more profound to say than "I'm sorry," which seemed somehow inadequate given all our efforts to acquire this visitation.

"What was his name?" I asked finally.

"What?"

"The man I killed. Do you know his name?" I had a terrible thought. "Do you know if he had a family? Any children who are now left orphaned?"

"I do not know," Mr. Hong said. "None of us here have the slightest idea of who the man was." He led us to a side door. "May I offer you tea?"

"That would be lovely," Astraia said, giving Mr. Hong her brightest smile.

"Lovely," I echoed, following them into a sitting room.

The space we entered was crowded with shelves and tables strewn with delicate vases, figurines and objects d'art. Precious Chinese silks in glorious colours topped every surface; a stack of incredible silk scarves lay piled like dirty laundry on a piano lid. I tried not to hyperventilate, thinking of all the damage I could do with one misplaced sweep of my crutch, and sank into the nearest chair despite the impoliteness of doing so without first being invited to sit.

A servant rolled in a tea trolley, impressing me with his dexterity in manoeuvring around the hazards. Mr. Hong nodded to Astraia to be mother, and she was happy to comply; evidently there were no women in this household.

"Will the minister be joining us here?" she asked as she handed him his cup.

"No, Ambassador Guo is out at present. He requested that I see you in his stead and hopes you will not be offended by the substitution."

"No, of course not," Astraia said with an intimate smile though I knew she must be disappointed. "We are delighted to meet with you, Mr. Hong. We heard you speak at the Fabian Society lecture a few weeks ago and were so impressed by your manner and your dexterity in traversing the translation challenges of the English and Chinese languages."

I waited to see if she would start fluttering her eyelashes at him but evidently, she was holding back the heavy artillery for a later barrage.

He studied her with narrowed eyes, then smiled back. "You were there? You heard Sir William Forrester Clydon's outrageous expiation for polluting my country with the opium poison? And then his physical attack on Ambassador Guo—that was indefensible. I am so sorry that you ladies had to witness that horrific spectacle. I was embarrassed on behalf of your country, on behalf of your Queen, that such a man should be seen as representing your interests."

As I recalled the incident, Mr. Guo had been the first to strike a blow. But I had no reason to defend Sir William, so stayed silent on the matter.

"We were moved to tears by Ambassador Guo's words," Astraia said, noting the fact that Minister Guo was to be known as an "Ambassador" despite the fact that the Chinese government had only a legation to England, not an actual embassy. "We have been struggling ever since on this issue, worrying about what we can do as Englishwomen to support your poor people. Should we stop drinking Chinese tea? It would be a terrible sacrifice but one we would gladly make if it would help." She took a sip of the high-quality tea, which had been served with neither sugar nor milk nor lemon. "So delicious," she said, breathing the steamy scent with feigned pleasure. I knew for a fact she could not tolerate an unadulterated brew.

"No, please do not stop drinking our tea," Mr. Hong said with a laugh. "Our farmers would be desolate and would likely take to growing opium poppies in its stead, which would make our current situation even worse! What you can do is, convince your Queen and your lawmakers to pay us properly for the commodity in good British silver, instead of trading for it with vile opium. That is all we ask."

"We will certainly do that," Astraia said, bravely taking another sip of her black refreshment. "We were so appalled by Sir William's contumelious conduct. Have he and the Ambassador known each other for many years?"

"I believe they became acquainted after the Margary affair fifteen years ago," Mr. Hong said. "You'll remember that unfortunate incident from the Ambassador's talk the other night. After Mr. Margary and his party were killed our two countries entered into a number of diplomatic exchanges and the Ambassador and Sir William became acquainted at that time. They have never been close, unfortunately, and their relationship has only further deteriorated since we've been in London."

"Such a shame," Astraia said.

"A shame," I echoed. I thought I should say something at least occasionally, since my purported remorse over the unknown Chinese dog-butcher's death was the pretext used for our visit here. Unfortunately, Astraia had not informed me of her objective, so I did not know how best to contribute to its achievement.

Her intent was soon made clear to me. "Mr. Hong, I understand some markings have been found in the Whitechapel area recently, near some horrific deaths; markings that imply the killers may have been members of a vicious Chinese criminal gang known as the Ya Zi society. Do you know anything about that iniquitous enterprise?"

He stared at her. "I beg your pardon?"

She realized she had conveyed too much assertiveness and quickly revised her tone. "I'm sorry if I sounded blunt," she said, her head bowed. "It's just that Miss Barquist and I both work in that neighbourhood and we've become very frightened lately." She lifted her head and gave him not only the eyelash flutter but also a tremulous lip.

Mr. Hong melted. "Oh Miss Holmes, how terrible! I wish there were something I could do to assure you. But I know nothing about the Ya Zi society operating here in Great Britain. I am surprised I have not heard these concerns before; I would have thought the local police would have contacted the ambassador if they had questions."

"Were you familiar with the Ya Zi society back home in China?"

"I'm familiar with Ya Zi lore, of course; the adventures of the nine sons of the dragon are a well-known myth in my country, like one of your fairy tales. But I am not convinced there is—or ever has been—a Ya Zi criminal society. And I cannot imagine what it would be doing here on the other side of the Earth, if it did exist. Let me tell you the Ya Zi story, to relieve your mind."

And like an uncle telling tales to the kiddies to keep them entertained on a rainy day, Mr. Hong launched into the story.

"The great and auspicious dragon king was blessed with many sons. Each of these sons was himself a dragon, and a particular manifestation of one of the dragon king's great qualities. He sent nine of his sons to assist the first Emperor to conquer the unruly tribes and bring the empire together. They were known as the nine sons of the dragon, and many astonishing stories and songs and art have been created about their glorious adventures and the favours they brought to those who invoked their assistance.

"The first son was Bi Xi, who looked like a turtle. His hard shell could carry any burden.

"The second son was Chi Wen, who looked like a fish. He could swallow any evil.

"The third was Pu Lao, who looked like a dog. His howl could scare away any enemy.

"The fourth was Bi An, with the face of a tiger. He was a fine guard for precious things.

"The fifth was Tao Tie, with the face of a wolf. He loved food, and brought abundance, even in times of famine.

"The sixth was Qiu Niu, with the face of a cow. He loved music, and emanated joy even in times of sorrow.

"The seventh was Suan Ni, with the face of a lion. He was a restful creature, who granted peace to the weary.

"The eighth was Jiao Tu, who looked like a snail. He was all-wise and held secrets both lofty and dangerous.

"And the last was Ya Zi, with the face of a jackal. He was a warrior filled with a lust for blood.

"Now of all of these nine sons of the dragon, the Emperor loved Ya Zi the most, because there was nothing Ya Zi enjoyed more than killing the Emperor's enemies. And because he had Ya Zi on his side, the Emperor became the most powerful ruler in all of the world. The Emperor's special guard was trained by the great Ya Zi himself, and any man lucky enough to be selected to serve in the guard dedicated himself to Ya Zi's emulation and veneration. Like Ya Zi, the guardsmen were fierce warriors, who loved to shed blood in the service of the Emperor, although over the centuries there were occasions when the guard had to choose between their loyalty to Ya Zi and their loyalty to a corrupt or undeserving ruler. But all this was thousands of years ago, and as the centuries passed the stories about the Emperor's special Ya Zi guard and their great deeds of slaughter and conquest devolved into unlikely rumours of a vicious criminal enterprise that runs the Chinese underworld to this day. They're like your English bogey-man stories, something you tell the children to make them behave—'if you don't obey your parents the warriors of the Ya Zi dragon will come and kill you'." He laughed. "Such nonsense."

Astraia gave a pretty tinkling laugh in response, which I tried to echo with less success. Tinkling has never been my forte.

"But you said that certain markings have been found near some horrific deaths, that have raised the spectre of the Ya Zi here in London," he said, his voice serious now. "What kind of markings, do you know?"

"A pictograph," Astraia said. "If you give me pen and paper, I will attempt to draw it for you."

Mr. Hong did not question how a well-bred young lady could have obtained sufficient access to police information to know how to duplicate markings found near murder victims. He simply brought over the requested writing implements and watched in silence as Astraia traced the design onto paper.

Up to this point he had been solicitous of us, even mildly flirtatious with Astraia, light and entertaining and perhaps a bit condescending. But when he saw the image Astraia drew on the paper his demeanour changed completely. A hardness entered both voice and manner.

"Is this some kind of joke?" he asked.

"Not at all," Astraia said. "Quite the contrary. To my knowledge this symbol has been found at two serious crime scenes during the last couple of weeks. Scenes of terrible carnage."

"How do you know?"

"I saw the dreadful image myself once—so did Miss Barquist; and we also saw it in a photograph taken at another scene. It is the Ya Zi symbol, is it not?"

"Hmm. What was the medium used? Chalked into the wall? A paper left at the scene, perhaps?"

"Nothing so genteel, Mr. Hong. In each case, the image was traced onto the filthy street near the body, using the victim's own blood. There was another murder as well, which might be related—Miss Barquist saw the victim, and we know it wasn't the same murderer, also there was no pictogram—but in that instance, the murderer wore a dragon mask."

She stared pointedly up at the wall behind us, and I turned to see what held her attention. On the wall, hanging above the door, was a huge wooden mask, a monster's face with beard and feathered hair.

A dragon mask. Yes, that was what I had seen running out of the alley in Limehouse, just before I found the dead Chinese man.

Mr. Hong's face screwed up into a momentary expression of angry desolation, then quickly smoothed back into the benevolent countenance he'd worn earlier in our visit—a guise I now knew to be only a shallow façade, the expression he showed for company.

"Well, this has been a most interesting and charming visit, ladies, but I'm afraid I have another engagement shortly," he said, folding the paper with the image and placing it in his coat pocket. He stood to his feet to lead us out of the room.

"That is the Ya Zi symbol, is it not?" Astraia repeated.

He shrugged, giving a light laugh. "There are some similarities, certainly—but I'm afraid someone is playing a cruel jest. There is no Ya Zi criminal society operating in London."

"And there is no Ya Zi dragon manifesting in the streets, slaughtering women with his vicious claws, claws so sharp and terrible as to engrave grooves even in brick walls? No Ya Zi dragon terrorizing Limehouse either, despite what Miss Barquist saw?" she asked as Mr. Hong practically pushed her out the door into the foyer. I followed after them both, still carefully employing my foot and my crutch—but I should have been paying greater attention to the movements of my other elbow. A careless shift with my arm knocked a small gewgaw off a delicate table. The crash was not loud—the floor was heavily carpeted, thank God—but I noticed a little ceramic head roll under a divan as I exited the horrible room.

I considered confessing to the destruction but took the coward's way out instead and stayed silent.

Not that anyone would have paid any attention to my words anyway at that moment.

"What the hell are you two doing here?" thundered a voice I knew only too well.

Detective Inspector Rankin stood in the foyer, a few steps ahead of a couple of bobbies who had just followed him into the building.

Chapter Ten

But Astraia was unruffled. "Good afternoon, Detective Inspector Rankin. Mr. Hong, let me introduce Detective Inspector Rankin of the Metropolitan Police, who is no doubt here to ask the Ambassador questions about the Ya Zi symbol that's been found at several crime scenes recently." Astraia looked pointedly at a sheaf of papers in the Inspector's hand, which I realized must include photographs of the pictograms left at the scenes where the women had been murdered— which Astraia had been required to point out to the man in the first place, since the police hadn't even noticed them.

"Miss Holmes, I told you to stay out of this case," Inspector Rankin seethed.

"Miss Barquist and I came here today so that she could make her formal apology to the Chinese people," Astraia said haughtily.

"Formal apology for what?"

"For killing one of their compatriots, of course," Astraia said. "Surely you can't have forgotten so soon Miss Barquist's traumatic experiences of the other night?" She accepted her coat and purse from a servant and tucked her arm into my free side. The servant offered my old battered bag to me and Astraia took possession of that as well. "Come, Miss Barquist. Mr. Hong has other visitors to see now."

She turned her back to the police and held her hand out to Mr. Hong. "Thank you so much for the delicious tea and the entertaining fairy story, Mr. Hong. So droll. Tell me, will we be seeing you at tomorrow night's meeting of the Anglo-Oriental Society for the Suppression of the Opium Trade?"

Mr. Hong shook her hand. "I expect so," he said. "I have the honour of being the guest speaker."

"What a marvellous coincidence," she said, her smile beaming and slightly triumphant. "We shall see you there, then."

She released my arm so that I too could shake hands with Mr. Hong. "Sorry about killing that man," I mumbled. "Please let me know if you learn anything about him."

"I will certainly do so," Mr. Hong said.

"Any information the legation obtains about the criminal who assaulted you will be shared with the police, Miss Barquist," Inspector Rankin said angrily. "You do not need to worry yourself about it."

We left the building. John had the carriage at the doorstep and was available to assist my nervous and wobbly self down the stairs.

"I'm going to lose my position," I bemoaned as we began a short carriage ride through the streets. Our destination was the nearest tearoom, so that Astraia could wash her mouth out with tea brewed and served in the "civilized British fashion," i.e. with plenty of milk.

"Nonsense," she said. "I'll speak to Mykie about it."

"Mykie?" I gave an inward groan. I had no inclination to visit Astraia's brother this afternoon. Either of them.

"Yes. He is dining with me tonight, a duty he feels obliged to effectuate at least once per quarter, on allowance day. I shall query him about Sir William and also inform him of what a good friend you have become to me, and how dreadful it would be for you to lose your post simply because Samuel Rankin is annoyed with me. My brothers have goaded me for years to develop female friendships; I'm certain they're both most grateful to you for being able to tolerant my eccentricities." She patted my hand. "Do not worry, Maddie. You won't lose your job."

We had a very satisfying tea after which John drove me back to the police veterinary stable—I hesitate to call it "home" although I suppose by this point that is what the place had become.

"Tomorrow night I will update you on what I've learned from Mykie," Astraia said. "I will collect you at six."

"Why? Where are we going?"

"To the meeting of the Anglo-Oriental Society for the Suppression of the Opium Trade, of course," Astraia said. "Don't you remember? Mr. Hong is speaking." She waved and they left, and I hobbled my way past several curious police constables to the stable where I found a newly injured horse awaiting my attention.

The animal didn't appear in much distress so I took time to change into work apparel before going into his stall. As unattractive as my day dress was, it was the best thing I had to wear to my newest engagement on the following night. I committed to make maintenance of my paltry wardrobe a priority, for a change.

*****

The next night's meeting of the Anglo-Oriental Society for the Suppression of the Opium Trade (Society for the Suppression of the Opium Trade—SSOT—for short) was held in a Quaker meeting house. This did not surprise me— Quakers had been both active and vocal for decades in their opposition to the evil business, as had the Anglican Church—

but I had not expected a political meeting to so closely approximate a church service.

We sang hymns. We prayed. We discussed pertinent Bible verses. I was glad for an opportunity to pray in a House of God for the four dead—Sarah Prentiss, the prostitute; Maria Murphy, the housemaid; the man I had found dead in the alley and the man I had myself killed. As someone who admittedly hadn't attended church in a long while, I found the whole thing very comforting—it alleviated some of the guilt that had been weighing on me for my repeated failure to attend services, for one thing—but I think Astraia found the meeting somewhat tedious. From some of the things she'd said from time to time, I'd gathered hers was not a religious family.

My mother had been quite a religious woman. Papa, obviously, had lacked that virtue. But worship services always remind me of my mother, and I promised myself again that night that I would make more of an effort to attend in future, as I had promised Mummy on her deathbed.

Sir Joseph Pease, who had debated with Sir William Forrester Clydon at the Fabian Society meeting that Astraia and I had attended a short fortnight ago, oversaw the order of the service. Sir Joseph had inherited the presidency of the SSOT from his brother and viewed his position as a sacred duty. This night he lead us in our hymns, our prayers, and our Bible verse readings before he spoke for a few minutes about the evils of the opium trade in language much less temperate than he'd used the other night in the more public venue, at one point actually referring to the men who'd gained wealth through opium as "greedy whoremongers destined for hell". Finally, he invited Mr. Hong to address the congregation, and it was clear from the cheers and affection of the group that

Mr. Hong needed no introduction to this particular collection of British citizens.

But the Mr. Hong who addressed this meeting was not the charming fellow of the day before nor the respectful gentleman of our first encounter. This Mr. Hong was distant, brunt, and threatening.

His declamation was short but minatory, beginning with "I can no longer restrain my fury at the recalcitrance of the British government to end its tyranny regarding Chinese sovereignty" and ending with a menacing ultimatum: "...and if the British Lion thinks it can continue to stomp its heavy paws down on the neck of the Chinese empire, then I warn you, ladies and gentlemen: we have agricultural and geological resources and talented, determined people, and someday we will gain our rightful place in the world. And then you will learn that we also have long memories, and we are slow to forgive," he said, almost hissing as he finished a terse discourse focused heavily on British greed and hypocrisy.

"Mr. Hong is very angry about something tonight," Astraia whispered during the half-hearted applause given to Mr. Hong as he sat down. The crowd had tapered in their enthusiasm for the man as his remarks went on. No one likes to be chastised or insulted, and Mr. Hong had been quite incendiary in his comments.

"Perhaps he's always like that when he's here, speaking with these SSOT people," I said. "Perhaps he feels comfortable here, where they're all in agreement with his beliefs."

"No," she said. "Look at these people—they're stunned by what he's said. Before he started, they were happy to have him speak. They are not happy now. They wanted to hear about the evils of the opium trade. They did not want to hear

170

about the evils of the British people. It is one thing to hear Sir Joseph, a respected Member of Parliament, rail against British greed. It is another thing entirely to take such abuse from a foreigner."

This was true. Several people were actually grumbling. And Sir Joseph now stood floundering at the dais, trying to figure out how to bring some positive closure to this disheartening meeting. Finally, he decided to give it up for a lost cause, reminded the congregation of the soirée musicale fund raiser planned for the following week, and called for a last hymn before ending the meeting early.

Mr. Hong rushed from the meeting house soon afterwards, before we could get a chance to speak with him. I know he saw us, and believe he intentionally left so soon in order to avoid Astraia and her incessant questions.

"Well, that was a waste of an evening," my friend said as we settled back into John's carriage for the long drive back to my neighbourhood.

"Not entirely," I said, holding up a copy of the society newspaper, *The Friend of China*. I thought I might attend a meeting again in the future—I agreed with both Sir Joseph and Mr. Hong about the greed that allowed the opium trade to continue, and my pride as an Englishwoman was not particularly pricked by rightful insults made to the British Lion. I thought the meeting had provided just enough church to satisfy my promises to Mummy, while yet appeasing the secular rather than spiritual fervour that abided within my own breast. And, I admit, I felt grateful to Mr. Hong for having given sanction the day before to our continued consumption of Chinese tea without guilt. Now I could sip my oolong with pleasure again, knowing that my consumption of the product supported Chinese farmers employed in righteous agricultural endeavours.

Astraia nodded to the newspaper in my hand. "Let me know if that periodical provides you with any insight into our current case," she said, a bit of snarkiness to her tone of voice.

"What did your brother Mycroft say when you spoke with him last night?" I asked. I had hoped she would tell me on our drive here, however she had been unusually quiet during the entire trip. But if she could vouchsafe that my continued employment was assured, I was anxious to hear about it.

"Mycroft was atypically close-mouthed last night," she said. "I believe he too has information about Ya Zi gang activities in the east harbour area, but he refused to share any of it with me. He also abjured providing me any insight into Sir William's household. Therefore, I will need to follow a different approach with my inquiries. I will probably be out of touch for the next several days. If you need anything, just contact John or Letty."

"All right," I said meekly, although I felt disquiet, wondering if I should insert myself into her business and just ask her outright what she had planned.

Such is life: we miss the small rolling stones that eventually join together to culminate in an avalanche.

"Did you say anything to your brother about the threats Detective Inspector Rankin has made regarding my employment at the police station?" I finally asked, since she seemed disinclined to raise the topic on her own.

She reached over and patted my hand. "Oh, my dear Maddie, I'm sorry; yes, all's well there—you needn't worry about your job."

I felt my eyes fill with relieved tears and was grateful for the darkness of the carriage as I covered my sniffles with a rough cough. If Astraia noticed, she was considerate enough not to say anything about it.

*****

Since Astraia had told me she'd be unavailable for a few days I was wary when I heard a polite knock on my office door the following mid-afternoon. The police and stable boys were not so genteel in announcing their visits; if my caller had been one of them he would have been bellowing at me to let him in or, more probably, would simply have entered without announcement, since the door was not locked.

So, the manner of notification, that simple polite door-knock, worried me from the start. And my anxiety did not improve once I discovered the identity of my visitor.

"Who is it, please?"

"It's Sherlock Holmes, Miss Barquist. May I enter?"

My breath caught in my throat, then sputtered out. I forced myself to calm down, then opened the door. "Of course, Mr. Holmes. You're quite welcome here," I said, lying for politeness sake just as my Mummy taught me.

Sherlock Holmes entered, shook my hand, and closed the door behind him. I did not inform him I was instructed to keep the door open whenever a man visited the stable. He made himself comfortable in a chair by the stove and lighted a pipe as I began preparing tea and a light snack, just as though this was an everyday visit by an ordinary caller.

"I understand you accompanied my sister to the SSOT meeting last evening," he said once we settled at the table with our refreshments. I found it difficult to sit with the man. I did not like the smell of pipe smoke, which reminded me of my father. I almost wished I had insisted the door be kept open, to help air out the place.

"Yes," I said. Old Vic whimpered and I went over to his basket to tend to him, grateful to have the excuse to distance myself from the man and his pipe. Although the dog didn't really need me—Juno lay beside him, licking up his discomfort.

"Is the dog healing adequately?" he asked.

"Yes."

"It's unfortunate you are not especially fond of dogs."

"He's growing on me." I was not going to ask him how he had deduced my limited enthusiasm for the animal. Perhaps because I was so hesitant about petting Old Vic, even as he lay panting pathetically in his basket (the dog did still have his teeth, after all).

"Do you know where my sister is?"

I looked up in surprise to see Mr. Holmes scrutinizing my expression. I determined to show a blank face. "No," I said. "I do not."

He continued to look at me, not saying a word, which I took as indication it was my responsibility to contribute something to the conversation.

"Your sister told me that she would be out of touch for several days, and if I wanted anything, I was to contact Letty or John."

"Letty and John do not know where she is."

"Have you informed the police?"

"No. She left a note. I am not particularly concerned about her welfare as I'm certain she meticulously planned every detail of this escapade. But I should like to remain apprised of her whereabouts."

Now it was my turn to examine his face in silence. I did not know where Astraia was. But I could have shared facts with her brother which perhaps he could have used to ferret her out. I could have told him that she had informed me she would be out of touch immediately after mentioning that she had been unable to obtain information about Sir William Forrester Clydon's household from Mr. Mycroft Holmes. I strongly suspected that Astraia's absence was associated in some way with her desire to gather the desired intelligence.

But wasn't this my first test, as her friend? Keeping her confidence? He said she had left a note. If she had wanted her brothers to know her destination she would have included that information in her correspondence.

"I'm sorry, Mr. Holmes," I said at last. "I do not know where Miss Holmes is. I only know that she expected to be unavailable for a couple of days."

"Are you not worried about her, Miss Barquist?"

I thought about it. Astraia Holmes was probably the smartest, most capable woman I had ever known. Fearless, yes, but also extremely competent. I decided to show faith in her.

"No, Mr. Holmes. I am not worried about her. I believe she will be just fine."

He nodded. "Thank you for the tea, Miss Barquist," he said, rising.

I walked him to the door.

"If you think of anything else, you will let me know, won't you Miss Barquist?" he asked.

"I will," I said. If Astraia did not appear within three days' time, I would tell her brother of her interest in Sir William and his household.

As soon as he left, I disposed of his pipe ashes in the refuse dump behind the stable, then left my office door open for several minutes, despite the cold, to air the noxious odour out of the place.

*****

The larder being depleted, and with no expectation of receiving replenishment from either generous friend or angry police colleague in the immediate future, I decided to struggle along to the market for a meat pie and perhaps some eggs, or apples or potatoes. I would also call on the Feinmans to see how their dray horse Tina was doing and see if they could spare a loaf of bread or a few day-old tea cakes.

A couple of police officers standing near the stable questioned the wisdom of my leaving the police station perimeter, one actually ordering me to remain until they could discuss it with the sergeant, but I refused to tolerate their nonsense. I had decided to go to the market, and that was that. The day was brisk and perambulating the streets with a roller cast remained challenging, but still it felt good to be out and about, and no doubt I would have enjoyed that hour was it not for two jarring incidents.

The first occurred when a short man in a mulberry cloth hat stopped me in the street to ask me if I was Madeleine Barquist, the police veterinarian. He looked harmless at first appearance, plus he was small enough in stature and build that I could have overpowered him were both of my feet and even my hands incapacitated. And this was a busy thoroughfare with plenty of witnesses. I admitted that yes, I was she.

"Can you walk me through the events of your midnight boudoir assault?" he asked. "Our readers are slavering to know more."

A light flashed in my face and I realized that a news photographer had just taken my picture. I raised my crutch to swing at the pair of them, and just before it connected with the nose of the reporter and the shoulder of the photographer the second incident occurred: I saw an emaciated beggar boy standing across the street, watching us intently. The streets of Whitechapel are infested with herds of emaciated beggar children, but this one specimen stood out for me because of the bright cerulean cloth he wore tied around his head, which reminded me of my Mummy's favourite scarf; as I completed my swing at the journalists with my crutch and started moving deeper into the market I wondered what had happened to Mummy's blue scarf after she died. Perhaps my Papa had sold it to Jenny and now it was experiencing reincarnation on the head of this filthy urchin.

Were it not for my ruminations on that scarf I would not have noticed the child again watching me when I exited the other end of the market, my crutch basket filled with meat pies and plums. Nor would I have taken note of him when Mr. Feinman escorted me from the bakery to the police station across the street, thoughtfully carrying both my market basket and two loaves of warm bread in his heavy arms.

"Do you know that child, Mr. Feinman?" I asked, tilting my head toward the blue beacon bobbing next to a flower cart at the street corner.

"Which child, Maddie?" he asked, a reasonable question since there were perhaps two dozen young punks visible in the vicinity.

But the blue vanguard had disappeared as quickly as my nod, reappearing multiple times over the following days, adding a new worry to my life.

Someone must have assigned this child—and possibly numerous other people I hadn't yet noticed—to spy on me. What was it they were hoping to see?

*****

"No doubt he's one of Sherlie's brats," Astraia said dismissively after I mentioned my worries on the matter when she visited late in the afternoon two days later. She had fortuitously appeared at my door just as I was plotting my

177

trip to 221B Baker Street to confess to her brother about her concerns over Sir William.

"Your brother has children?" I asked, confused by her attitude toward her nephews and troubled that the great Sherlock Holmes would allow his progeny to dress in rags and run around the worst parts of town without adult accompaniment.

"No—his Baker Street Irregulars," she said. "His army of street urchin spies. Haven't you read about them in Dr. Watson's chronicle?"

Now that she mentioned it, I did seem to recall something about Mr. Holmes using street children as his own intelligence force.

This identification of my blue-scarfed stalker alleviated some of my tension. I did not anticipate doing anything requiring secrecy—patricide is a once-in-a-lifetime sin—so if accounts of my regular daily activities were relayed to Mr. Holmes, I did not see any particular harm to it. My bigger concern with the matter was simply this: that I had become so important to Sherlock Holmes that he was spending money now to monitor my movements.

Once again, I questioned my common sense in allowing myself to become friends with Astraia, a decision that could lead to disaster for me should her brother uncover my secrets. Ah well, too late now. But I couldn't help wishing my friend had been simple Miss Astraia Smith, instead of Miss Astraia Holmes.

"Where have you been these last three days?" I asked again, for of course that had been the first thing I had said to her when she'd arrived at my stable office. She had fobbed me off then, saying she would tell me the whole thing over a nice cup of tea if that wouldn't be too much trouble; and she fobbed me off again now as she sipped at the sweetened, milky brew, saying she had been out of touch these last few days and needed to finish perusing the newspapers stacked on my table before she could tell me of her own adventures.

"That photograph of you is not terribly flattering," was her comment on the latest news article about me. The heated story accompanying the ghastly image implied that my passions were so wild that I thought nothing of attacking innocent men on the street.

"I have never taken a good photograph," I said.

"Did you see this?" she asked, pointing a chipped nail at an article in yesterday morning's newspaper. I read the headline: *Chinaman Killed in Whitechapel Alley.*

"I didn't have anything to do with this one," I protested. "I never saw him."

"You think not? Read the description."

No identification had been found on the unknown man's body, and there was little description of the fellow provided in the article except that the man had been dressed in stylish English apparel and lacked the traditional Chinese queue.

I had only ever seen one Chinese man with short hair.

"Mr. Hong?" I said in horror.

"I believe so," Astraia said. She stared at me with her penetrating brown eyes. "We need to find out."

"All right," I said. "How will we obtain the necessary information?" In my mind I pictured us breaking into the morgue or some such thing. But she did not have anything so dramatic in mind.

"His body was found in this neighbourhood," she said. "You are an employee of this police station. Go ask someone."

I acquiesced. I rolled myself out of the stable and over to the station office where I spent a few enlightening minutes speaking with the desk sergeant.

I returned to the stable, shivering with cold.

"Yes," I told Astraia with a sigh. "It was Mr. Hong." I huddled over the stove to warm myself. I had not taken time to put on a coat before rushing out.

"How did he die?" she asked.

"Same as the others," I said. "Like the two women. Slashed. Eviscerated." It deeply saddened me to think that someone I had so admired, someone I had spoken with just a short time ago, had been killed in such a gruesome fashion. "I asked about the pictogram, but some other officers entered, and the sergeant suddenly remembered they aren't supposed to talk with me about police matters any more. And of course, he wouldn't tell me if the knife wounds were symmetrical or not."

"We need more information before we can make deductions about his killer," she said. "For example, Mr. Hong may have been killed because he asked the wrong questions of the wrong people."

"What do you mean?"

"You saw how he behaved when we told him about the Ya Zi killings," she said. "He knew something and was disturbed by it. So disturbed that he was not able to maintain his usual calm demeanour at the SSOT meeting the next night. Maddie, I am very much afraid that Mr. Hong might have been killed because he began his own investigation into these crimes, after our visit to the legation."

"He died because of us, because of what we told him?" I asked, stricken.

"He died because of us," she affirmed. "Or perhaps because of some information he gleaned from his interrogation by the police." She set the last newspaper back down on the table. "All right," she said. "I will now tell you about what I've been doing for the past three days.

"You will recall from the conversation we overheard at the Savoy Theatre that Maria Murphy, Sir William and Lady Clydon's late maid, came to their employ from the Monroe Agency, and that Lady Clydon said that she would hire her replacement from Madame Hollande's establishment."

I began to have a very bad feeling about where this was going. "Don't tell me you entered into the Clydon's service?" I said.

"Don't interrupt," she said. "First, I went to Monroe's, to see what I could find out about Maria's background. They were unwilling to answer my questions, so I was forced to enter their office after hours to search their files."

She saw the expression on my face. "Yes, Maddie, I broke into their office. Don't worry—I didn't steal anything. I used my lock-picks; I am confident they remain unaware anyone was even there. Can I continue now?"

"Where did you stay at night?"

"The first couple of nights I stayed in my bolt-hole. Sherlie is not the only one who maintains a hidden sanctuary, you know. Of course, mine is more respectable, just a cheap room in a lady boarding house, really."

I had no response to that. Astraia Holmes was even more audacious and reckless than I had ever imagined. It did occur to me that her cheap rooming house bolthole was probably also more respectable than anyplace I'd lived in since Mummy died. Noting my silence, she went on.

"Their file on Maria provided nothing of consequence except that she had no relatives in this part of England. So, the next day I went to Madame Hollande's to inquire after employment. I was Bridget O'Malley, a housemaid in Miss Astraia Holmes's household until this week, when that good lady was called to attend to an ailing friend on the continent. Bridget also carried a glowing character reference from Miss

Madeleine Barquist, a respectable employee of the Metropolitan Police. I was sure you wouldn't mind."

"No, of course not," I mumbled, numb by now at this woman's nerve.

For the first time I began to consider that she might be the one person in the world who could perhaps accept my heinous family and criminal history without criticism.

"Madame Hollande had several open postings to recommend to me. I of course found ways to respectfully decline them all until she mentioned the position at Sir William Forrester Clydon's London home. I agreed to be interviewed by Lady Clydon's housekeeper.

"Mrs. Humphrey, Lady Clydon's housekeeper, is quite the martinet; I shouldn't be able to work for her for a single hour under any other circumstance. But I was revoltingly deferential to her during the interview, obsequious to the point of Uriah Heep, and she offered me the job, beginning that very hour.

"I was hired immediately because apparently I am the same size Maria was, so I could save the household money by wearing her old uniforms. I wouldn't be surprised to see two fingers pinching a penny on the family coat of arms, so obsessed do they seem with frugality. Sir William is not short of funds, as I found when I searched his desk. He is simply a miser. And Mrs. Humphrey is his pinchpenny partner.

"They even gave me Maria's bed, a cot in a draughty garret shared with two other housemaids. I searched around but any meagre items she may have possessed had been appropriated by others, probably within hours of her death. I found remnants of an old nosegay lovingly pressed beneath the mattress of her bed. But of course that provided no lead to her killer, nor did it give much information on her life other than she had treasured this small gift, received, presumably, from some unknown person since she would never have wasted the pittance she earned in wages buying such a frivolous item for herself.

"I wanted to explore the house last night, pry out all the secrets and hidden places while everyone slept, but this proved impossible with my two roommates, who were very light sleepers and also terribly inquisitive—which is often the case in the lower orders.

"This morning too was wasted; I was required to spend the whole time cleaning the multitude of hearths in that house—most of which, I am convinced, had not been cleaned in an age. Just look at my nails. No doubt there is still a trace of charcoal on my face and hair, since I cannot abide washing in cold water and that's all Sir William's staff are permitted to access—and very little of that. One must expend money to maintain a clean and well-fed staff, you know, and as I've said that is not the practice in the Clydon household below stairs, although I gather Lady Clydon does not share her husband's parsimony when it comes to funding her unique personal interests. Believe it or not, as much as the staff dislikes Sir William, they detest Lady Clydon even more. But her oddities were not part of my investigation.

"This afternoon proved much more fruitful to our case. I was assigned to clean Sir William's desk."

At this she opened a ragged portmanteau she had brought in with her. And for the first time I noticed the shabby apparel she wore. Her brown-and-grey dress was simple in both material and design, and darned in a few places; her hat looked almost as bad as the one I had bought from Jenny. I realized her apparel was a disguise, no doubt her Bridget O'Malley façade.

"Astraia, don't tell me you came straight here from Sir William's establishment?"

"Of course, I did," she said. "I had to show you what I found."

"But what about your brothers, and Letty and John? Shouldn't you tell them you've returned safe? You have returned, haven't you—you're not going back there?"

"Good God, no—I'm not going back. And as for telling my family—didn't you just say that Sherlie's spies are watching you? No doubt he has already been apprised of my materialization here... Now, I had better show you what I discovered before John appears to haul me off back home."

She reached into the valise to pull out a sheaf of papers. She set them with a flourish on the table, a victorious smile on her face.

"What are those?" I asked, referring to the pile of disparate documents, including paper in a variety of types and sizes, from fine linen stationary to scraps of the cheap wood-based paper used in newssheets.

"These are from Sir William's love letter collection," she said. "The important one is here."

She selected one of the flimsiest sheets and handed it to me. The paper was so poor and ancient I had to handle it carefully lest it flake apart. Written with pencil and dated just three weeks ago, I assumed the writer had used some old discarded paper since even the lowest-grade pulp shouldn't disintegrate this soon.

My deerst Billy,

Yu havnt bin to see me in an age and yur valt wont let me in to see yu so im leeving yu this not. I must see yu rite a way it is URGENT. I dunt want to tell yur wife but I will if yu dunt see me rite a way.

I love yu so much.

Yrs,

Maria

I looked at Astraia. "This is the important one?"

"Maddie, this stack of missives includes romantic epistles written from countesses and from washerwomen. And this is only the top layer from the man's love letter drawer—it seemed overkill to grab everything. Evidently Sir William takes a great deal of pleasure out of receiving billets doux from his paramours and no doubt strongly encourages his chères amie to write them."

"This doesn't read much like a love letter to me."

She scrambled through the pile and handed me two others of similar paper quality. "No, but these will."

I began reading but quickly put them down, my face reddening with embarrassment and not just from the poor spelling. "She wasn't exactly Elizabeth Barrett Browning."

"No, Maria's letters remind one of Moll Flanders, only bawdier. And Maria's are among the tamest of the bunch; some written by others are explicit to the point of pornography."

"I'm surprised that Sir William possesses the capacity to so inflame the passions of these women," I said. In our two encounters I had observed only a fat, rich old man lacking any sort of attraction.

"I gather from these that he can be quite charming when he sets his mind to it," Astraia remarked.

"Why did you take so many of the letters?" I asked. "Why didn't you just take Maria's missives?"

"Because I didn't want him to know I was investigating his relationship with Maria, of course," she said. "This way, he won't know which of his inamoratas was the focus of my interest."

"You believe he'll know you took them?"

185

"I'm certain of it. Especially since I had to club him over the head."

"What?!"

"He discovered me riffling through his drawer and caught me reading his correspondence. I presume he viewed that as an attempt at flirtation on my part, since then he tried to kiss me. Luckily, he keeps a bust of Lord Nelson near at hand on the desk, which I immediately ascertained would make an effective cosh. I utilized it."

Chapter Eleven

"Oh my God."

"Don't worry, he isn't dead."

"Oh my God."

"Just bleeding a little bit."

"Oh my—what on earth is that?"

She had taken another item out of her portmanteau. "Sir William also collects weapons," she said. "I found this one particularly interesting."

She handed me a dagger to examine. I recognized the symbol on the thick handle, and gasped.

"It's the Ya Zi pictogram," I said.

"The gold dragon handle on his black lacquered cane holds the same image," she said. "But I didn't dare take his cane, since it is too big to hide in the bag."

"What other incriminating items did he have in his home?"

"Unfortunately, I have no idea. I had to leave the establishment quickly, since I had just knocked out the master of the house and there was no telling how soon he'd gain consciousness or be found by Mrs. Humphrey or one of the other housemaids. I almost didn't go back to my room to retrieve my valise but was suddenly fearful that I might have left a clue in there that could give a hint to my identity. But I needn't have worried—I was sufficiently careful when I packed. I need to stop doubting myself. Sherlie and Mykie never doubt themselves."

I looked at the stack of letters again. "I gather it's your hypothesis that Sir William was the father of Maria's baby."

"That seems the obvious deduction, yes."

"So, do you think Sir William is the murderer? He has that dagger, and used to live in China—perhaps he's associated with the Ya Zi society in some way?"

"We are still in the information-gathering stage of our investigation," she said. "It's too early to draw conclusions." She placed the letters and dagger back in the portmanteau. "I wonder where Sherlie is? Well, I can't wait for him any longer—I need to get back to my house, to be ready to receive my visitors."

"Your visitors?"

"Certainly. As soon as Sir William's household found him injured and they ascertained that Bridget O'Malley was missing, Mrs. Humphrey will have sent a request to Madame Hollande for more information about that upstart girl. Very soon now, someone will visit Astraia Holmes to ask if she ever had a housemaid by that name. She will of course inform them that she never heard of this person. You too should be prepared to receive visitors making these same types of queries."

She stood and handed me the portmanteau. "Please keep this here. I do not have time to haul it back to my boarding house for safekeeping. I recommend that you install it some place where nosy detective inspectors won't be likely to stumble over it."

She moved to the door. "It's such a nuisance to be a woman on one's own; I had the devil's own time getting a hackney to bring me here. I will ask one of your nice policeman friends to find me a cab. When Sherlie arrives, please tell him I went home. Tell him I refused to tell you where I've been for these last three days. He may not believe you, but I'm confident you'll muddle through his inquisition."

In the end, I was not subjected to Mr. Holmes's inquiries. He did not come looking for his sister after all.

But one of Sir William's agents did appear, no more than a few hours after I had safely stashed the valise containing the tawdry evidence in a corner of my bedroom next to my own shabby handbag. I assured the man, quite convincingly, that I had certainly never written a letter of recommendation for anyone named Bridget O'Malley and gave him a copy of my handwriting to take back to his employers for comparison purposes.

I inscribed a bible verse as my handwriting example. My father, who had not been a religious man, would nevertheless frequently cite some of the more inflammatory verses during his diatribes, so I had any number of selections to choose, from memory. I opted for this gem from Jeremiah:

The Lord make thee like Zedekiah and like Ahab, whom the king of Babylon roasted in the fire because they have committed villainy in Israel, and have committed adultery with their neighbours' wives, and have spoken lying words in my name, which I have not commanded them; even I know, and am a witness, saith the Lord.

I felt confident that my note would never find a place in Sir William's billets doux drawer.

*****

The next morning, I received a letter from Astraia requesting that I accompany her to visit her brother Sherlock

189

Holmes and informing me that John would come by in mid-afternoon to collect me.

I enjoyed assisting Astraia in her investigations. But I was the woman who had killed Jack the Ripper, my own father, and I wanted to keep this information to myself. And the last thing I desired to do was socialize with Sherlock Holmes. I considered simply telling John upon his arrival that no, I did not have a job like Astraia's and could not take time off from work in the middle of the day to join his mistress on a visit to her brother. But that wasn't precisely true, was it? Frank Froest had verified that Mycroft Holmes had arranged my situation with my employers so that I could do precisely that.

Frank also told me that having the government insert itself in local police employment decisions had not gone over well with headquarters. I accepted this censure as my due: I could not even be annoyed with Astraia for speaking with her brother about my situation since she had done so with my encouragement, in response to my expressed fear over losing my job.

As one might guess, I was not in the best of moods when John came to the stable door to collect me early that afternoon. I was treating a horse for colic, so told Astraia's manservant that I needed to continue working for another hour and afterwards would require time to clean up. I suggested that he go back home to tell his mistress that I was unavailable today.

But he said no, he was happy to wait, and although it was nearly 3 o'clock before I was ready to leave, he seemed perfectly content when I finally rolled myself out to his cab.

Astraia was less happy when we reached her home several hours late to collect her. But once I informed her that I could not leave a horse in dire distress she calmed down, saying only that she wished I did not have to work so much.

I refrained from asking her who had overseen the library for these last four days, which I felt showed significant forbearance on my part.

She was still broody, however, and recalcitrant to talk during the trip to 221B Baker Street, which suited me just fine. Usually I was glad enough to join Astraia on her investigations, but I did not want to visit Sherlock Holmes and did not see any reason why I should put on a show of wishing to do so.

His housekeeper showed us to his rooms. He was alone, his amanuensis Dr. Watson off attending to personal errands, possibly earning his daily wage. Under other circumstances I might have felt sorry for Mr. Holmes, being forced to host two disgruntled women on his own, but to be honest I was not certain he even noticed our poor humours.

After acknowledging me with cordiality and kissing his sister on the cheek, Mr. Holmes asked his housekeeper to bring in the nuncheon she had prepared for this visit. We settled down to bread, cheese and meats, and I eat perhaps more than my share since I had not had time to consume anything else today. Although I didn't think Mr. Holmes noticed that, either. He ate very little, himself.

Happily, he did not elect to smoke a pipe at any time during our visit, though there was evidence of his regular indulgence all over the room.

He sat patiently in his chair until his sister had taken several sips of his housekeeper's excellent tea, then asked "What did you wish to see me about, Astraia?"

This question surprised me, since I had assumed, we were here at Mr. Holmes's behest. I would not have imagined Astraia would have come to see her brother of her own accord.

"I am desirous of sharing information," she said. "I believe you know things that would aid in my investigations. And I may be able to assist you in your inquiries as well."

I caught my breath. Astraia was here to ask for her brother's help.

No wonder she was in a bad mood.

He smiled. "I doubt you know anything about which I am ignorant."

"Did you know that Maria Murphy was pregnant with Sir William Forrester Clydon's baby when she was killed?"

He was silent for a few moments. "No, I confess that piece of information had eluded me. How interesting." He held his hand in a way that seemed to cup a pipe, and I waited for him to light one, but he continued to refrain from doing so.

"I should like to know more about the Ya Zi society," Astraia said, almost defiantly, and I knew that it was very difficult for her to ask her brother for this information. I conjectured that only her guilt over the death of Mr. Hong could have brought her to such action.

"What do you already know?"

"I know about the legend of the nine sons of the dragon. I know Mr. Wu's grandmother used to terrorize children with tales of a creature with huge claws that left piles of bodies in its wake. I know the pictogram which has been found etched in blood in at least two murder sites is the ideograph of the Ya Zi dragon. I know the noble Ya Zi warriors of old have degenerated into a Chinese criminal society that has now spread to the London harbour neighbourhoods."

She also knew that the late Mr. Hong had been troubled by, and perhaps been investigating, the Ya Zi society's recent appearance in London. But I noticed she didn't share this information with her brother.

"You know quite a bit, it seems," Sherlock Holmes said. "I had not heard of the old grandmother's fable. What do you wish to learn from me?"

"I wish to determine the connection between the Ya Zi society and the deaths of Sarah Prentiss, prostitute, and Maria Murphy, housemaid. I also wish to—" She took a deep breath. "I wish to know if you agree with me that the person who killed these individuals is not the same person, possibly Mr. Wu, who killed a man in a Limehouse alley while wearing a dragon mask. In addition, I am concerned about which murderer is responsible for the death of Mr. Hong."

"You have deduced no connection between the Ya Zi society and the deaths of the two women? I believe that's premature of you."

"Granted. It is possible that there is no connection between the Ya Zi Society and those deaths. But there is certainly a connection between all four of the deaths and the Ya Zi legend."

"I concur. All right. I will tell you what I know about the Ya Zi society.

"The Ya Zi society in London is led by a career criminal named Zhu Wei. He controls the opium and Chinese prostitution trades, as well as a variety of criminal enterprises such as extortion and fencing of stolen goods. He may also be involved in the white slave trade—if there actually is such a thing, which I am not at all convinced about; I believe those lurid stories are likely inventions of the British press, salacious fables created to sell papers. Either way, Zhu Wei prefers to limit his scope of control to the Chinese community, desiring to avoid capturing the interest of Scotland Yard. And of me. Frankly I am dubious that his organization has anything whatsoever to do with the deaths of those two women or Mr. Hong. They are probably responsible for most of the violent deaths that occur in the Limehouse district, however."

"Then you do not believe that the Ya Zi criminal society is involved with this case?"

Her brother stared out the window for a long while, as though by peering through the glass he could gain insight into his own soul. Finally, he spoke. "Not precisely. I do not believe they were involved in those deaths. But it is my gravest fear that the Ya Zi society has now taken an interest in you, Astraia, and in you too, Miss Barquist. That is why I have been so concerned that you remove yourselves from this investigation. Poor Samuel Rankin has become quite agitated about it and for once I agree with him."

"Agitated. About. What?" Astraia enunciated slowly.

"The man who tortured Miss Barquist's dog has been identified," her brother said with a sigh. "His name was Zhu Lei. He was a brother or a cousin of Zhu Wei. Perhaps an uncle. Chinese familial ties can be confusing."

I began breathing rapidly, without control, and knew I would soon black out. I had killed the brother/cousin/uncle of a Chinese gang leader? I would have laughed hysterically, except that now I could not breathe at all.

My first murder had been Jack the Ripper. My second had been a member of a notorious international criminal gang.

I had turned into quite the community vigilante.

Mr. Holmes strode over to my chair and unceremoniously pushed my head down between my knees. "Calm down, Miss Barquist. Astraia, please get a cool damp cloth and place it on the back of Miss Barquist's neck."

His strong hand held my head down—an action that threatened to send me into even greater hysterics, though the concerned man could not know that—but when I felt the

194

chilled wet cloth touch the back of my neck, raising goose bumps up and down my spine, I quickly recovered.

I began to breathe normally. Mr. Holmes removed his hand, I lifted my head, and Astraia took the wet cloth away. I used my serviette to dab at a few drops that had trickled down the side of my neck to puddle at the base of my throat and gave a large sigh. "Thank you," I said. "I am fine now."

"Is Maddie in danger, Sherlie?" Astraia asked with concern.

He snorted. "Of course, she's in danger, you idiot," he said. "You're both in danger. You need to stay out of my case!"

She stood. "Fine," she said. "You have convinced me. We will stay out of your case. Come along, Maddie. Thank you for the information, Sherlie." She went up on tiptoes to give her brother a kiss, then hustled me quickly out of the place. As John assisted me into the cab, I looked back up at 221B Baker Street and saw Mr. Holmes standing at the window watching me, a frown on his face.

"Well, that was useful," Astraia said with a triumphant grin. "I am sorry that you received that scare, Maddie—although certainly it's better to know the identity of the man you killed than to remain in ignorance. In fact, I can't believe no one told us before now."

"Perhaps it's a recent discovery."

"I doubt it. I suspect Samuel Rankin knew all about Zhu Lei's identity when we saw him at the Chinese legation the other day."

I nodded. This seemed likely. It also made better sense than blaming anger at the press for the plethora of police patrolling around the stable in recent days. I remembered the officer who had tried to keep me from going to the market the other day, and felt my lips thinning in annoyance.

Those fools! For years they had treated me like a colleague, like just one of the boys—comfortable and teasing and a little bit dismissive; they would joke about their cases and never worry about my delicate feminine sensibilities. But now, it seemed, they had decided I needed to be treated like a...like a woman.

Now they were protecting me. Which meant they were keeping secrets from me. I had become a victim of the conspiracy of men to protect women from the harshness of the world by keeping them in ignorance of the Base Nature of Man.

It was my own fault. It was because I had screamed, that night when Hubert Cranston woke me with his mouth on my neck, his hand on my shoulder. Everything had changed that night.

Astraia was still smiling, which added to my annoyance. "What do you mean, that visit to your brother was useful?" I asked.

"Now we won't waste any more time investigating the Ya Zi society. We can narrow our focus of enquiry."

"I thought you told your brother you would quit the case."

"I told my brother I would stay out of *his* case. He is investigating the Ya Zi criminal gang. We now know they do not have anything to do with our murders—or at least we know that Sherlock Holmes thinks they don't have anything to do with them, which is sufficient for me. He really is a very good detective."

"I think he probably meant that you were to stay out of everything associated with Ya Zi—whether it's the society or the pictogram or the dragon itself," I said.

"Then he should have said so, shouldn't he? Not that I would have paid him any mind if he had, and well he knows it. But we will certainly stay out of his Ya Zi society

196

investigations, and so I have promised him. You must stay out of Limehouse, lest you wander into another Ya Zi society killing. They must have sent Zhu Lei out to threaten you, using Mr. Wu's identification of you."

"Why do you say Zhu Lei was sent to threaten me? You don't believe his intent was to kill me?"

"Of course not. If he wanted to kill you, he would not have spent all that effort hurting your dear little doggie. He would have just killed you."

I had been a veterinarian for over ten years. I could have told her that the world was filled with people who took pleasure in hurting dear little doggies. At first I thought to leave her in ignorance—and even as I made that decision, I realized that I too was participating in that insidious conspiracy to protect the womenfolk from knowing all about the big evil world in which we live.

"Astraia, there are people who actually enjoy hurting animals," I said.

She looked thoughtful for a few moments, then said "Of course there are. How foolish of me. Well, perhaps he was there to injure or kill you—but there haven't been any other attempts since then, have there?"

"No. But there are a lot more policemen loitering around the stable now, to scare any miscreants away."

"Are there? Well that's good then," she said, dismissing any remaining concern about my safety. "That is probably why Sherlie put his Baker Street Irregulars on the case, to watch over you as well. I should have inquired about them, found out how many he's assigned as your guard."

We continued the ride back toward H Division in silence. Shortly before the turn to Leman Street, Astraia, who had been looking out the window, yelled at John to slow down the cab so she could buy an afternoon newspaper. John obeyed this directive and soon a young news boy was handing the latest edition into Astraia's hand and accepting his payment from her driver.

Astraia perused the article which had grabbed her attention, then slapped the paper over to me, snarling "Damn them all! I'll bet they have known about this for days, all of them, and they never had any intention of telling us about it! Thank god for nosy newspapermen!"

I finally saw the headline that had drawn Astraia's ire: *"Dragon Murder Witness!"* Some inquisitive newspaperman had uncovered the fact the police had a witness to Mr. Hong's murder who said the murderer was a Chinese man who had turned into a giant dragon.

"They can't have known about this witness for too long," I said mildly. "Mr. Hong has only been dead for three days."

"I'll bet my brother Sherlie knew all about it, even as he pretended he was telling me everything he knew. And I'll bet that officer you spoke to at the desk yesterday knew all about it—even while you were asking him questions about Mr. Hong, trying to find out how the poor man died, that officer was keeping this little titbit of information quiet from you."

"Be fair, Astraia. They're under orders not to talk to me."

"And whose fault is that? Samuel Rankin's, that is who. I could have solved this thing by now, if he'd only kept his interfering nose out of my business."

I had seen Astraia Holmes miffed, resentful, annoyed and even angry, but this was the first time I ever saw her truly in a rage. As the cab pulled up to the police station, I hoped DI Rankin would be nowhere in sight, because I feared for his life if Astraia saw him now.

"We have to finish this thing, Maddie," she said, her teeth gritted.

"Yes." I only concurred to calm her down.

"Before there are any more deaths."

"All right." I was at a complete loss as to what the two of us could possibly do to prevent any more deaths, other perhaps than my staying away from mallets.

"We need to interview this witness ourselves."

"To be sure." There was no way the police were going to let us near any witness.

"I'll leave it in your hands to find him."

"Me?" I expostulated, but to no avail. Having settled on our next step—me finding this unknown witness, who might not even exist, might only be an invention to sell newspapers—Astraia leaned her head back against the bolster and closed her eyes as I exited the cab.

I rolled slowly toward my stable, painfully aware now of all the police eyes watching my every movement. Before I entered the courtyard, I turned my head to peer down the street—and yes, there he was, the scruffy child with a blue scarf tied around his head. I turned to look the other way down the street and saw, just for a moment, the unlovely face of Hubert Cranston glaring at me before he stepped through a door into a competitor's pub.

He did not look jolly today.

I hurried into my temporary home, careful to inspect all the window closures and lock the doors before I started the stove or looked in on the animals.

*****

The next morning Frank Froest came for tea, for the first time in days. I knew he had been avoiding me in order to elude my questions. Part of me was sorry that he came by this morning, because I hated putting him in such a position. The other part was grateful that I was going to be able to get this over with, because I knew Astraia wouldn't rest until I completed the task she had set before me.

"Come in, Frank, sit down and warm yourself up," I said, smiling brightly and pouring the boiling water immediately into the chipped chicken tea pot. Several pieces of the Feinmans' freshest gingerbread had been arranged on a plate, a paltry bribe—or perhaps a meagre apology for what I was about to put my old friend through.

He eyed me with suspicion. "This looks good, Maddie," he said. "I hope you don't plan on asking me any questions this morning that I won't be able to answer." He took a bite of gingerbread and settled down at the table to await his tea.

I laughed, unconvincingly. "Oh Frank, you are so droll. Why would you say such a thing?"

"Because I know you were out with Astraia Holmes yesterday, and as much as I like the girl, I don't trust her not to lead you into trouble."

I nodded and sat down at the table with him, pouring his tea and handing him another piece of gingerbread. "I appreciate that, Frank. You are a good friend to me."

"I am, Maddie; that's a fact. You have no idea."

"Then why don't we just get the questions out of the way, so then we can enjoy our time together like the old friends we are."

He sighed. "All right, Madeleine. Ask your questions so that I can refuse to answer and we can get on with our day. Good tea, by the way."

"Thank you." I was usually stingy with the tea, using one leaf when two was prescribed, but not today. Today I made it the way my Mummy taught me, back when we had the funds for good strong tea three times a day. I waited for Frank to finish his first cup, then poured him a second and handed him a third piece of gingerbread before beginning my interrogation.

"There was an interesting story reported in the paper yesterday afternoon," I said. I took a bit of gingerbread over to the dog basket, where Juno would share it with her convalescing friend.

"Was there?"

"The reporter indicated there was a witness to Mr. Hong's murder. Did you hear that story as well?" I petted the two animals, avoiding Frank's eyes.

"I heard tell of such a thing," he said slowly, eyeing me under his brows as he drank his tea.

"Did you hear that the slasher serpent has now metamorphosed into a dragon?"

"To be honest, two earlier witnesses described a dragon. We just didn't take them seriously, at that time."

"You're taking these dragon stories seriously now?"

He shrugged, not answering my question. I needed to find a less overt way to gain the necessary information.

"Are you keeping this witness in custody, for his own protection?"

"We want to, but Dr. Inskip is insistent that we release him. And since he did not do anything illegal—he was actually walking home from mass when he witnessed the murder; the priest has vouched for him—we will probably need to let him go home this afternoon."

I nodded. "I hope he'll be safe."

"We'll send an officer home with him, to make sure he arrives there without harm."

"That's good of you," I said, and to my friend's very great relief I changed the subject, encouraging him to grouse about a corrupt local politician who had tried to extort money from the owner of a local ladies boarding house—or madam, as she no doubt really was.

The moment Frank left I slipped on my coat, grabbed my crutch, and rolled myself down the road to the beautiful new Whitechapel Library building. I had never been there before, and almost lost my nerve when I entered and was faced with a steep stone staircase; but I persevered and dragged myself up the thing, clinging to the iron balustrade with every placement of my roller cast, taking what comfort I could in the knowledge that if I fell, at least I would take the policeman who had followed me from headquarters tumbling down the stairs as well. Still, it was a significant physical endeavor and I sincerely hoped that today, for once, Astraia would have deemed it worth her time to come to work.

When I finally reached the main desk, I found Letty, not Astraia, in attendance. She told me that Astraia was around somewhere, but that she wouldn't go looking for her until after I had registered myself as a member in the library ledger (something she had been nagging me about almost since we'd met). I agreed readily to this extortion; I expected that once my foot was healed I would probably enjoy spending time in this library, perusing the stacks of books, papers and periodicals that grew in number with each succeeding day.

I provided the registration information and Letty scurried away, returning in just a few minutes with Astraia, a linen apron covering most of her lacy yellow day dress.

"Forgive my appearance, Maddie; I've been digging through boxes of donated periodicals and am simply filthy," Astraia said, wiping her bare hands off on the front of her apron before she took my hand in her own and shook it.

I looked down at my own apparel. I wasn't covered with horse manure for a change, but that was about the best that could be said for me.

"I need to update you on that task you assigned me yesterday," I said.

"Splendid!" she said. "Let's find a reading table and you can tell me all you learned."

It didn't take long to share my meagre morsels of information with her, but even so she was satisfied.

"Dr. Inskip will be leaving the police station this afternoon, accompanied by an officer," she mused.

"Yes. I do not know what he looks like, or what kind of doctor he is—he might be a dentist or a theologian rather than a medical man—but at any rate I would expect him to be more respectable than the usual miscreants released from jail, since he encountered the dreadful killing on his way home from church."

"Yes, I shall keep that in mind as well," she said.

"Do you intend to follow him home?" I asked.

"Of course. Did you ever doubt it?"

No. I had known that would be her response. That was why I had hurried here, because I knew she would want time to make her surveillance arrangements.

"Did you wish to accompany me?" she asked.

I considered it, then shook my head no with regret. "I do not believe I could do so without encountering obstruction from the police," I said. "They are watching me quite vigilantly. PC Perkins even followed me to the library. See him, over in that corner?"

Astraia waved at PC Perkins, who cowered back behind the stacks. I think he had actually believed I hadn't noticed him scuttling behind me all the way here.

"That is unfortunate. But perhaps I can determine some way to get around them. Would you be available this afternoon, if I come by to get you?"

"I could break away for a while," I said after a short consideration of my workload. "I will be prepared to leave if you come by."

"Excellent," she said. "And Maddie?"

"Yes?"

She grinned. "Good work."

I nodded and left, walking over to where PC Perkins shrank behind a stack of children's books. I told the bobby that since he was following me anyway he might as well make himself useful and allowed him to assist me to climb down the staircase without mishap. He accompanied me back to the precinct, walking beside me, chatting all the while, and I found him to be a very droll and entertaining fellow, and not too tall for my comfort.

I was feeling quite at my ease, enjoying the walk back, when a large man stepped in front of us, blocking our path.

"Hello Maddie," he said with a sly smile.

"Mr. Cranston," I said, gripping PC Perkins's arm like a vise.

The officer responded to my obvious distress. "You're blocking our egress. Please move out of our way," PC Perkins told Jolly Bert.

"I want to speak with you Maddie," the repulsive publican demanded, ignoring the constable. "You have something I want. You give it to me, or I'll come get it."

Chapter Twelve

"Move out of our way or I'll place you under arrest," PC Perkins ordered.

With great ceremony Jolly Bert shifted his bulk to the edge of the sidewalk, allowing his arm to brush suggestively against my torso as we stepped past him.

"You know what I want Maddie," he yelled at our backs. "You know where to find me. Don't make me come to you to get it."

I continued to grip PC Perkins's arm as we hurried down the road, me rolling my cast as quickly as the little wheels could manage.

"That was him, wasn't it?" PC Perkins said. "That was the man who attacked you that night. The one I chased—in fact, it was very near here that I lost him."

"He probably ducked into his pub," I said. "That's it—the Grey Stallion." I pointed to the dingy establishment across the street. That was where Bert wanted me to deliver the journal. I had never entered the place and had sworn I never would. After witnessing the murder of Miss Kelly, I knew the kind of meat Bert sometimes served in his pies.

Perkins nodded. I realized I was still clinging to his arm and forced myself to release him.

"Jolly Bert is a terrible, terrible man, Constable Perkins," I said. And fearless too, I now realized—he had no compunction about molesting me in front of a policeman! He must feel very confident. Did he have friends in high places who would protect him?

"We won't let him hurt you again, Miss Maddie," Constable Perkins vowed, and the determined tone in his voice almost brought me to tears. If Jolly Bert had friends in the police force, Constable Perkins was not among their number.

I wondered how Astraia would emancipate me from my police guard but had no doubt that she would manage it. Consequently, I was ready when John came to the stable door in mid-afternoon to tell me Miss Holmes was delivering books of interest to library subscribers unable to obtain them personally and wondered if I would care to accompany her.

"Yes," I said. "That would be lovely," though in truth I could imagine few activities less appealing than driving all over the East End transporting books to invalid library patrons.

"The library has two subscribers named Doctor Inskip," Astraia explained after I hauled myself into the seat of the hansom and John returned to the horses. "However, Dr. Martin Inskip is the only one whose address is near both a Catholic church and the alley where Mr. Hong was killed."

I had accidently sat down on a book. I moved it. Books were stacked in piles all over the seats and floor of the cab. "Very clever deduction," I said. "And he had some books on order?"

"Well, no. But I was able to determine the types of books he is most interested in from a perusal of his past selections, and found some recent tomes in the same genre which he had not yet seen because I had balked at setting them out on the shelves, mostly because they're ludicrous trumpery. Libraries should be for the furtherance of science and history, and education in the literary arts. Phrenology is a crackpot discipline."

"Phrenology?"

"Yes. Our Dr. Inskip is a phrenologist. He assesses the mental faculties and propensities of individuals by measuring their skulls and counting the bumps on their head."

I lifted a book from the seat beside me. "*The Woman in White*?" I had read Wilkie Collins's novel of love, lunacy and Freemasonry many years ago; I did not recall anything about phrenology.

Astraia sighed. "John is already suspicious, because dropping off books is a task I usually force on Letty. In order to add verisimilitude to our story, we must visit a few other subscribers first," she said. "Miss Ermentrude Binkley is a devotee of Wilkie Collins and Charles Dickens."

We visited Miss Binkley to drop off several beloved novels she wished to re-read. And Mr. Pipestone to give him the collection of sermons on the Epistles of John he had requested. And Mrs. Newbury to hand her a worn copy of *Mother's Home Remedies.* And numerous others. At each stop we each got out of the cab to hand the books to their intended recipients (and get a receipt in return), and we each accepted a cup of tea if offered, although by the third such offering I was beginning to experience some discomfort. After exiting the home of Miss Sarissa Jones, delighted to have obtained the first five volumes of Thomas Bowdler's *The Family Shakespeare* (*"in which nothing is added to the original text; but those words and expressions are omitted which cannot with propriety be read aloud in a family"*), Astraia whispered "I believe we've lulled the suspicions of both John and the constable who's been following us."

I looked around and noticed Police Constable Hemings, yawning as he leaned on a lamp post down the street.

Astraia rummaged amongst the books in the cab just as she had a half-dozen times before, emerging to hand John a new address card.

He did not question it, but merely assisted us into the vehicle and began the next slog of the afternoon.

Dr. Inskip's respectable housekeeper didn't interrogate the two ladies standing on her doorstep, arms full of books; she simply showed us to the library where the murder witness, a hale man of middle years, freshly washed, dressed in smoking jacket, trembling hand holding a glass of golden liquid, angrily paced.

"Blast it, Mrs. Woodruff, you know I—" Then he saw us follow the housekeeper into the room. And he saw the books in our arms.

"The library just received a copy of the latest edition of Samuel Roberts Wells's *How to Read Character: A New Illustrated Hand-Book of Phrenology and Physiognomy, for Students and Examiners; with A Descriptive Chart*, so I added it to the pile of books I had been saving for you, Dr. Inskip," Astraia said sweetly. "But if this is a bad time, we can return at a later date." Of course she had no intention of returning at a later date; she had recognized the gleam of avarice in the good doctor's eye when she mentioned this new edition of a popular work in his field, so knew he would receive us.

"Excellent, excellent," the man said, setting down his glass of whisky and taking the books from our arms. After placing them on a table he signed Astraia's receipt and said "Would you ladies like tea? Of course, you would—I can tell from the structure of your faces that you enjoy your tea—Mrs.

Woodruff!" He walked to the door. "Mrs. Woodruff, can you bring tea for my visitors, Misses—"

"Miss Holmes and Miss Barquist," Astraia supplied.

"Miss Holmes and Miss Barquist," he repeated. "You I recognize from the library," he said, pointing to Astraia. "But I don't believe we've ever met before," he said to me. "Remind me to measure your head." He walked back to the table and picked up the Wells book, not listening for a response from either of us or, for that matter, from Mrs. Woodruff. I hoped Mrs. Woodruff had not heard his call, but no such luck; within a few short minutes she had returned with a complete tea setting. I was glad to see cakes, because I really needed something solid to sop up all the fluid sloshing within, anxious to exit.

"I have been desirous to see this edition," Dr. Inskip said, turning the book over in his hands. "I understand it contains an expanded section on the characteristics of Suavity."

But Astraia had no intention of allowing Dr. Inskip to misdirect the conversation.

"You seemed so agitated when we arrived, Dr. Inskip," she said. "Is this a bad time?"

He snorted. "Can you believe it, I witnessed a murder the other night and instead of respecting the fact that I came forward with important information, the police kept me in custody while they, as they put it, 'sorted out my alibi'. I tell you, my days are over as a public-minded citizen intent on sharing crucial information with the authorities. I am a very busy man, Miss Holmes. The next time I come upon a gruesome murder being committed by a mythical beast I will just walk on past without informing anyone."

During this diatribe Dr. Inskip had picked up a pair of callipers from his desk. He now came over to where I sat chewing my cake and began measuring my head. I glanced at

Astraia, who nodded. So, I let him continue, despite my extreme dislike of having gentlemen touch my head, since the exercise seemed to calm him.

We allowed him to rail at the police while he appraised my head fore and aft with the instrument, then ran his fingers around the various nodules and indentations life and nature had formed on my scalp. It was a good thing I did not wear an elaborate hairstyle, but only a simple braid; otherwise, I might have been quite annoyed with the mess he made of it. Instead I merely gritted my teeth as I allowed this strange man to touch me, something I certainly would not have permitted under any circumstance had Astraia not been there with me.

Eventually he got around to telling us his story.

"I was walking home from late mass at St. Mary of Perpetual Help when I heard a terrible cry emit from a nearby alley," he said. "London is a dangerous place, ladies, and I normally would not have left the lighted pathway to follow an alley cry no matter how pathetic, but I had been ruminating just a few minutes before on the name of the patron saint of my church and so this opportunity to provide help to someone in need seemed to me in that moment like a divine directive. Although had I known the victim was not a British Christian but rather a pagan Chinese I certainly would not have made the effort.

"Your Veneration lobe is quite pronounced, Miss Barquist. That speaks well of you. You must be a devoted daughter."

The growl I had been suppressing since the doctor mentioned his disregard of *Chinee* pagans now sought to escape. I clamped it down.

"Assuming that the person making the horrible cries was a Christian rather than an unworthy pagan, I ran into the dark alley with no thought for my own safety," the doctor continued.

"How magnanimous of you," Astraia said sweetly.

"Thank you, Miss Holmes. I felt it was my Christian duty to assist my brother in need. *The Good Samaritan*, you know. I entered the alley and immediately encountered a thick, almost glutinous smoke that completely stupefied me—I lost track of place, of balance and of time."

To my mind, this was the first interesting thing he said. There had been no such smoke at the murder I encountered in the Limehouse district. From his description, it sounded as though he had been drugged.

There was a particular area low behind my ear that he seemed to find especially compelling; at least one finger managed to rub there almost continually during his examination of my scalp. His thumbs and forefingers moved to my eye sockets, so my head was completely enveloped in his hands. This close to his quilted waist, I smelled the tobacco whose use gave the term *smoking jacket* its name.

"I'm impressed by your lobe of Order, Miss Barquist," he said. "You would make an excellent housewife."

"That's what I'm always telling her," Astraia said. "But do go on with your amazing tale, Dr. Inskip. I believe you mentioned a mythical beast and a murder?"

"I began moving in the direction I assumed, in my dazed mind, to be forward, and hit an obstacle with my foot that I recognized immediately, due to my professional expertise, as a human head. I bent down to help the person, whom I quickly realized was Chinese even though he was dressed in British garb. But as I leaned down I saw, blazing through the slowly dissipating smoke, two huge red eyes."

His fingers returned to their favourite part, that area toward the back of my head below the ears. As he spoke, he rubbed the skin there as though it were a lucky rabbit's foot or a child's favourite blanket. "Then I heard a blood-curdling cry and the face with the red eyes raised itself above me, looming at least ten feet. As the smoke continued to evanesce, I recognized a dreadful creature from my favourite childhood picture book, a fiercesome dragon! And then, almost as soon as I saw it, it disappeared, and I saw a Chinese man run out of the alley."

"A dragon!" Astraia said in horrified tones. "Oh, Dr. Inskip! How dreadful!"

"How did you know the running man was Chinese?" I asked, my only contribution to this conversation.

"He wore a Chinese robe and long hair plaited into a queue down his back," the phrenologist said.

"That could have been a disguise," Astraia said. "Did you see the man's face?"

"No. I opted to assist the man on the ground rather than chase after a crazed murderer. Of course, I quickly realized the man was quite dead, what with the torrents of blood everywhere." Then, strangely, he giggled almost nervously, focusing all his fingers on that special area of my head.

"Did you see any claws on the creature? Or claw marks on any nearby buildings?" Astraia asked.

"Strange, the police asked me that question too. It was dark, Miss Holmes. All I saw were the flaming red eyes of the monster. I did not pause to examine the scenery."

He certainly would not have noticed if a pictograph had been etched in the ground in Mr. Hong's blood. Nor would he have examined Mr. Hong's wounds closely enough to know if they were symmetrical.

Then he giggled again. "You have an unusually large Conjugal Love lobe, Miss Barquist. Are you walking out with anyone?"

Astraia stood. "We've distracted you from your work long enough, Dr. Inskip. Thank you for the tea, and for sharing your fascinating story." She grabbed my hand, pulling me out of my chair and away from the phrenologist's enthusiastic massage of my lobe of Conjugal Love.

Dr. Inskip walked us to the door. He handed me his card. "Miss Barquist, your head is quite remarkable. I would like to see you again. Where can I reach you?"

I could just imagine the police response if they saw me spending time with a witness in their murder investigation.

"You can leave her a message at the library," Astraia said. "Come along, Miss Barquist—we have other patrons to visit."

Dr. Inskip frowned at this; perhaps he thought I would allow others to touch my scalp as he had.

"Don't worry. I won't let her visit any other phrenologists," Astraia told him, a touch of acerbity in her voice. We hurried back to the cab. Astraia reached in to procure another address for John, and soon we were back to our book delivery service.

"We must go visit the murder site ourselves tomorrow," Astraia said as the horses clopped down the road to the next library patron's home. "We must see if any claw marks are carved into the alley wall."

I nodded. "Did you notice he said the eyes of his dragon were red? Didn't the snake Mr. Harris saw have green eyes? The dragon mask I saw also had green eyes."

"Yes. I noticed that discrepancy as well."

We were both silent for a moment while I tried to repair the mess to my hair. "At least being able to feel my head bumps while he vented his anger appeared to calm him," I said.

"Being able to feel your head bumps certainly did *something* to him," Astraia remarked dryly. "It's unfortunate there are no doctors on the subscribers list who specialize in female hysteria paroxysm treatments. After watching Dr. Inskip spend so much time and enthusiasm rubbing your Conjugal Love lobe, I feel we could both use a treatment."

"Well, at any rate, I believe we coaxed him into a better humour, so perhaps in future he will not actually leave corpses on the ground unreported, as he had indicated during his initial castigations toward the police," I said.

"Very civic minded of you," she commented.

When the books were all finally delivered, Astraia instructed John to drop me off at home. Before I exited the cab, she reminded me of the SSOT soirée musicale we were attending the following evening and said John would be by to pick me up at five o'clock so that we could have supper first together at her home.

As I entered the stable, I remembered that this event would be a fundraiser. Happily, so many other people had paid for my meals this month I had an excess of grocery funds that I could use to make a donation. Then my focus turned to other pressing matters and I rolled hurriedly down the hall to retrieve the china pot from underneath my bed.

✳✳✳✳✳

DI Rankin and PC Perkins came to the office together the next day to question me again about Jolly Bert. Hubert Cranston had badly miscalculated PC Perkins's compliance when he stood arrogant and immobile in the sidewalk yesterday, blocking the young constable's path.

"PC Perkins is now confidant that Hubert Cranston was the man he chased when he fled from this office that night you were attacked," DI Rankin said. "The first night you were attacked," he amended.

Upon hearing the detective inspector's voice, Old Vic began to growl. It wasn't the fearsome growl of his pre-laceration days, but I knew he meant it as a threat. I wondered where Juno was; her loving attention usually soothed his rancour. But she seemed to be out, no doubt attending to her own feline affairs.

"Yes," I said, eyeing the cur to see if he would attempt to climb out of his basket and bite the handsome officer. He did not do so, but he did keep growling for the remainder of DI Rankin's visit. I believe he remembered Inspector Rankin as the person who had spoken in harsh tones to his beloved Astraia Holmes. Old Vic was as smart as he was surly.

"PC Perkins said that in addition to that attempted assault, Mr. Cranston threatened you on the street yesterday."

"Yes."

"Can you explain to us what that threat was about? PC Perkins says that Cranston said you have something he wants. The night you were assaulted, you told me you didn't know why you were attacked by him. Do you now have some idea about why he might be threatening you? What does he want you to give him, Miss Maddie? Does it have anything to do with Chinese goods or Chinese people?"

I tried to remember the story I had told to Astraia. That's the trouble with telling stories: one needs to be consistent, in case one's various listeners decide to exchange notes. "Nothing Chinese, Inspector Rankin. Bert and my father were great friends. I remember now that Papa kept a journal, although I never paid much attention to it. I always assumed it was a log of his veterinary cases. But after Papa died, Bert told me he wanted this journal for sentimental reasons. He became quite insistent, which is why I believe my father must have documented some unsavoury things about him in it. I

215

told Bert I never saw it, I never had it, and I did not know where it was—but Bert wouldn't let up. That was a year ago and I believe he left town for a time, but now he has come back and he's at it again. I didn't think about that when he attacked me in here—it was late, and I was so tired when I spoke with you. I'm scared of him." I did my best Astraia-Holmes-vulnerable-female-talking-to-the-big-strong-man impression, but I don't think I was very convincing.

"And you don't know where this journal is?"

"No."

"You don't know what your father might have written about Cranston?"

"No."

"It must have been something truly heinous," PC Perkins said. "Your father died a year ago...that was about the time of the Ripper killings."

"I think you're right," I said, my tone a shocked whisper.

"I wish we had that journal," DI Rankin said. "Are you certain you looked everywhere?"

"Yes," I said. "I went through all of Papa's things after he died. But if you or some of your officers wish to do your own search of his belongings, you're welcome to do so." I waved to the cabinet and to shelves still covered with my father's possessions. I knew I should clear out everything, but it made me ill to touch things that he had once touched. Perhaps Letty and John would help me.

DI Rankin nodded. "I think we probably will do a thorough search," he said. "I'll let you know." I would need to make arrangements with Astraia to take the portmanteau full of love letters back, just in case they decided to search the entire building.

The two of them left and I rolled myself over to Old Vic's basket to provide food and reassurance. DI Rankin may have

216

been the one person in the world Old Vic disliked even more than me, no doubt because the detective inspector was always yelling at Astraia, Old Vic's goddess.

That afternoon the stable boys tried to bring me a mare nearing her time, but I declined to accept responsibility for her, the first time I ever refused to assume a duty that properly belonged to them. The horse had foaled before and knew perfectly well what to do, all by herself. I told them to take her back to their stable and said I would look in on her when I returned from my evening out, but that I did not anticipate any trouble for her.

They did not even argue, which demonstrated to me better than anything else the heavy hand of Mycroft Holmes.

*****

I attired myself in the same dress I had worn to the Fabian Society lecture, a faded, darned thing but still relatively respectable. Letty had tried to improve the dress with new lace, but there is only so much one can do to spiff up patches. As I primped, I happily sang Christmas carols to myself and any listening beasts, although the holiday was a month gone. I had just finished styling my hair when I heard Old Vic growl ominously, along with Juno's hiss. I hoped the two animals hadn't decided to recommence hostilities.

"What's going on, you two?" I yelled. There was no answer, of course. I moved quickly but cautiously down the hall toward the office.

A frightening sight awaited me.

"Hello, Maddie," Bert said. "You look very nice this evening." He sat in my chair, pawing through my father's medical bag. At my table. In my stable. Which had been locked.

217

"How did you get in?" I asked.

He shrugged and showed me a key. "I have friends on the force," he said. "You know why I'm here. I want your father's journal."

"I have no idea what you're talking about." I tried to ignore my anxiety as I looked around the room for a weapon. I saw several possibilities but didn't know if I could reach any of them in time. Unfortunately, the police had kept my mallet.

"I do not know why you're being so unfriendly," he complained. "You used to be nicer to me. Much nicer. You will be nice again, before this night's over. And you will gladly hand over the journal, just to make it stop."

"I'll scream," I said.

"They won't come," he said confidently. "Not the boys on guard tonight. Nor will the stable lads next door. I have seen to that, with a brew I concocted special and sent over just for them, for tonight's supper. And when they all finally wake up, why, I'll be at home in my pub, where I've been all evening—where I am right now, you know—but sadly you will have disappeared from London. I've made arrangements with some friends of mine down at the docks who pay top dollar for white women."

I thought I would retch. Feeling my apprehension, the animals' growls and hisses became louder.

"If you don't shut up that dog, I may have to kill him," Bert said. Apparently, he did not fear an enraged cat.

Up until this moment I had been terribly afraid of this man; I had, in fact, spent my entire life fearing him. But when he said those words, I snapped.

Never again would anyone hurt my dog.

I hobbled over to the stove, to Old Vic's basket. "Hush now," I said, patting the animals reassuringly. Juno ran out of the room. Old Vic continued to growl, though not as loud. I wondered how soon John would arrive to deliver me to the musicale. He was a strong man, younger than Bert, but lacked the older man's size and bulk.

"I'm going to make some tea," I said. I lifted the kettle to see if there was still sufficient hot water or if I would need to refill it. I deemed the hot water to be adequate for my immediate needs.

"I brought my own refreshment," Bert said, lifting a bottle to his lips.

As he drank, I hefted the hot kettle and swung it as hard as I could against Bert's head. He turned at the last minute so only got a clip across his jaw, but that was enough to send him, his chair and his bottle sprawling to the ground.

He was dizzy, but alert enough. He started to stand, swearing furiously.

I poured the boiling water on him. He screamed, perhaps the loudest scream I've ever heard. And he was right—no one came running.

Dripping water, Bert stood, murder in his eyes. He lunged toward me, the neck of the broken bottle in his hand. I grabbed one of my father's scalpels from the open medical bag on the table and held it out toward Bert's eyes. "Do not think for an instant that I won't use this," I said. "I would slice you to pieces without compunction." Old Vic growled in agreement.

My father's friend hesitated for just a moment, his red face already beginning to blister, no doubt wracked with extraordinary pain—and I realized for the first time in my adult life that he wasn't the huge man I had always thought him to be, ever since I was a child frightened of the monster looming over me in the dark. Why, he wasn't actually any taller than I was. I was assessing my chances of perhaps even beating him in a knife and broken bottle fight when John knocked on the stable door.

"Miss Maddie, are you ready?"

Furious at the interruption, Bert turned his head to the door. I whacked him again with the still hot but no longer heavy kettle.

"John!" I yelled. "I need your assistance!"

As the good man rushed in, the bad one rushed out. John was torn between chasing after the villain and staying to see if I was all right.

"There's no point following him, John," I said. "He knows this neighbourhood too well. No doubt he's already lost in the warrens." I set the knife and kettle down on the table, and bent to pet Old Vic once more, my hand shaking. "You were a good dog," I said. His growling stopped and he settled back into an uneasy sleep.

"Did that devil hurt you, Miss Maddie?" John knew Bert for a blackguard, having spent several recent days following him around on Astraia's orders.

I retrieved the stable door key from the floor where Bert had dropped it when I clobbered him the first time. "He just scared me," I said. "Truthfully, he came off the worse for our confrontation. However, I believe he may have drugged the stable boys with an adulterated beverage, and perhaps even the police constables. Can you check on them while I freshen up?" I hoped the officers, once roused, would not inflict on me yet another interrogation. I worried that if it became a question of who had assaulted whom, charges might be pressed on me instead of on Bert—for I was not the one whose face was blistered in the encounter.

"I will more than check on them—I will let them know that once again, they have failed to protect you while you've been attacked," John said angrily. "And this time, I myself can give witness as to your attacker."

Strangely, the short brush with my nemesis had not even mussed my hair. I quickly completed my interrupted toilette, then woke the dog to take him outside to perform his evening duty. I left him with food, water and another appreciative pat before I walked over to the precinct to check on the condition of the officers myself.

I was more determined than ever to attend tonight's planned entertainment. Perhaps a more delicate woman would have chosen to stay home to wail and wring her hands over her ordeal—but frankly I wanted the comfort of being with a group of people tonight. I did not want to sit at home by myself while Bert was free to come terrorize me again. And I wanted to tell my friend Astraia what had happened.

Unfortunately I missed my dinner at Astraia's because the sceptical night watch, once awoken from their stupor, insisted on getting my statement while the outraged John lodged his complaint against Bert and against the officers who were supposed to be guarding the stable from intruders.

However, my statement was not a lengthy one. The policemen who had been awoken by John were far more interested in rousing their fellow officers and finding Jolly Bert than in questioning me tonight. They were furious with the man for drugging their ale and determined to hunt him down—more to make him answer for what he had inexplicably done to them than for what he had purportedly done to me, though they were angry about that as well and now inclined to believe me when I spoke ill of him.

So eventually we were allowed to leave, something that probably would not have happened had Deputy Inspector Rankin, out on another case this evening, been present to interrogate me on details. As John assisted me into the carriage before we left to pick up Astraia, he said he thought that we would make the soirée musicale in time, or perhaps be just a few minutes late—and reminded me that at events like this, they always served refreshments.

This would be an evening spent sitting in a large room listening to music. I would not be running around town, for a change. I felt comfortable enough with the wheeled cast by now that I left both crutches at home. I also left my large ratty handbag in my room next to Astraia's valise of billets doux, opting to carry my donation money in a small knitted reticule of my Mummy's instead, along with one of her lace hankies. Upon rethinking the matter, I shoved both bags beneath the bed. I doubted that Jolly Bert would be doing anything this evening other than hiding out from the police while he nursed his sore face with cold compresses, but I wanted to ensure the documents were kept away from the prying eyes of any other intruders who might succeed in sneaking in.

After carefully locking the veterinary stable building, John escorted me to the carriage. I saw, through open windows and doors, that all of the stable lads and careless constables had been successfully prodded awake from their beverage-induced torpor. None of them looked very energetic, however. I hoped I was right about the mare being able to manage the birth by herself, because she would receive only minimal help from the boys in the stable tonight.

As we pulled away from the police headquarters, I looked through the carriage windows to see if any blue-headed urchins followed. I did not see the child—but I did notice a policeman on a horse, riding close by, someone I did not recognize. I wondered if there had been a police escort when Astraia and I visited her brother Sherlock Holmes. There had certainly been one yesterday while Astraia and I traipsed all over the East End delivering books. It seemed logical to assume that I had probably been accompanied by policemen on all of my excursions ever since Zhu Lei's identity had been uncovered and the police realized the Ya Zi gang were interested in me. And I wondered where this officer had been while Bert tried to attack me tonight. Mounted constables usually avoided the plebeian work of foot officers. Perhaps he had been currying his horse. Or maybe he had been sleeping too.

I did not mind the escorts. I did mind the fact that no one had asked my permission or even bothered to tell me about them. And I certainly minded that they had ignored my warnings about Bert Cranston. But DI Rankin had believed me as had PC Perkins. They would be furious about tonight's scuffle. No doubt they would take some action.

The public soirée musicale would be held in a meeting hall far distant in the West End. I wondered if the officer escort would follow us the entire way, then wait around with John all evening until the event ended and it was time to deliver me home.

I also wondered how the police knew to have an officer ready to follow me this evening. It seemed likely that one of Astraia's brothers had instructed John to keep the police informed of all of our outings together. I decided to discuss this with Astraia later. Probably she would not accede to this type of treatment. Once Bert was arrested, we might have to devise a way to move around town without John's accompaniment. But for right now, I was grateful for John's escort. He had been a good friend to me tonight.

When we collected Astraia she looked lovely as usual, this evening in blue satin with a grey fox collar. She informed me that Ramsay MacDonald would be meeting us there, as the meeting hall was near his place of work.

She had been worried when I missed supper but confident there was a good reason for it. I told her about the disturbance at the stable, downplaying my fear and elaborating on Bert Cranston's painful injuries. She said that she would go with me the next day to check on my complaint against the horrid man, and said that if the miscreant was still free we would insist on his immediate arrest and incarceration. We also discussed our strategy for our trip out to the site where Mr. Hong had been murdered. It was not far from either her work place or mine, but when I reminded her about my dedicated police escort and said that I believed John was sharing the details of all of our expeditions with local law enforcement, and she had verified this for herself by looking out the window of the carriage and espying the policeman on horseback, she said we would need to avoid either walking to the place or having John drive us.

"The police will never let us examine the murder scene," she said. "Especially if they have realized that one of the people we visited yesterday was Dr. Inskip."

She sat in silence for a few moments, but soon I saw her pearly teeth glittering in the passing lamp light. "There is a new ready-made apparel shop very near to the mouth of the alley where Mr. Hong was killed," she said. "Madame Estelle's, I believe it is called. As I have told you repeatedly, you need new clothes. You and I will meet at this establishment tomorrow at 2 o'clock; I will attend you as your fashion advisor. I will come by myself because Letty will be needed to supervise the library, plus she won't mind not going as she detests the very notion of ready-to-wear clothing. Be prepared for her to berate you about it."

I could not conceive of Letty ever berating anyone about anything. The most she might do is give me a sad, disappointed look before hauling my new clothes off in order to tailor them to better fit me.

But before I met with Astraia at Madame Estelle's I would need to go to the bank to withdraw some of my precious savings. At least I needn't fear that anyone might try to rob me afterward, since I would no doubt be accompanied by my own police escort.

Strange that I should feel safer walking the streets of London than I felt in my own home on the grounds of the police precinct.

Astraia continued. "Once inside Madame Estelle's, we will use the back exit to leave the building and then enter the alley surreptitiously to observe whether or not any claw marks or any other clues are apparent. That should not take more than a few minutes. Then we'll re-enter the building, again through the back, you will make your purchases, and we will leave properly through the front door with the bonus of having our various guards available to haul your parcels. I hope you buy many things. John always looks so ridiculous carrying women's hatboxes."

"Does Madame Estelle sell hats and shoes in addition to clothing?" I asked.

"Perhaps not. But if they don't, we'll find a shoe shop and a milliner's as well."

I could see no flaw in her plan other than the bite into my savings. I could not argue that my wardrobe did not need replenishing. Now or later made little difference to me, and at least this shopping excursion was for a good cause, i.e. to throw our guards off the scent while we gathered necessary information.

I had never attended a soirée musicale before so did not know what to expect. But if I'd had expectations, I am sure the entertainment that night would have exceeded them.

The meeting hall was quite crowded and most of the chairs already bespoken by the time we arrived. Happily, Ramsay had saved two seats for us near the front, right on the aisle so I didn't have to roll over anyone, which I considered very thoughtful of him.

Perhaps that evening was typical of the soirée musicale format; I cannot say, having never attended such a thing in the past. A chorus, pianist, harpist and six soloists entertained us with ballads, madrigals, arias, and folk songs in both English and French; there were even two comic songs from Gilbert and Sullivan operettas I wanted to hear in full someday. I promised myself I would buy the vocal scores, excited to learn new songs to serenade the horses. As I listened to the pianist play a thrilling Liszt polonaise, I regretted once again that my mother's death had necessitated the termination of my piano lessons. Most of the performers were highly talented artistes, and if a few seemed to fall short it was only because they had the misfortune of being on the same program with true masters of the musical arts.

The Anglo-Oriental Society for the Suppression of the Opium Trade had daringly arranged for authentic Chinese refreshments to be served during the intermission before the second act. I had never before experienced Chinese foodstuffs, and found this a strange but thrilling treat, and most satisfying for someone who had missed her evening meal. This being a fundraiser for the SSOT, Sir Joseph Pease spoke after the break about the goals of that worthy organization. But he was wise enough to know we were all there to hear angelic music, not a lecture on earthly evils, so he kept his words brief. He took a moment to recognize the Chinese Minister to Britain, Guo Jiegang, who received a stirring round of applause from the audience for his work in trying to eradicate the evils of opium from his country's shores. Sir Joseph did not invite the minister to speak, perhaps because Mr. Guo's translator had suffered his dreadful demise just days before and the envoy did not wish to speak in English.

Astraia elbowed me while Sir Joseph was speaking. "Look over there," she whispered with a nod.

I peered toward the direction indicated, a large display of indoor plants, and saw a man standing behind them. "Sir William Forrester Clydon! What is he doing here? This crowd would excoriate him if they knew his identity and vile purposes!" I was appalled to see he was audaciously nibbling on one of the Chinese stuffed biscuits, purchased through funds donated tonight to the SSOT.

"I expect that's why he's skulking in the foliage, the cowardly cur. He hopes no one will recognize him."

"Let's expose him!" I cried. "Let him face public censure for his greed and villainy and licentious behaviour."

"No," she said. "We need to ascertain his purpose here. If he leaves, we shall follow him."

"Are you ladies enjoying yourselves?" Ramsay asked, leaning toward our huddle. We had ignored him for too long. A coloratura glided across the floor to stand near the piano, preparing to sing her second aria of the evening.

"Oh, yes, James," Astraia gushed. "The music this evening has been quite magical. Thank you for bringing us," she said, although of course he had done no such thing.

But he settled back in his chair, satisfied, as the second act began.

Employees from several reputable Chinese restaurants began moving through the crowd, gathering the remaining refuse. As the coloratura opened her mouth to sing and the Chinese servers moved rapidly back into the shadows, I noticed a familiar face among the workers.

"Mr. Wu!" I gasped.

"What?" Astraia said urgently, leaning over me.

"Hush!" said the woman behind me, annoyed because we were talking over the music.

I pointed the direction for Astraia, but Mr. Wu had now disappeared behind a wall of Chinese faces.

"What on Earth is going on here?" Astraia breathed.

"Hush," Ramsay said, though more politely than the woman sitting behind us. Astraia and I went silent and watched, nervously awaiting the next jolt of the evening. First Sir William, then Mr. Wu. What should we expect next?

It occurred several songs later, while the choir was singing a collection of fifteenth-century madrigals. Someone screamed "Fire!" and we turned our attention away from the vocalists to see smoke billowing out from an area at the side of the room leading to the kitchen.

Ramsay immediately stood to take charge. "Astraia, you and Maddie exit quickly and quietly," he ordered before he rushed toward the fire area in order to ascertain its severity.

Astraia and I assisted a few elderly women to leave the building. Soon we stood out in front, street lamplight our only illumination in the cloud-filled night, watching the activity as John and our police officer escort entered the building to assist with rescue or support fire-fighting efforts or indulge in some other heroic type of behaviour.

"That was unfortunate," Astraia said.

"I agree. I quite enjoyed listening to that choir," I said.

She scowled at me. "Not that," she said. "I mean it's unfortunate that the evening ended before we could discover what brought both Sir Joseph and Mr. Wu out here tonight. Wait—did you see him?" she asked, suddenly excited.

"Who?" I asked. I looked around but could see no one I recognized in the smoke and confusion.

"Come along," she ordered, and quickly ran toward the side of the building, the skirts of her pretty blue dress tracking through the filth on the ground.

I followed as rapidly as my wheeled appendage would allow, but she had disappeared around the corner of the building. I finally reached the dark side street. Smoky mist drifted toward me. "Astraia!" I yelled in fear, knowing full well the crazy woman had felt no compunction whatsoever about running straight into a wall of thick, dark smoke.

"Damn it!" I followed her into the heart of hell.

Chapter Thirteen

Immediately upon entering the thick mist I knew this was not normal smoke from a fire. It had a sweeter odour than fire smoke and didn't burn my eyes or throat. It made my head swim, violently, and I quickly became completely lost, my mind muddled, almost inaccessible. Fear began racing through my body.

"Astraia!" I yelled, disturbed to hear an old yet familiar frightened quaver in my voice, absent since my father's death.

"Over here, Maddie. Watch your step!" she yelled back; her voice reedy yet determined.

"Can you keep speaking, Astraia, so I can find you?" I asked, moving farther into the vapor, aware despite my befuddlement of my vulnerability as I rolled my broken foot over ground I could not see. I was horrified to realize there were tears in my eyes and my voice. I had not felt this scared since witnessing my father butcher poor Mary Kelly. Even when Jolly Bert woke me with his nasty lips on my neck, and tonight when I found him sitting at my table, I hadn't responded with such panic. I knew my extreme response was irrational, but I couldn't control it. I wanted desperately to know where Astraia was.

"We're not alone, Maddie," she said from the dark, her voice steady, but intense with anxiety.

I froze, and despite my terror and dizziness became aware of two things. First, I began to perceive a vague coppery odour, a sickening smell I know better than most people ever will. And second, my fractured senses became attuned to the sound of someone—or something—moving very near.

The clouds above us parted and the moon appeared, illuminating a dreadful, inexplicable scene. A viridian dragon rose up in front of me, at least ten feet tall, air congealing into scaly muscle, smoke pouring out of his enormous nostrils, his mouth open in a wide, cruel grin. His huge eyes blazed bright, ruby-blood-fire red. He extended an arm from his snake-like body and I saw the sharp, blood-encrusted claws that would soon eviscerate me.

This was no simple dragon mask, lit by lanterns and held upright by human strength.

Naturally I screamed, the sharp high A I had honed over recent weeks. Unfortunately, my shout was lost in the wails, alarms and frenzied noises still surging from the throng of people milling in front of the burning building.

An explosion roared nearby. Acrid smoke from a discharged firearm replaced the rapidly dissipating vapor that had so disorientated my senses. The dragon disappeared, popping out of existence as quickly as it had materialized. I felt my quivering body relax, but then a creature ran past me, breathing heavily.

"Follow him, Maddie!" Astraia ordered.

I obeyed, turning to follow the wretched villain out of the alley. My pursuit continued almost to the lighted street but then my cursed foot—my healthy, normally dependable one—slipped in a puddle of filth and I fell, sprawled onto the ground, face flat in the muck.

Slowly I forced myself to stand, taking stock of myself. My face hurt and would no doubt exhibit colourful bruises by tomorrow morning, but I seemed to suffer no other physical injuries. However, the front half of my body was soddened with feculence. Even Letty would be unwilling to clean my dress after this mephitic drenching. I would burn the thing, as soon as I returned home.

I took my mother's hankie out of my reticule, to wipe the worst of the ooze off my face, wincing as I touched the new bruises, then rolled and heaved myself back to Astraia, whom I could see fairly well now that the dragon smoke had subsided. She knelt down by a body, identifiable only in occasional flashes of moonlight.

"I must confess I'm surprised," I said, staring down at the brutally—and symmetrically—slashed corpse of Sir William Forrester Clydon.

"I'm not," my friend said. "There were only two possibilities, after all. But I am deeply sorry it's turned out this way." She moved away from the body to collect an item from the ground.

"Come along," she said, striding with determination toward the street.

"Are we returning to the carriage?" I asked. John would probably prefer that I sit on top, to avoid my filthy apparel contaminating the cushions.

"Not at all," she said. "We're going to capture a murderer."

"But I lost him," I said.

"I know where he went."

"Shouldn't we tell our police officer, so he can accompany us?" Also, common decency would be to inform someone of Sir William's murder.

"That's not necessary," she said, striding toward the people and lights. "You and I are sufficient to conclude this business. If Samuel Rankin or my brothers or my own

232

servants had bothered to tell us that we would be accompanied by bodyguards everywhere we went, I might feel obligated to share information with our entourage. But if we aren't even supposed to know they exist, how can we be expected to keep them informed of our plans? Let someone else find Sir William; you and I have more important matters to attend to."

We reached the crowd outside of the meeting hall. Flames now billowed out of the doors and windows. We merged into the horde for a few moments—not quite unnoticed, due to my reek—then pushed our way through to continue walking down the street.

I had no argument to make. If Astraia Holmes felt the two of us were adequate force to apprehend the criminal, I trusted that this was true.

Hadn't she just frightened off a dragon?

"What was that explosion I heard?" I asked. My ears still rang from the force of it.

"I always carry a loaded revolver in my reticule," she said. Of course, she did.

"Letty always scolds me about it. She does not feel it's proper for a lady. But she will not excoriate me about it anymore after tonight, since it saved your life."

"Thank you for that," I said.

"You're welcome."

"Do we have far to go?" I asked, panting. Astraia was much shorter than I, but tonight she was a woman with a purpose and easily outstrode my awkward wheeled gait. I wished I had brought my crutches tonight but had become quite prideful lately about my ability to manoeuvre without them. Foolish me.

"Not at all," she said. "Don't you recognize where we are?"

It took a few more minutes, but soon I did indeed recognize where we were. My head swam with the awareness, almost as dizzy as it had been when drugged with dragon mist, as I pulled myself up the steps of the brightly lit headquarters building of the Chinese legation. Astraia forged into the edifice without even attempting to knock at the door. Happily, it was unlatched, though I have no doubt she would have picked the lock had it been secured.

I followed her into the foyer.

"Ambassador Guo!" she yelled. "We know you're here! We followed your blood trail."

We had followed a blood trail?

A clock sounded the hour, the only noise in the otherwise silent building. Then I heard a door creak and turned my head to see Minister Guo step out of the same parlour where the late Mr. Hong had entertained us with a fanciful tale about dragons, just a few short days ago.

He was no longer the elegant Chinese gentleman. His robes were torn and filthy. His arm hung limp, his shoulder drenched in blood. He looked old, hurt, and exhausted.

Then I thought about what he must see when he looked at us. I appeared—and smelled—like something that had crawled out of a sewer. Astraia was a miniature Boadicea, her red hair streaming down her back, one hand gripping a black lacquer cane with a gold dragon handle, the other one holding a gun in steady precision, her face and bodice and skirt covered in Sir William's blood.

The old man started yelling at us in Chinese, but Astraia interrupted his unintelligible tirade.

"We know you speak English, Ambassador," she said. "We know why you killed Sir William. But why did you kill Mr. Hong?"

We knew why he killed Sir William. Astraia gave me too much credit, I'm afraid.

"He killed Mr. Hong?" I asked, horrified. Mr. Hong had been devoted to Mr. Guo.

"Of course," Astraia said. "That's the only possible deduction."

The murderer pulled himself together. "Would you ladies care to join me in the parlour?" he asked dryly, with perfect upper-class British enunciation. "Perhaps you can wait for me while I find a servant to attend to my wound." The monster had abated, allowing the diplomat to evince.

"We will join you in the parlour," Astraia said, "but I expect your servants may not return for some time, if at all. Madeleine is a doctor. She can tend to your wound."

He looked at me in askance.

"I'll wash my hands first," I assured him.

We followed him into the parlour, Astraia first handing me the black lacquered cane she had picked up at the murder site.

"You should use this," she said, and I gratefully took the implement, happy for its assistance and sorry neither of us had thought of this before. I had expected to spend the evening sitting listening to music, not running through the streets. Both of my lower extremities felt the strain.

I glanced around at the gimcracks and what-nots still cluttering every surface and shuddered, wondering if anyone had even noticed the piece I'd broken the last time I had been in this room.

Minister Guo waved to the pile of exotic silk scarves dangling off the closed lid of a piano. "You can use one of those to tie up my wound until my attendants return," he said.

"You believe your attendants are still at the scene of the fire they set at the meeting hall?" Astraia said.

"I presume."

"Are you aware that there were also members of the Ya Zi society present tonight?" she asked. "They may impede your servants' return."

"Perhaps." I did not see his expression, as I was using the water in a basin at the side of the room to wash my hands and face, but from his voice I gathered he had not actually been aware that Ya Zi gang members had also been at the hall.

I had noticed Mr. Wu tonight—but hadn't thought what that meant about the Ya Zi society. I looked around for something to wipe the dampness away, then sighed and used one of the beautiful scarves to remove the remains of the alleyway slop from my hands and face. I was glad that Letty was not here to see me rub feculence into exquisite specimens of the world's most expensive cloth.

I recognized the design on one panel as a representation of the nine sons of the dragon king, which seemed entirely appropriate in the circumstance. I brought the swath of red silk shot through with green and gold embroidery over to where Minister Guo stood.

"I will apply pressure to the wound and bandage it up to stop the bleeding," I said. "Your servants can tend it properly later."

"I don't think so," Astraia said. "I expect it will be the police doctor who will care for the ambassador's wound."

"We shall see," Minister Guo said, but stood still in order to allow me to tend to his injury.

I tore the silk lengthwise, folding half to use as a bandage and the other half to secure it onto his upper arm and shoulder. From what I could see through the blood and the man's torn robes, the bullet had been small in calibre and had gone straight through the flesh, completely missing his humerus. The injury had already almost stopped bleeding.

Neither Astraia nor Minister Guo spoke. I thought each was probably trying to wait the other out. I did not possess such patience.

"Tell me, Miss Holmes, why did the ambassador kill Sir William?" I asked.

"Because he found out that Sir William was employing his Ya Zi cane—the cane you are currently using, Maddie—to manifest the dragon," she said.

His wound now dressed, Minister Guo walked over to a sideboard and poured himself a glass of red liquid. He did not offer any to us. Astraia continued her explanation.

"Sir William's first victim, Sarah Prentiss, was just target practice, since he'd never produced the thing before. The cuts he made to Maria Murphy's body were shallower than the deep carvings he made in Miss Prentiss, because by then he had learned to better control his power; I knew this when I saw the cuts in the alley building where the maid was found, which were shallower and more restrained than the grooves in Mr. Wu's building. Sir William's intended victim all along was Miss Murphy, who was pregnant with his child and threatened to make this fact public. Lady Clydon, the chairwoman of the London Social Purity Society, would not have tolerated such notoriety—and for a short time I wondered if Lady Clydon herself might be the murderer. But when I inspected the financial records in Sir William's desk, I discovered that in fact most of the real wealth in the family is hers—and his high station in life is a direct result of her connections to the nobility. Probably he had been caught straying before and she had warned him against any future missteps. He carved the claw marks into the buildings and wrote the Ya Zi pictograph in the victims' blood to misdirect the police toward the criminal gang, never dreaming that law enforcement would not even notice the clues until someone pointed them out."

This cane I held in my hand could be used to manifest dragons? I looked down at the bulky handle of the thing. It seemed absurd. "How did he obtain the dragon cane in the first place?" I asked.

"He stole it!" Minister Guo said, goaded beyond control, dropping his diplomat mask. "From my family in China! We guarded the emperor and the Ya Zi tradition for thousands of years—safekeeping the daggers and swords and other arcane relics is our sacred responsibility—and then that man entered my family's home as a guest and plundered it of its treasures!"

"How did you convince Sir William to meet you tonight?" Astraia asked.

"Easily. I told him that I had proof that he had killed two women using the Ya Zi weapons, and that I intended to share that proof with his government unless he helped me to end the opium trade. He agreed to meet me to discuss it, but of course he intended to betray me."

"Why did you kill Mr. Hong?" Astraia asked.

"Because he accused me—me! —of being one of those so-called Ya Zi thugs, that filth who profit from selling that poison that's destroying our people! He knew of my family's Ya Zi warrior history—yet he thought I was capable of being involved in these murders! He accused me of working with that creature Zhu Wei! I could not believe it—Hong Guofan, whom I had trusted as a son, accusing me and threatening me! Of course, I killed him. My family honour demanded it.

"We—my family—are the true Ya Zi warriors, guardians of the traditions from time immemorial—not those thugs selling opium in the streets, calling themselves Ya Zi, using

238

murder and dragon masks to terrorize and control the masses! They pollute our name as that bastard Clydon polluted our sacred rituals! And we will eliminate them as well!"

He set his wine glass down carelessly on a priceless Chinese platter, not even noticing when it fell over, spilling red fluid over the ceramic and the teak table below it. He turned to us; a dagger held in his good hand.

"But first," he said, "unfortunately, I have to eliminate the two of you."

He moved toward Astraia, the tip of his dagger pointed in her direction, assuming her to be the more dangerous of us. He winced as he lifted the hand of his wounded arm to the dagger as well, mumbling incomprehensible ritualistic words as he used his fumbling fingers to fiddle with the hilt of the vicious implement.

Cloying clouds of gas began seeping out of the dagger tip. I saw Astraia's eyes start to glaze over, her mouth gaping open, her hand with the gun dropping to her side as the head of a monster with red eyes began to form in the noxious syrupy mist. And now that I knew the legend, I realized the muzzle of the dragon resembled that of a jackal. I imagined I saw the silhouette of claws grasping out toward her in curling clouds of smoke. I was terrified for the life of my friend, frozen in the grip of the creature's lure as its scalpel-sharp misty claws neared her blood-flecked blue satin bosom.

Well, what could I do? I clubbed the old man over the head with the handle of Sir William's black-lacquered cane, with such forced that I quite nearly tipped over, making him the second man I clobbered on the head that night. This one lacked the stamina of Bert Cranston. He collapsed to the ground. Immediately the incipient dragon dissipated and vanished.

Astraia collected Minister Guo's dagger from where it fell while I bent down to assure myself, he wasn't dead. He still breathed, but just barely. His eyes sank in heavy pools in his face; his skin was damp and pallid. It seemed unlikely he'd last out the hour. I sighed; at this rate I would soon surpass my father in number of kills.

I dragged the old man a few steps to the nearby sofa and heaved him up onto its cushions; he moaned as something sharp jabbed out, ripping his robe. I lifted him again and called to Astraia to examine the silken pillows. "What's there?" I asked.

Astraia reached over to remove a heavy glove hidden in the plump clouds of silk, three sharp tines poking out through the centre fingertips like vicious claws. Setting the old man gently down, I felt his head where I had struck him. There was a bump there now—a sizeable one, in fact—but no blood. Sub-cutaneous hematoma. Perhaps even brain haemorrhage.

"Ah," Astraia said with satisfaction, holding up the lethal glove. "That's another mystery solved." She looked around until she espied the pile of silks on the piano. "That will do," she said. "Maddie, I'm afraid I must reclaim that cane. But don't worry—you won't need to walk anywhere else tonight."

I handed the cane to her and watched as she carefully wrapped the relics—cane, dagger and glove—inside one of the exquisite silken swaths, then placed the silk-wrapped weapons parcel amidst the other glorious scarves covering the piano lid.

"Maddie, I must leave you for a short while. The last time James MacDonald saw us we were exiting a burning building. By now he will have noticed we're missing, and I hate to worry him, even if I don't mind worrying the rest of them. You stay here with Mr. Guo and I'll go fetch the authorities."

"What if the ambassador's servants return?"

"They won't. You saw Mr. Wu at the meeting hall. If the legation servants have not returned by now, it's because the Ya Zi gang scared them away. Or worse."

I could still hardly think of Mr. Wu as inspiring fear but supposed it must be true.

"And even if they do return, it won't matter," my friend continued. "That poison Mr. Guo took should kill him quite soon, I imagine."

She left, and I turned back to the sofa to feel the thready, weak pulse, and ponder that which Astraia had apparently already noticed: bloody bubbles now forming from faint breaths barely emitted between the parted lips of the dying man. I used my fingers to open one eye and peer at a black pupil so large as to almost fill the iris. The other pupil was also dilated, but not to such a degree. Mr. Guo's unequal pupil dilation might be a result of his head injury—but my wallop hadn't caused his lungs to rupture.

Frowning, I glanced at the wine decanter, then dragged my tired feet over to examine Mr. Guo's spilled wine, now dripping with a barely-perceptible sizzle onto the carpet, the narrow rivulet following a slight groove the acid of the beverage had etched into the teak. The rich red fluid appeared quite thick, more reminiscent of mercury—or clotted blood—than the distilled vintage of the grape.

Perhaps my assault wasn't wholly responsible for the man's impending doom.

Why had Mr. Guo taken such a chance trying to manifest a dragon at us when all he had to do was offer us a glass of the same poisoned wine he was drinking? Was it because as a dying man, the last survivor of his warrior lineage, he wanted to manifest his family dragon one last time? Or maybe it was something as simple as a cultural taboo regarding a Chinese nobleman sharing a libation with a western woman covered in excreta.

Wait—why was I assuming Mr. Guo was the last of his line? Hadn't he said the Ya Zi criminal gang would be eliminated? He had already consumed the deadly potion when he made that comment—how could he be so confident the gang would meet its doom?

Was there yet a third person manifesting smoke dragons in the streets of London?

*****

An hour later Astraia and I sat beside each other in John's carriage, swaths of glorious Chinese silks piled on the seat across from us. I was fading into exhausted sleep when Astraia spoke.

"I am sincerely disappointed about Mr. Guo. I had such admiration for his devotion to his homeland. I hope his ministerial replacement works as hard as he did against the evil opium trade."

"Hmm," I said groggily.

"Did I tell you they hadn't even discovered Sir William's body yet? PC Browning began chastising me for disappearing, and then I took him around to the side of the building and showed him the corpse. I had to wait for him to collect some other officers to examine that crime locale before I could bring him over to the legation building to see Mr. Guo's body. That is why it took me so long to get back, Maddie. I am sorry."

"Hmm."

242

"They'd be interrogating us now like mad if I hadn't told John we needed to see Mycroft immediately. Just that one name, and he was able to whisk us away. Amazing."

I groaned. "We aren't going over to your brother's club now, are we?"

"That's what I wanted to do, but John persuaded me that it would be preferable for us to wash up prior to meeting with my brother. He will take us home, then go to the Diogenes Club himself to fetch Mykie while we perform our ablutions. I must admit you are rather feculent."

I did not grace this comment with a response. I slept for the rest of the long ride to Astraia's townhouse.

The best thing about washing up at Astraia's was the ease and quantity of hot water made available to me. I used the opportunity to bathe parts of my body that hadn't been thoroughly cleansed since I'd been in this same room preparing for the operetta.

Letty, God bless her, had been primping and repairing some of my discarded work dresses for me, so I was actually able to meet Astraia's acclaimed brother Mycroft Holmes in a gown of my own that looked reasonably respectable and didn't smell like a sewer.

"Mykie, I want you to meet my dearest friend Madeleine Barquist," Astraia said after greeting a large man who lumbered into the parlour where we were enjoying a well-deserved tea. "Maddie, this is Mykie."

Standing, I held my hand out to a man whom I was confident I would never dare call by a diminutive. "I'm very happy to meet you, Mr. Holmes." As large as my hand was, his engulfed it. I was grateful when he gently released me.

"I'm happy to meet you, Miss Barquist. We feel you've become quite a member of our family," he said graciously in his deep voice, his large grey eyes boring into mine, so intense

I feared irrationally he must be able to see into my every secret. I turned away to return to the tea table.

"Come sit down, Mykie, and have some tea. Or would you like John to bring you something stronger?"

"What I would like, little minx, is my bed. Do you realize it is almost one o'clock in the morning? So, show me what John dragged me over here to see."

"First I need to tell you about the Ya Zi dragon."

"I'm familiar already with both the myth and the criminal gang," he said impatiently.

"Then I'll start by telling you how and why Sir William Forrester Clydon used the Ya Zi ritual to murder two women."

One of Mr. Holmes's eyebrows lifted at this interesting preface to the story and he joined us at the tea table. The sandwiches disappeared as he absorbed her words. Happily, for me, Letty brought in cakes as replacement.

Astraia told her brother almost everything—most of which he already knew; even having deduced that she must have gained entry into Sir William's household—but he allowed her to complete her tale as she chose without interruption before saying "Now let us examine these weapons you've collected."

Astraia carefully rummaged through the pile of silks John had left on a table. "Those damned claws in the glove are so sharp they've damaged most of the scarves. Such a shame. Mykie—I'm afraid I stole all of these from the legation. I told the police that before Mr. Guo's heart failed him he gave all this silk to Maddie and me as a gift to express his gratitude for assisting him home after the fire started in the meeting hall. I wouldn't have taken them all, but it was easier to hide the weapons that way."

"Don't worry about it," Mr. Holmes said. "I'll take them with me."

"Can't Letty keep just two, to make shawls for Maddie and me?"

"No," Mr. Holmes said. "I'm a very lenient brother. But I cannot allow you to profit from your theft, even when said theft was done for a noble purpose."

She frowned but unwrapped the weapons and brought them over to the tea table. I hurried to clear a space for the items.

"The dagger and cane both contain dual technologies, a magic lantern shows which projects a dragon onto a wall or, when necessary, onto the hallucinogenic gas which is also emitted through the device," she told her brother. "Maddie has another one at her office, in the portmanteau with Sir William's letters." She also set out the glove, razor-sharp claws attached to the fingertips. I now noticed that the claws were blood encrusted.

"I do not know how the technology works precisely," Astraia said. "But I'm sure I will be able to ascertain the methodology once I've studied the matter."

"That won't be necessary, Astrie," Mr. Holmes said. "You must leave the government something to do."

"I thought you could focus on how those two old men, Sir William and Mr. Guo, were able to garner sufficient strength to eviscerate their victims. Even with the claws as sharp as they are on this glove, it would take immense strength to cut through a human chest like butter. Not to mention the incisions Sir William made in the alleyway buildings at the crime scenes."

"I expect they ingested some sort of drug. We will find it. We will also need to find Sir William's claw glove, since it appears you did not bother to collect that vital item."

She hung her head. "I must have missed it when I investigated his home," she said in embarrassment. "I'm sorry, Mykie."

He patted her hand. "It's all right, my dear," he said jovially, and I wondered if her sudden atypical meekness was yet another fabrication, put on to appease her brother.

I had been thinking quite a bit about that wine Mr. Guo had drunk without offering any to us. He had not seemed to me like a man on the verge of suicide.

"Mr. Guo had that bullet wound," I said slowly.

"Bullet wound?" Mr. Holmes inquired.

"I forgot to mention that," Astraia said, giving me an exasperated look. "I shot him."

"But my point is: Mr. Guo was suffering that bullet wound, which meant his body was already heavily stressed," I said. "Is it possible that the adulteration in the wine he consumed at the legation, so acidic as to etch a groove into the teak table, was not poison but rather this strength drug you mention? Perhaps his toxic response occurred after I knocked him unconscious; maybe the chemicals reacted against his body because he was unable to exert the burst of physical prowess granted by the drug. Or perhaps he simply ingested too much of the drug in a short period of time and it killed him—he would also have ingested it prior to killing Sir William, after all."

The two siblings stared at me, then Astraia grinned. "Maddie, how clever of you!"

Mycroft Holmes stood, setting his serviette onto the table. "I may have underestimated you, Miss Barquist. I'd better have John drive me to the legation to ensure that all samples of that wine and the drug have been secured. There must be some at Sir William's home as well—the official who informs Lady Clydon of her husband's death must be instructed to obtain his dragon claw glove and the strength drug as well as any other associated paraphernalia." He called for John as he and his hostess walked to the door, then addressed us once again. "Ladies, I occasionally hear of a case that might be best served by lady investigators, crimes that would not require you shooting anyone, Astraia—we'll discuss that later—non-violent crimes such as servants stealing from important families and similar petty thefts. We can talk about that another time." He bent down to kiss his sister good-bye. "John can deliver the silks and weaponry to me tomorrow. Come along, Miss Barquist; I will drop you off at the police stables on my way. You must be exhausted."

I looked toward Astraia for direction, but she just shrugged, saying "By the way, I don't think either of us will be up to going to the ready-made clothing store tomorrow, Maddie. Perhaps next week." I was surprised; I thought the only reason she wanted to go shopping with me was to disguise our now-unnecessary visit to the alley where Mr. Hong had been killed. Was it possible she actually wanted to spend time with me in a non-investigatory pursuit? I smiled.

"But I still plan to come by to assist you with your charge against Hubert Cranston," she continued. "That wicked rascal will be very sorry he decided to mess with a friend of Astraia Holmes." She gave me a hug goodnight, and we parted.

Grabbing the replacement reticule Letty had given me, I followed Mr. Holmes out to John's cab. I had to scurry to keep up; he moved more quickly than I would have expected in such a large man, particularly someone whom his own sister described as "lazy" and "indolent".

I worried that he would spend the ride time interrogating me, but such was not the case. He closed his eyes and in minutes was emitting the loudest snores I had ever heard outside of a horse stall.

He awoke when John came to the door to assist me out of the cab upon arrival at police headquarters.

"John, please accompany Miss Barquist to her rooms and procure the dagger and letters my sister left with her." John nodded and walked with me to the stable, holding onto my arm to provide support as for some reason I was almost unable to propel myself forward of my own accord.

The door to my office was unlocked. Again, I cursed myself for not having my crutch this evening. But John surprised me by pulling a pistol out of his waistcoat. "Don't worry, Miss Maddie. Just stay behind me."

We entered a warm dark room. I did not hear any of Old Vic's customary growls, and I thought: that monster has killed him, just as he threatened. My anger surged and I rushed in, pushing John aside.

I smelled just a hint of the familiar dragon gas before I saw a fierce bearded dragon with flaming green eyes swaying high against the stable wall, its head lowering toward me in threat.

I gasped, and the image disappeared. It had been simply a magic lantern trick, an ingenious design built into a dagger and projected onto mist.

A man stood up from the table and approached me.

"Miss Barquist, please let me help you to sit," Sherlock Holmes said. "I believe we should have a physician come around tomorrow to examine your foot. So much running around as you have been doing cannot have aided in its healing. Light the lamps, John. I believe I have caused Miss Barquist a bit of a fright."

Chapter Fourteen

He helped me into a chair as John, sliding his pistol back into his waistcoat, said "Mr. Sherlock, Mr. Mycroft instructed me to collect some things that Miss Astraia left in Miss Barquist's care."

"Tell my brother that I have taken charge of the items in question and will make delivery to him as appropriate in a day or so when I have completed my examination of the mechanism."

John nodded, lit every lamp in the place, and left.

"Would you like me to make you a cup of tea?" Sherlock Holmes asked mildly.

I stared at the dragon dagger now resting innocuously on the tabletop. I wanted the thing out of my home and out of my life. "No," I said. "I have had enough tea for the night." I looked pointedly at the clock, which indicated almost half-two in the morning.

"I won't keep you long, Miss Barquist," he said. "Can I induce you to indulge in a glass of whisky with me?"

"I don't have any whisky."

"I brought my own." He slipped the dagger into his coat then removed a flask from the same pocket. He poured a fair measure of the golden fluid into two teacups, topping mine up with water.

He raised his glass in a toast. "To the successful end of a difficult case," he said, then took an appreciative sip.

I nodded and tasted my drink. It was very good whisky, on par with that which Astraia had obtained for me from her other brother, that day I had broken my foot.

"Did you just complete a difficult case, Mr. Holmes?"

"Not I. I understand you and my sister did, however."

"Mr. Holmes, I am far too tired tonight to tell you about that."

"You do not need to tell me anything, Miss Barquist. Samuel Rankin came to see me tonight and told me the whole."

I doubted Samuel Rankin knew the whole—but perhaps Sherlock Holmes had been able to piece the thing together from what he heard.

Old Vic made a snuffling sound from his bed, emitting a horrific stench. I thought please stay asleep, Old Vic—I am too tired to deal with you tonight.

"Do not fret yourself over the dog, Miss Barquist. I took care of his needs for you," Mr. Holmes said.

"Thank you," I said, feeling guilty that I had not thought once all night about Old Vic's needs. Bert Cranston's intrusion at the beginning of the evening had rattled me; had I even left food for the poor animal? Probably, but I couldn't quite remember...

Fortunately, I could see remnants of fresh food in his bowl. "Did he bite you?" I asked Mr. Holmes. Old Vic had no patience with the old proverb about not biting the hand that feeds you.

"Not at all. We're quite good friends now."

I nodded, not surprised. This was Astraia's brother, after all. I felt my eyes drooping and wished he'd go away.

"I waited around for you tonight because I wanted to assure you of something," he said.

"Oh?"

He stood and gathered the hat and coat he had evidently removed earlier in the evening after the room heated sufficiently. Really, I could not remember the office ever feeling this toasty.

I wondered how much of my precious coal he had fed to the stove.

"I wanted to tell you that you can stop worrying about Hubert Cranston," Sherlock Holmes said. "I must commend you; you have done very well in fighting him off for yourself. But the man won't be around to bother anyone anymore."

I stared at him, stunned. Had they captured Bert? Were they sending him away? Mr. Holmes opened the door, and I suddenly noticed he held Astraia's portmanteau in his hand. I frowned to see him holding that item. I was very tired, but surely, I hadn't given it to him and then forgotten?

"It will be a great relief to have him gone," I said. I stood to follow Mr. Holmes to the door, despite his motions to me that I should remain seated. "Will you tell your children to stop following me around now?"

He frowned. "What do you mean?"

"Your Baker Street Irregulars," I said. "The children who've been following me around."

"Miss Barquist, I put no Baker Street Irregulars on this case," he said. "Lock the door behind me."

It was so warm in here I was tempted to fall asleep at the table. I assumed Mr. Holmes had not been here long since there was no indication, by tobacco remains or miasma, that he had smoked his pipe while waiting for my return. But I discovered evidence to the contrary, indicating he had been here for quite a while, when I walked over to the stove to see how much charcoal he had left me and noticed bits of paper ash covering the top of the stove and littering the floor. I lifted the stove lid to peer inside and recognized three distinct types of combustible materials in the ashes.

Charcoal.

Sir William's collection of love letters.

And my father's journal, which had documented in hideous detail the butchery and monstrosities committed by him and his friend Jolly Bert.

Which I had kept in my bulky ancient handbag ever since I'd discovered the thing the morning after Papa's death. The handbag I had hidden under my bed this evening, next to Astraia's portmanteau—the valise which her brother had taken with him tonight though it was now empty of both dragon dagger and letters.

At first panicked, I grabbed the fire tongs automatically, to extract the remains of the journal. But then I set the tool back into the bucket. Mr. Holmes was right. The fire was the best place for the horrid thing.

I sat at the table sipping my whisky, deep in thought as the stove continued to blaze. The smell of the dragon gas had completely dissipated. Eventually I fell asleep.

*****

At ten the next morning PC Frank Froest brought a physician by to see me, an arrangement made by Sherlock Holmes, concerned not just about my foot but also with the bad bruise I had received on my face from my fall in the alley where Sir William was killed. I was not too unhappy about this visit, since my ambulation this morning was quite poor, and I had started to wonder if I had caused permanent damage to my extremities by forcing my broken foot to so much exertion.

The physician certainly seemed to think it possible. He chastised me for all of my *"gadding about"*, threatening to remove the wheels from my cast altogether if I did not begin to rest my foot and the limb above it (which was quite swollen) for at least twenty of the twenty-four hours of the day. In other words, I was to move from my office chair to my bed and back, and not do much else, for the next four weeks. When I objected that I would not be able to accomplish my work, Frank said that I would be provided with my own assistant, starting tomorrow.

"I will not have one of those stable wastrels loitering in here day-in and day-out," I insisted.

"No, not one of them. We picked up a young girl on the street, fighting with a pimp from Madam DuBarry's house who was trying to steer her into their particular line of work. She is fresh off the farm and seems a nice girl, and I thought you might like having someone to train, someone who can manage things for you when you need to leave the office. If you do not like her, we can get you someone else. But I think she'll fit in well here."

I stared at him. The Metropolitan Police was going to pay for me to have an assistant? I thought I saw the magic wand of Mycroft Holmes at work in this decision.

And best of all, if I had a companion here with me—my own Letty, so to speak, only focused on medicating horses instead of more homely duties—I could continue to live here without being required to keep the door open even in inclement weather (like today) whenever I had masculine visitors.

Frank also told me that Bert had been found and arrested. I wasn't to worry about him anymore, he said. "You won't need to testify against him either, not after all he did," Frank said.

"You mean drugging the police?" I asked.

"The case has become more complicated than that," Frank said. But he refused to speak any further about it, just reiterated that Bert was no longer any concern for me.

With everything else that was happening I had not thought to look in on the pregnant mare last night. This morning she foaled on her own—and I did not examine her baby either. And no one from the stable argued with me about it. I sat in my warm office all day, updating paperwork, stroking the cat purring on my lap and reading the adventure novels Letty had so kindly loaned to me from the library.

*****

I went to bed that night relatively content. It would never have been my choice for Mr. Sherlock Holmes to know my deepest, most dangerous and most humiliating secrets— quite the contrary—but what was done was done. Not that the fact I had killed my father had been included in his journal, of course—but I assumed Mr. Holmes had deduced that for himself after reading about Papa's career as Jack the Ripper, not to mention the things he had written about me.

Mr. Holmes did not seem horrified when he left. He never threatened me with incarceration. He hadn't even taken the journal with him as evidence. Instead he'd burned the nasty diary and sent a physician to examine my abused foot. And Hubert "Jolly Bert" Cranston had been arrested. It appeared that everything would turn out fine. I did not need to worry anymore. I would be safe.

I was awakened a few hours later by a knife held to my throat.

"What now?" I groaned. I was tired of all these intrusions. Tired of all these knives.

"Don't scream, Miss Maddie," a vaguely familiar voice said. I opened my eyes and saw three men in my room, two of them holding lanterns. The only one I recognized was Mr. Wu.

"Are you going to scream, Miss Maddie?" he asked me.

"Not immediately, Mr. Wu. How did you get in here?"

"Your police guard is gone this evening," he said. "I guess they thought you were safe from harm now. You have changed this room since I spent the night here. It's much nicer than I remember."

Why had the police removed the watch they'd set on me? Was it because of the deaths of Mr. Guo and Sir William? Bert Cranston had been arrested—perhaps that was why they had removed my guard. "Am I safe from harm?" I asked.

"Of course, you are," a strange yet soothing voice said, a voice belonging to the best-dressed man in the group. His robes could almost rival Minister Guo's in elegance, so I assumed him to be the leader. "Qin will remove his knife from your throat now." The leader spoke in Chinese to the man holding the weapon to my person. The fellow immediately stepped back, bowing to me.

I sat up in bed, glad I wore my heaviest nightgown, and looked at the leader with polite enquiry. I was nervous, of course, but did not feel that I was in danger. If they had wanted to kill me, surely, they wouldn't have bothered to wake me up first.

Mr. Wu spoke. "Miss Maddie, this is Zhu Wei. Perhaps you have heard of him."

I was facing the man whose cousin/brother/uncle I had killed? I began to worry that I might be in more danger than

I had originally thought. "I have heard of you, of course Mr. Zhu. I am sorry about the death of your relative Zhu Lei."

He shrugged. "I too am sorry. No doubt you had good reason to kill him."

"He hurt my dog."

Zhu Wei stared at me, his dark eyes unreadable. "He was never fond of animals," he said finally.

"Why are you here, Mr. Zhu?" I asked.

"I understand you and your friend Miss Holmes have taken possession of some arcane relics which I want," he said. "Specifically, two daggers, a dragon-headed cane, and two very special gloves."

I do not believe I have ever felt more vulnerable than I did in that moment, sitting in my bed late at night, confronted by three members of a dangerous criminal gang, knowing I was about to tell them something they would not want to hear.

"Mr. Zhu, I'm afraid the Ya Zi appurtenances have been claimed by Miss Holmes's brother Mycroft, on behalf of Her Majesty's government. Neither Miss Holmes nor I expect to ever see them again."

"I don't believe you." At his angry tone, the man with the knife started twisting it in my direction again.

"Mr. Zhu, you can search this entire place. I assure you; you will not find that which you seek."

He nodded at the knife-wielder, who moved closer toward me.

"Miss Maddie, please tell us what we want to know," pleaded Mr. Wu.

I stared at the knife nearing my face. "I already told you the truth, Mr. Wu. I don't have anything to add to that."

As I prepared to release a loud high A from my throat, a small boy ran into the room. He wore a cerulean blue scarf tied around his head. "The police are returning, Mr. Zhu," he panted. Now that the street urchin was only feet away, I could see his features bore an Eastern cast.

Mr. Zhu waved at the knife man, who retreated again. "I believe you, Miss Maddie," Mr. Zhu said. "And I am grateful to you and to Miss Holmes for disposing of Ambassador Guo Jiegang, who has long been a thorn in my side, trying to shut down my opium business... I am going to leave you now with a friendly warning, which you will pass on to your friend Mycroft Holmes. Let him know that if the ritual items aren't provided to me very soon his sister Astraia might find herself an exceedingly unhappy passenger on a boat to the Orient, one more unfortunate victim of the dreaded white slave trade."

The three men and their young friend walked to the door. "Go back to sleep, Miss Maddie," Zhu Wei said. "Whenever you see little Chan here, think of me." He left, followed by the knife-wielder and the boy.

"Goodbye, Miss Maddie," Mr. Wu said. "I'm sorry I won't be able to do business with you anymore, but I have moved my little store into a different neighbourhood." He followed his evil master out.

I lay in bed for a few minutes, then leapt up as I realized I hadn't heard a sound from Old Vic. Had they injured my dog again?

Despite the doctor's strictures I ran as quickly as I could into the office, almost bursting into tears when I saw that Old Vic lay flatulating in his dog basket, fast asleep, Juno the cat wrapped around him. I lifted both animals from the basket and carried them back into my bedroom, to sleep at the foot of my bed.

Morpheus did not embrace me for a long while. I had much to ponder. A ruthless criminal gang leader, a man who threatened Astraia with a fate worse than death if we did not give him the tools he needed to subjugate his community in his thrall, was nevertheless grateful to Astraia and me for killing Mr. Guo, because he had impeded the gang's immoral enterprise. Life was very complicated sometimes.

*****

Early the next morning I wrote a letter to Mycroft Holmes, informing him of my visitors of the night before and their demands. I would give her brother a chance to tell Astraia about the threats levied against her and the actions he planned to take to protect her. If he did not discuss the matter with her within a few days, I would tell her about the menace myself, since she had every right to know she might be in danger.

"Miss Maddie, are you decent?" a voice yelled from the other side of the door as I was finishing the letter.

"Come on in, Detective Inspector Rankin," I yelled. I hoped he brought something to eat, as I hadn't prepared anything for breakfast yet.

He entered, his hands empty. Well, Frank Froest hadn't been by yet today, so I could still hope.

I had become very reliant lately on other people providing my meals.

"How are you doing after your adventure the other night, Miss Maddie?" he asked. He sat at the table and poured himself a cup of tea. I was discomfited to realize he felt so comfortable with me. I did notice he kept the outside door open, however. I sighed and went to add more coal to the stove.

"I know I have you to thank for my visit from Sherlock Holmes after the events at the SSOT fundraiser and at the legation," I said. "I had another adventure last night as well."

I told him about my criminal gang visitors, although I didn't mention the dragon weapons they sought since I did not know if Mr. Mycroft Holmes would want that information shared.

"You would recognize Zhu Wei if you saw him again?" DI Rankin asked excitedly after my story was completed. I realized he knew all about the Ya Zi gang operating in the area. No doubt he had known from the beginning that I had witnessed a Ya Zi gang murder that day in the Limehouse neighbourhood—perhaps one of many the villains had committed using the dragon mask.

"I suppose," I said, annoyed to think how much investigative work Astraia and I could have saved—well, Astraia, mostly—if only this man had been open with us about what he knew.

"No one on the police force has ever seen him. We might need to ask you to identify him sometime. Don't worry—I wouldn't put you in danger."

"Fine," I said. I handed him the letter I wrote to Mycroft Holmes. "Could you see that this is delivered to Astraia's brother Mycroft right away? He needs to know about Zhu Wei's threats to his sister."

He took it and stood. "Certainly," he said. "Since I have a conference scheduled with Mycroft this morning anyway, I'll deliver it myself. And in the meantime, I'll arrange for a police guard to watch his sister's house."

Astraia would not be happy about that. I realized I had better tell her soon about the Ya Zi gang threats, not wait for Mr. Holmes to give her the news.

"I also need to discover what happened to your guard last night—there was no instruction given for them to decrease their diligence." He scowled, and I knew he worried that somehow the Chinese gang influence had infiltrated the police force. I suspected it was more likely a case of my wardens having decided that standing guard outside of the police stable was an unnecessary curtailment of their regular evening pub inspection duty. The officers working the night watch were known as the least reliable men on the force—one reason my father had never been caught.

I walked DI Rankin to the door. I expected him to leave, but was taken aback when he stopped at the door and turned to face me, just inches away from my arm and hand prepared to shut out the cold wind. He stood so close I was fully aware of his height, feeling almost petite beside him—not an awareness I enjoyed.

"Miss Maddie, do you like music?"

"Yes," I said, thinking *what an odd question—he knows I went to that soirée musicale the other night. And the Gilbert and Sullivan Operetta not long ago—he saw me in the green taffeta dress with the peacock feathers falling out of my hair.*

"I thought you might. I have heard you singing while you work. You have a lovely voice. I was just wondering..."

"Yes?"

"You get half-Sundays off, do you not?"

"Yes." Actually, I had been taking so much time off lately I hadn't been paying much attention to my official free time— my formerly highly-anticipated half-Sunday off had become almost irrelevant.

"I like music too, but don't enjoy going to entertainments by myself. I was wondering if you would like to accompany me to the music hall on Sunday, and perhaps go out for a meal afterward."

I stared up at him. Although I had never heard them speak even a single kind word to each other, somehow, I had always thought that Samuel Rankin was one of Astraia's beaux.

"Um, I could do that," I said finally. "Yes. That would be nice."

He smiled at me, the first smile I ever saw on his face. He had a glorious smile, and I would have continued staring at it, but we were interrupted by Astraia's voice nearby.

"Hello, Samuel, Maddie. Samuel, you should either leave or go inside, but do not make Maddie continue holding the door open like that. It's freezing out here."

He quickly stepped aside to allow her to enter. "I'm leaving now."

"Good," she said.

He didn't rise to her bait. "Goodbye, Miss Maddie. I'll see you later." He hurried away.

"Goodbye, Detective Inspector." I closed the door behind him. Astraia slipped off coat and gloves then peered into the old china chicken tea pot, frowned, and began to brew a new potful of tea. I was glad to see she, at least, had not arrived empty-handed.

"I'm sorry I didn't get over here yesterday," she said. "But Mykie told me Jolly Bert has been arrested and your testimony won't be needed after all."

"I've been told," I said. "Where's Letty?" I moved to the sink to wash my hands prior to setting out the food Astraia had brought.

"At the library. I had so much to tell you I just couldn't go to work this morning."

"I have much to tell you as well." Would I tell her about my Sunday plans with DI Rankin? Of course, I would, though maybe not today. But I would certainly tell her about all of my nighttime visitors—including her brother Sherlock two nights ago.

I probably wouldn't tell her about the burnt journal, though. I still wasn't ready to discuss that part of my life with anyone. I doubted I ever would, unless somehow Sherlock Holmes made it necessary through some words or action of his own.

I scowled to remember that my deepest secrets were now shared with another person. Assuming he had deduced that I killed my father. Which he probably had.

"My news first," she said. "My brother Mycroft came to see me this morning, the third time he's been to my door in a month, which I know is a great annoyance to him since he prefers to conduct all of his business at his club. But the club doesn't allow ladies to enter, therefore, he must go out of his way in order to see me. He was very grumpy, poor dear; I do not think he'd fallen asleep these last few nights at all. I pity anyone who has to interact with him today."

I thought sympathetically about DI Rankin, now on his way to meet with the man.

"Anyway," she continued, "he told me that Lady Deborah Peacham has been found murdered. You know who that is, of course."

I nodded. Lady Peacham was a leader of the Central Committee of the National Society for Women's Suffrage. She had been arrested last week, after trying to interrupt a committee meeting of the House of Commons.

"Mykie said the police are questioning her husband Sir John about it, but that he expects the truth behind her death lies in a stratum of society that male policemen cannot infiltrate."

She smiled in excited anticipation. "Maddie—how would you like to become a suffragist?"

An hour later Astraia left. I had told her about my visit from Mr. Wu, Zhu Wei and Qin the knife wielder, and the threats Zhu Wei had made against her. She said it sounded quite exciting and that she hoped to meet the man someday, although she expected Mykie would have him arrested long before she got the chance.

But my day's visits were not over yet. Almost as soon as she had gone, Frank Froest came to join me for tea, with extraordinary news he was now able to share.

Yesterday, acting on orders from Scotland Yard, the police had inspected Jolly Bert Cranston's pub larder. He had been charged last night with using human meat in his pub pies. If found guilty, he would hang.

I knew the investigation on this charge had occurred because Mr. Holmes learned from Papa's journal that Bert took organs from Jack the Ripper's murder victims. I considered writing a thank-you note to Sherlock Holmes for taking Jolly Bert off the streets permanently but dismissed that idea as an inadequate expression of my gratitude and relief. I tried to remember if *A Study in Scarlet* had ever mentioned if the detective owned a horse or dog that might occasionally need medical treatment. I thought not. Perhaps there would be some other way I could show my appreciation.

Although I still anticipated keeping company with Samuel Rankin on Sunday, I couldn't help but feel annoyed that he had failed to tell me about these latest charges filed against Bert. Of which he certainly must have been thoroughly cognizant when he spoke with me this morning.

My mind was soon engaged in other matters, however. Frank introduced me to Susie, my new assistant. An injured horse was brought in for surgery. The buckshot donkey was released. Despite all of my worries and plans, I managed to spend the rest of the day earning my keep as the police horse doctor.

And when I slept that night with my dog and cat on my bed, I enjoyed my first peaceful dreams in years.

THE END

The first time Melanie Bacon ever heard the phrase "Jack of all trades, master of none" was in reference to herself. A few of the many trades she worked at but mastered regardless were Indian casino investigator, bookstore owner, chair of a city planning commission, and former manager for a Fortune 500 corporation. Currently, she lives on an island in Washington state just north of Seattle with her lazy kitty and her partner Michael, and on top of all that, she is a candidate for local county commissioner.

For more information on Melanie and her books visit:
http://dragonrippernovel.com/

Visit Melanie on Facebook, too:
https://www.facebook.com/thedetectivists/

Can't wait for the next installment in the Dragon Ripper series? Join Melanie's review team to get news, updates and the chance to read an advance copy of Book 2 of The Detectivists for free!

Sign up at MelanieBacon@delsolpress.org

Printed in Great Britain
by Amazon